R

SUMMER BY THE SEA

SUMMER BY THE SEA

Ann Cliff

CHIVERS

British Library Cataloguing in Publication Data available

This Large Print edition published by BBC Audiobooks Ltd, Bath, 2010.
Published by arrangement with Robert Hale Limited.

U.K. Hardcover ISBN 978 1 408 49257 4
U.K. Softcover ISBN 978 1 408 49258 1

AudioG◉ -1 SEP 2010

Printed and bound in Great Britain by
CPI Antony Rowe, Chippenham and Eastbourne

For Peter and Irene, Jill and Martin, with thanks for your encouragement and the happy times at Bridlington.

ONE

Bridlington, Yorkshire: 1890

'Wind's coming up, and seas are high already. I wish lads were home.' Mary Baker's hands moved automatically as her four needles clicked, measuring the evening hours with another gansey. She was knitting the traditional garment in dark-blue oiled wool, a jersey with the distinctive pattern of the Bridlington fishermen in the design.

Helen looked round the kitchen as the fire flared up in a sudden draught and the wind howled down the chimney, rattling the windows. Here they were cosy, warm and safe, but on the sea in a storm it would be very different. Although it was April, the night had darkened early as black clouds blotted out the sunset. 'I never realized, when we came here for holidays, what a hard life fishing must be for the men on a night like this.' She had a vision of a little boat tossed about by the wind, towering waves crashing down on it, spray flying. Poor lads, how would they survive? Helen had too much imagination, her mother said, for her own good. Her secret worry was that she had too much emotion, threatening to spill out sometimes and shame her. Yorkshire folk by tradition distrusted emotion.

1

'It's hard for the women, too. Not just the waiting, but the work. Think on then, never marry a fisherman.' Mary's lined face was quite serious. 'You're bright enough to do better than marry a local lad, and your ma won't thank me for encouraging it.' She sighed. 'My poor Fred had a coble, a little boat like Dan's. He was one of the best. Fred never drank, he brought all his money home, although fish-buyers often paid out in the public house. But sometimes it was too rough to go out. And then again, the fish might not run. It's a chancy business, fishing.'

'But life is easier now?' To Helen Mrs Baker seemed quite comfortable; mistress of Seaview and very well organized, with a little maid to help her and now Helen to work there as well, just for the season.

'Ay, well, you could say so. Now that I've a boarding house, it's easy to forget how hard it was then, except that the lad reminds me.' The frown relaxed for a moment into an ironic smile as the bony fingers flew on. 'Mind you, looking after visitors is no bed of roses. You'll see, you're working here for the summer. You'll be run off your feet, some days. Season hasn't started yet.'

As Helen had said when she began, if you came from a farm you were used to hard work. 'What happened to your husband, Mrs Baker? Is it rude to ask? But I'm new and there's a lot I don't know.'

2

The older woman paused before answering, but the needles clicked on. 'You wouldn't remember. How old are you? Eighteen? It was the year before you were born then, the big storm of seventy-one. Twenty-three vessels were lost in the bay here, lass. A lot were overloaded, colliers they were; a shameful business. And Fred, he wasn't fishing by then, he worked in the harbour after his leg was broken, but he went out with the lifeboat; he died trying to save folks from the sea.' Mary shook her head. 'I never wanted our Daniel to go to sea, but what can you do? You can't hold 'em back.' Another pause. 'You've not seen my lad yet. He has shares in a coble and they went out today. I'm feared for them, now.'

No wonder she worried, the poor woman, and no wonder she was so stern. It was time to find something cheerful to say. 'But the bay's usually quite safe, isn't it? Flamborough Head shelters us from storms, I thought.' Helen pushed her dark curls back and adjusted her little white cap. She remembered being told that the chalk cliffs of Flamborough jutted out nearly six miles into the North Sea. You could see those gleaming cliffs from the front windows of the boarding house, curving out to shelter Bridlington Bay.

There was silence for a while, apart from the howling wind in the chimney. Helen tried again. 'So if your son is out in the bay . . . he should be safe.'

3

Mary tutted impatiently. 'Depends on the wind, lass. If gale's from north or west, we're sheltered, right enough. Bay of Safety, the Scotchmen call us when they run down the coast in summer after the herring. But Bridlington Bay can be a deathtrap with an easterly, believe me. Breaking surf, see.' She took another ball of wool and joined the threads. 'This coast is the worst in England, they say.'

Bay of Safety; well, from her point of view she should be safe here. But the wind was from the east tonight; Helen had noticed that when she took in the washing from the yard. On the farm at home cold easterlies were dreaded when the ewes were lambing. The Yorkshire Wolds were exposed chalk hills and when the winds came whipping in across the North Sea they could freeze a newborn lamb to death before it had time to dry out. Thinking of home made tears prick her eyes. Helen already missed her home, Mother and Father, the animals—and the lad she would never kiss again. Charlie had never been serious about her, but she loved him: his curly hair and cheeky smile. She swallowed the ache in her throat. Talk about something else . . . 'Are we —are you expecting any more guests this week, Mrs Baker?'

The needles clicked on as Mary looked at the girl over her glasses. 'Mary'll do. No need for Missus. Well, we might get more folks in.

4

When you run a boarding house you never know who might turn up. You have to be ready for anything, lass. Beds ready, plenty of food and good fires. We're in April now, folks will be coming to the seaside before long.' She came to the end of a row and moved the knitting over. 'When spring comes they all want to get out of those smoky West Riding towns for a breath of fresh air. That's how we make a living, here in Bridlington. Sea air is good for you, the doctors say, though I reckon it's just that we've less smoke.'

Seaview was so different from the farm! Of course, the kitchen was similar; the big scrubbed table in the centre, the red tiled floor and the huge coal cooking range made it look like a farmhouse kitchen. There was a cat called Kipper, sitting on the rug in front of the fire. But this was a boarding house, one of the better such establishments; as her mother had explained, more like a guest house or small hotel. The rooms were spacious, with high ceilings and the big solid doors had brass handles. 'You'll learn a lot, Helen,' Mother had told her. 'Make sure to mind your manners, they'll be well-to-do people who stay there.'

'My manners are perfect, Mother. You made sure of that,' Helen had replied demurely and they'd both laughed. It had only been last week, but it seemed ages ago.

Mary continued, 'There's a family from

5

Leeds booked in for Saturday; they'll be coming by train. I'll do some baking. First thing tomorrow you can get the bottled gooseberries for pies, and you can get bedrooms ready. It pays to be ready in good time, and young Susie will be in to help us.'

Two days ago Helen had started to work for Mrs Baker. The first ordeal on that Monday morning had been walking into the dining-room with a loaded tray. Three guests were sitting expectantly round the huge mahogany dining table: two men and a middle aged woman. Helen had managed not to spill the coffee and she was rewarded by a faint smile from Miss Burton, the schoolteacher who boarded at Seaview during the week. The men had been buried in their newspapers, but Helen knew that one was a travelling salesman, staying only a night or two, and that the other was Mr Kirby, a regular guest. Mrs Baker knew him well and called him James; she was unconventional in some ways.

Mary now looked at the clock and pulled the kettle onto the fire. 'Time for James's cup of tea, he likes it at nine o'clock. Make a pot, there's a good girl, black of course. And take it to the sitting-room for him. The china cups are on the dresser there.' The knitting needles clicked on.

How stuffy, to have a cup of tea at the same time every night. The stuffy Mr Kirby was reading by the fire when Helen carried in the

6

tray carefully and set it down on a low table. 'Will there be anything else, Mr Kirby?' The gaslight was bright, a contrast with the softer glow of the paraffin lamp in the kitchen. Seaview had gaslights in the public rooms and Helen thought that they made everybody look slightly green.

'Thank you . . . what's your name again?' He took off his reading glasses and smiled at her, and Helen realized that he was quite young. Men sitting by the fire in slippers were usually old, like her father, but this one looked athletic, with broad shoulders and a sort of sad look in his dark eyes. Helen's susceptible heart missed a beat, but only until she remembered she was on duty and a servant. 'It's a bad night and I suppose young Dan is still out fishing, is he? Mary will be worried about him.' Mr Kirby had a quiet, deep voice.

'I'm Helen, sir, and yes, Mrs Baker is worried. I hope . . .' She broke off as they heard a crash in the hall. The wind howled as though the storm had come out of the dark night, right into the house. James Kirby got out of his chair in one smooth movement. He and Helen ran out of the room and they nearly fell over a pair of legs in big leather sea boots. A young man was lying on the floor, wet through and gasping for breath. Another lad stood over him, just as wet. The wind tore through the open door and the lights flickered in the draught.

7

'Here he is, his ma can look after him. You'd better tell her we've lost Robbie. I think he's gone, we lost sight of him in the dark . . . there was nowt we could do.' The young man shook his head. 'I'm off home. I've never seen seas like that, never.'

Mary came out into the hall and she looked grim. 'Help me with him, lass,' she said, but Helen was frozen with horror and it was James Kirby who moved first, to put his arm under the lad's wet shoulders and link arms with Mary, lifting him up. Together they half carried, half dragged him across the tiled floor. 'Bring him into the kitchen. Steady now . . . put him down here. Thank you, James.' Helen, overcoming her shock, helped to draw off the heavy boots. 'Now Dan, off with your things. Bring some towels, Helen.'

Dan was barely conscious. Helen gently pulled the gansey over his head and Kirby slid him out of the waterlogged trousers. Horrified at the thought of seeing a man naked, Helen hurried off to the linen closet. But when she got back, there was the lad still like a skinned rabbit and it was her job to put the towels round him. His pale skin was covered with red welts. It was the first time she had seen Mary's beloved son and she was seeing far too much of him.

Dan had evidently been dragged out of the sea to safety; Seaview was only a few yards from the shore. He lay gazing at the ceiling and his breathing was still heavy. Mr Kirby gently turned him over onto his stomach and water dribbled out of his mouth; he must have swallowed quantities of sea water. Kirby put pressure on his lungs, trying to express more water.

Mary stood looking down at her son for a while. Then she heated up a pan of milk and added cubes of bread to it, with a little sugar. After a while Dan coughed, spluttered and sat up. 'Get this down you,' Mary muttered as she fed him with a spoon as though he were a baby.

Mr Kirby went back to the sitting-room with a smile at Helen and there was silence apart from the crackling of the fire. Dan seemed to be totally exhausted. 'Wind dropped just enough, or we'd have been done for,' he mumbled, but that was all.

When the lad had been taken to his bed in the basement and wrapped in a woollen blanket with a hot brick at his feet Mary sighed and sat down, as though weary herself. 'Who brought him home?'

'Another lad . . . he said they'd lost Robbie.' It had to be said, although Helen hated to say it. One of the lads had not come home.

Mary shook her head. 'I knew it. They should never ha' gone out. It would be Dave who brought him back; they were three in the boat. Robbie, he was the third. The youngest, he would be.' She seemed to be biting back

9

tears.

Helen tried not to think about the poor lost lad. There was so much to learn about the sea. 'I thought there would be more men in the boat than that? For a fishing boat?'

'Nay, herring-fishing's not till later. You'll know about it when herring boats come in, the whole of Bridlington harbour's alight. The lads were off long-lining in a coble. They try to make a living out of that in winter up till the end of May. Then there's crab and lobster pots. That's what they do in the spring.' Mary sighed. 'They might have lost boat as well. No doubt he'll tell us in the morning. Away to your bed, lass.'

Helen went wearily up the stairs to her attic bedroom under the roof. She looked out through the window at the sea raging and churning, the breakers white with foam in the faint light from the shore. The tide was ebbing and she could see wet sand. Far out on the headland, the Flamborough lighthouse sent its unique signal into the night, one red and two white flashes. Dan had said the wind had just dropped enough to let the boats come in, but it was still blowing. The Bay of Safety had shown its treacherous side tonight. How could his mother ever let Dan go out to sea again?

It was time to close the curtains on the dark. Helen's little room was neat; it was good to have things tidy, that was what housekeeping was all about. She put down her candle on the washstand and took out the journal that she tried to write every day.

A wild night and one of the fishing boats was wrecked. Two men came home, one still missing. Daniel, Mrs Baker's son, is safe.

She stopped and chewed the end of her pencil.

He was wet and cold and I helped to dry him. Fishermen are brave and very tough, they are often in danger. The coast of Yorkshire is famous for wrecking ships. How can they call this the Bay of Safety?

The sea was just as romantic, but darker and more dangerous than she had realized.

Mr James Kirby helped with Dan, he is a guest, he is probably stuffy but I think he is not as old as he seems.

After jumping into bed Helen did not cry with homesickness as she had for the first two nights. She was still thinking of poor Robbie. 'God, if you do exist, save the poor lad. Why do you let such bad things happen?' She had never met the fisher lad, but for some time she thought about him and wondered whether he suffered, whether his death had been an easy one. How terrible to die out there in the cold

11

water, without your friends, with no one to hold your hand! The only deaths Helen had seen had been of her grandparents: peaceful, sad but inevitable, after a long and full life. This lad must have been at the beginning of his adult life . . . Eventually, she fell asleep.

Somebody must have looked after Robbie that night, because morning brought better news. Mary went out early, wrapped in a shawl and came back with a smile. 'Robbie's home, I saw his ma. He got back somehow and the boat's staved in, but they reckon they can mend it.' She went down to wake Daniel with the story and Helen heard a shout of triumph. Daniel would recover quickly now. Helen was surprised how happy she felt; after all, she had never known Robbie. But the whole household was lighter and even the guests in the dining-room were happier, brighter than before when they heard the news.

Mary's son appeared in the kitchen at mid-morning, clean, dressed and much less like the skinned rabbit of the night before. Seen in his gansey and trousers, Daniel Baker was slim and handsome, with a brown face, fair hair and bright blue eyes full of mischief, which he applied to Helen as soon as his breakfast was over. 'Now tell me, Miss Moore, where do you come from?' He was persuasive, as though he really wanted to know.

Helen picked up his empty plate and poured him another mug of tea. 'I'm Helen, usually.'

Should she call him Mr Daniel? 'My folks have a farm out Pocklington way. They sent me here for the summer.'

Daniel treated her to the full bore of the blue eyes. 'Now why did they do that?'

'I'm not sure. To get experience, I suppose.' The Moores had plenty of work for their two daughters in the dairy at home. 'For me to see how other folks live—and to learn housekeeping. Excuse me, Mr Daniel, I have to work.'

The lad laughed, a pleasant carefree sound from one who had been so close to death last night. He was wearing his bruises lightly. 'Nay, Dan's the name.' He suddenly leaned forward and tickled her under the chin. 'You're not a bad-looking lass, are you? Quite bonny when you smile.'

It was time to be firm. 'Now less of that, if you please. I take no nonsense from the farm lads at home and I'm taking none from you. Just behave yourself, young man. Stroke the cat instead.' Helen glared at him. Her parents had discouraged her from vanity and made her tie the dark curls back severely. She knew how to look severe.

'Sorry Miss Moore, I'm sure.' Another laugh and Dan picked up Kipper the cat and sat her on his knee. 'You're quite right, I should show more respect. We all have to get along somehow, don't we, Kipper?' The cat purred.

'Why do you call her Kipper?' Helen was curious in spite of herself.

'She was a little flat-sided stray when she came here, flat as a kipper, she was. You'd never think it now. But that orange tinge in her fur, that's still kipper-colour.' The lad seemed to be quite attached to the animal. *'She shall have a fishy in a little dishy, she shall have a fishy when the boat comes in,'* he sang to Kipper, who was unmoved. 'That's what the lads from up north sing. You'll have to watch out for the northern lads when herring boats are in, Miss Moore! They love a bonny lass. Well, I must be off. Got a job to do.' With a wink Dan set down the cat, pulled on his cap and went out. The kitchen seemed quiet without him.

Helen went upstairs to make the beds and dust the bedrooms, wondering what to do with the afternoon. 'You can have a half-day off on a Wednesday, lass,' Mary had said when she started. 'And Sundays we'll do as little as maybe, depending on how many guests are in. You might want to go to church.' At home there had been outings and holidays from time to time, but never a fixed afternoon off. First she would write up her diary, and then . . . perhaps go round the town and look at the shops, although she had no money. Living on a farm, you saw very few shops. Yesterday's storm had blown itself out and the day was fine, although the breeze was cold.

14

Of the seven guest-rooms at Seaview, only three were in use. When summer came there would be more folks about and much more work. Susie the maid had been in to do some of the work and Helen had met her briefly; she seemed to be about fourteen and quite cheerful. There was an older woman, Freda, who came in when things got busy, Mary said.

Having put the bedrooms to rights, Helen dusted down the wide staircase and went into the dining-room. In the large bay window James Kirby sat at a table with books and papers spread all around him. Mary was polishing the dining table. 'There you are, Helen. You can peel the potatoes for tonight; we'll have a bite to eat and then, as I said before, you can have the rest of the day off. I told your ma I'd treat you right and give you time off, but it might be different when the house is full. So make the most of it while you can.'

James Kirby looked at Helen, then back to Mary. 'Helen could come with me, if you think her mother would not object.' Then to Helen he said, 'This afternoon I'm taking a trip over to the cliffs yonder, just for an hour or two, for my research. It's only a few miles. You can come for the ride if you like . . . but of course you may have planned something else.' He was giving her the chance to refuse.

With Mary nodding and smiling approval it seemed harmless enough. 'Thank you, Mr

15

Kirby. I'd like to come.' This was so unlike the stories she had heard of girls in service: kept down, starved and even beaten. It would be fun to go out, unless Mr Kirby had Ulterior Motives. Helen knew to beware of these, but Mary would know if there was likely to be any danger in his company.

At home on the farm they had always eaten dinner at midday, a large meal with suet duff or Yorkshire puddings and hearty, filling stews. At Seaview things were different and the main meal was served in the evening, when the guests had come in. Lunch was a light meal; today Mary put oatcakes and cheese on the table, while Helen made a pot of tea.

'James is a very respectable young gentleman, you'll come to no harm with him,' Mary told her. 'He's here to write a book—that's why there are so many papers in the dining-room.'

'Doesn't he work?' Helen put down her teacup.

'Well, he has a business in York; he lives there, but stays here when he can. He wanted to be here in the spring this year for some reason. Now off you go. Dry the dishes and then you can have a wash, there's soot on your face. You can use one of the guest bathrooms at this time of day, it will save carrying water. Make sure you leave it tidy, though.' The two guest bathrooms were a great luxury, with hot and cold running water and even a water

16

closet. Staff had a water closet, but it was outside, across the yard. Helen had to carry up water to her attic when she wanted to wash.

'Mrs Baker—Mary, why are you so good to me? Most girls in service have a hard life, I've always thought.'

'Nay, lass, you've got to treat folks right these days, or they won't stay. It's maybe different on the farms but here in Brid—and all along the coast a smart young lass can get a job anywhere in summer. Besides,' and Mary looked suddenly cunning, 'I've got an arrangement with your ma. You're not exactly a maid, Helen. You're a sort of apprentice housekeeper and entitled to be treated like family.' She laughed shortly. 'I was glad you spoke sharply to young Dan, this morn—ay, I heard you both, right enough. Dan needs to be kept in his place, he does.'

'You know my mother?' This might partly explain why Helen had been sent to Seaview.

'Ay. Your ma and me, we go back a long way.' Mary smiled. 'I was in service with her, before I married Fred. Well before your time of course, and your ma was only young. But she never forgot me.'

That was like Mother; she never forgot anything, for better or worse.

TWO

Punctually at one o'clock a smart horse and trap rolled up to the front door. James Kirby was in the hall, a notebook sticking out of his pocket. 'Back by four at the latest,' he said briskly to Mary. 'Good day, John, we want to go to Bempton today, if you please.' The driver touched his cap and helped Helen up into the vehicle.

'I like to drive with John, he keeps up a good pace,' Mr Kirby explained as they bowled briskly along the esplanade towards the faraway arm of Flamborough Head. 'I like a good turn of speed.' He looked much younger than the man who drank tea by the fire at Seaview.

'So do I, but of course, if you go too fast you don't have time to see things.' Helen nodded. 'What sort of things are you looking for, sir? Mary said you are writing a book.' She smiled. 'I suppose I am too, in a way. I write a sort of journal, every day if I can. And put little drawings into it, there's usually more drawings than words . . .' she tailed off, conscious that she was chattering, and drew her shawl more closely round her.

James turned to look at her, his dark curly hair blowing in the breeze. 'Do you, now? Perhaps I could see it some time? That is, unless it's private, you know. Some young ladies would die rather than let anyone see their private journals!'

Did she want anyone else to see her thoughts and sketches? 'I—I'm not sure. But my book is full of small things, birds and wildflowers in the different seasons . . . and things like how to make really good blackberry jam. I don't know whether it would interest you, Mr Kirby.' No, a man like this wouldn't be interested in jam. A gentleman from York, especially one with a strong, square face would concentrate on the important things in life.

'Small things can be important, though. I carry a notebook with me everywhere I go, ready to write things down as I find them. A small book, some folks get uneasy if they see you writing down what they say.' Kirby pointed upwards. 'Look, Helen, here's a gannet. Big birds, aren't they? They would make a good drawing.' The bird's six-foot wingspan was impressive as it swooped over the trap, casting a black shadow, and Helen flinched. More followed, but the horse was obviously used to them and ignored the birds. It was a young, glossy horse with a lively trot, most unlike the bored and jaded animals that normally ambled round the town.

Helen was conscious that Kirby glanced once or twice at her as they went along. After a while he said thoughtfully, 'So what are you doing at Seaview, Helen?'

19

'Well, Mother thought it would do me good to get away from home, and that this would be good experience.' *And she wanted to get me away from a certain young man, but I'm not going to talk about that.* Helen shut her mouth firmly in case anything unwise escaped.

'And do you think it will?' Kirby looked at her again with his dark eyes. 'You will meet a great variety of people. Farming families often wrap up their daughters in cotton wool and they never leave home until they marry.'

Helen smiled. 'I somehow can't imagine being married. Can you?' There was something about travelling like this that seemed to allow the freedom to talk naturally.

There was a pause before Kirby said quietly, 'I was married . . . my wife died.'

'How—dreadful.' Helen spoke impulsively. What was the proper thing to say?

Suddenly she understood a little more about him. 'You came to Bridlington—to get away from York for a while.' It explained the sadness in his eyes.

'Exactly. That's just it, Helen—a complete change of scene.'

Helen thought for a while. 'Excuse me, Mr Kirby, but do you often talk to . . . servants, like this?' She was used to the independent life of a farmer's family, but had been ready to take her place meekly in the kitchen at Seaview and speak when she was spoken to. Why should a writer bother with her? It was a

20

puzzle.

'My book's about workers of all kinds, Helen. I find them rather more interesting than the . . . er, the leisured classes.' Kirby laughed. 'And it's pleasant to have company, you know. I'm glad Mary approved.'

'So that's it!' Helen beamed. 'You talk to everybody. It's easier for a man, of course,' she added wistfully.

The trap left the coast for a while, passed through a small village and then took a stony road almost to the edge of the Bempton cliffs; towers of chalk rising sheer from the sea on the north side of Flamborough Head. Helen hardly dared look down to where, far below, white-capped waves lapped the shore, looking tiny from where they were. They would be high seas to a fishing boat. The North Sea was a steely grey underneath scudding clouds. A fishing coble off the shore looked like a miniature, a toy boat with a tiny sail. The headland cut off their view of the bay. Down on the rocky beach there were caves, indentations in the chalky buttresses.

'Four hundred feet sheer drop,' said Mr Kirby cheerfully. 'This is the nesting time of course, and there are thousands of seabirds breeding here. Do you know your seabirds, Helen?'

'Er . . . some of them. The herring gulls of course; they are everywhere. And the little puffins with bright beaks; I like them best.

21

There're others of course, only I can't remember them. I'm a farm girl, Mr Kirby. I know our birds fairly well, of course.'

'Razorbills, guillemots . . . and kittiwakes, that's what we'll see. Come this way.' They got out of the trap and walked to a point on the cliffs where they could see the curving face below them. The noise was deafening, thousands of birds clamouring at once. Every ledge had its birds, wherever they could gain a foothold, but the air was never still. All the time birds were taking off, wheeling out to sea, returning, soaring over their heads and swooping to the rocks again. As they watched birds dived into the sea for fish, their wings folded back as they plummeted into the water. There was a pungent odour of fish and bird droppings. It must be much worse down there on the ledges. Poor little chicks, how did they survive in such a harsh nursery?

'This must be one of the biggest breeding grounds in England,' James called above the din. Helen nodded. She would record this scene in her journal. Flocks of gulls came inland to the farm, especially in the winter, wheeling in clouds above the plough. There they were graceful, like dancers in an intricate ballet. Helen loved to watch them. Here at Bempton they were raucously at home, busy with domestic squabbles, frantic to feed their offspring.

It was soon apparent that the birds were not

all they had come to see. A few hundred yards along the cliff was a small knot of men, fishermen by the look of them. Two men were hauling on a contraption with a rope which disappeared over the side of the cliff. In a few minutes, a head appeared. They were pulling another man up from the drop, a figure splashed with white bird-droppings.

'Has there been an accident?' Helen asked, nervous at the thought.

'No . . . not yet, anyhow. These men are called cimmers,' James said briefly. 'Probably a dialect form of climbers.'

'Whatever are they doing?' They looked intent, but too cheerful to be taking part in a rescue.

'It's a risky job. They collect the seabirds' eggs, you see, just for a couple of weeks in the spring.' The man gradually clambered up and onto the turf, puffing a little. Two large canvas bags attached to his harness were full of eggs. Very carefully he took off the harness and lowered the bags gently to the ground.

It was a strange new world to a girl from a farm. Helen was used to discomfort and she knew there could be danger in a frisky bull, or a carthorse's hoofs. But to put yourself deliberately over a drop like this was . . . well, it was daft. Were the eggs worth it?

It was the next cimmer's turn to go over. With a gasp, Helen realized that she recognized the man. It was Dan, Mary's son, in

23

his close-fitting blue gansey and a rather large hat. As they strapped him into the harness he saw Helen and grinned at her. 'Don't tell my ma!' Then he was over the side, abseiling down the sheer chalkface confidently. Helen hardly dared to watch as Dan kicked himself off from an overhang and somehow found a foothold on a ledge below. Small stones sprayed out beneath him as he landed.

It was clear that these young men thrived on danger. They were showing off to each other and to whoever stood by to watch them. Helen was the only woman on the cliff top; perhaps the wives and sweethearts of these men were too afraid to watch. Or perhaps they didn't want to encourage the showing-off, the daredevil spirit.

Dan was risking his life again, after nearly losing it last night. Helen could imagine his rope breaking, sending the slim body falling, tumbling down the rocks, his laughing, handsome face smashed, gone for ever; just for a few eggs. 'It's terrifying. I don't want to see him killed! Did you know Dan would be here?' Helen shuddered.

'Of course, it was Dan who told me they were collecting today. Naturally Mary would be horrified if she knew about this,' Kirby said quietly. He looked over the edge. 'Especially that!' Dan was swinging in an arc, grabbing eggs from far to the left and the right of him. The angry birds flew round him in a cloud.

From time to time he gave a hand signal and the men at the top let out the rope a little for him to drop to a lower ledge.

'What if the winch slips and lets him go? I can't watch!' Shaking, Helen turned her back on the cliffs and the restless sea. She would try not to think about Dan, down there among the birds. Nothing he did was safe, it seemed.

In the normal world, a pale sun had come out from behind the clouds and the short turf had the green tinge of spring. Not far inland a skylark spiralled, singing its heart out as it rose higher and higher. A few bees hovered in the gorse bushes. It was a safe, peaceful scene, just like home. At home there would be lambs playing in the fields and her father would be riding round the farm, checking on the growth of the corn. Helen walked for a few yards inland, away from the treacherous cliffs. Vivid red campions grew in the short grass and in the tangle of bushes beyond there was a clamour of nesting birds, small inland birds rejoicing in the spring. For a moment she felt intensely homesick. How could she spend the glorious summer months in a boarding house? How could she work in a hot kitchen instead of being outside with the spiralling larks, out in the pastures and the hay meadows in the sunshine? What had her mother been thinking of? The lark's song held an aching sadness.

In her heart Helen knew why she was there, far from home and it was not just the problem of falling in love with Charlie. Little had been said, but last winter her father had been ill with pneumonia. It frequently killed farmers in the cold northern winters and the doctors were powerless to stop it. David Moore had survived, but they all knew that if he died or was unable to work they would lose the rented farm. His lordship, the owner of the estate, did not accept women tenants. That was the reason why the Moores thought that Helen needed to learn to be a housekeeper; to be able to obtain respectable employment if the worst came to the worst. If all went well, she would marry a prosperous farmer and the housekeeping experience would be useful there, too.

There was a cheer from the group of men and Helen turned as someone came up behind her. Dan was back, up from the brink and the silly lad was laughing. 'Would you like some eggs, Miss Moore?' Dan's face was scratched and he had bird droppings on his shoulders. The cap was removed politely and she could see that inside it he carried a tightly rolled pair of socks. 'Those guillemots kick the eggs off the ledge sometimes when we go down and you can get hit by a falling egg—they're very hard,' he explained. 'Or falling rock, of course. So I pad out the cap. Have some gulls' eggs, lass.'

Helen would have liked some of the bright-blue eggs, but she saw a snag. 'How can I take them back to Seaview? Your mother would guess you'd been risking your life again. Why do you do it, Daniel?' She was still feeling shaky.

James was laughing now. 'Because men must work and women must weep, as the poet said. And I think he loves taking risks.'

'Go on, Helen. Ma needn't know I've been here. She likes gulls' eggs.' The blue eyes twinkled and Helen found herself smiling at Dan. 'Dealers only want kittiwake and guillemot eggs. So we keep gulls' for home, they make good pancakes.'

Eventually Kirby took a few, although Helen couldn't work out how he would get them home. 'Look, a razorbill's egg.' He showed it to Helen, an elongated shape with a pointed end. 'They probably roll around the ledge, rather than falling off.'

Kirby went over to speak to another 'cimmer', who grinned at him. 'Fancy a dangle on a rope?' the man asked jovially.

To the man's surprise, James agreed. 'Why not?' He gave his notebook to Helen, took an ancient cap from his pocket and jammed it on his head. The other men helped him into the harness. 'Give me a basket, there's a good chap.' Then he was off over the side, looking quite at ease.

The men on the ropes looked at each other. 'First time I've seen a visitor go over,' one said. 'Never thought he'd have a go, or I wouldn't have offered.'

'Let's hope he doesn't panic or we're done for.' The second man looked grim.

Helen herself was near to panic, for the second time that day. What if they lost Mr Kirby? She walked away from the edge, not daring to look down. Didn't he realize the danger—or was he incredibly brave? It must take a lot of courage to launch into space, but Kirby had no need to take risks and he wouldn't have the fishermen's experience of hard physical effort.

There was a sudden flurry and the rope flew out; the winch must have slipped for a moment or two. Several men ran to it and hauled on the rope, but James would have been violently decanted down, bumping on the ledges. Helen shuddered. In seconds the winch had been secured, but the damage was done. The lads on the rope continued to look worried and Helen found she was holding her breath. Dan hailed Kirby from the top and was obviously relieved when there was an answering shout. He was still conscious.

'Should never have let him go down,' an older man grumbled. 'Will get us a bad name, for sure, if we . . . lose him.'

If we lose him! They were preparing for the worst. Helen's imagination began to race and she wondered whether this was Kirby's way of letting go of life, a meaningless life after the loss of his wife. But to do such a thing was surely selfish? What about Dan and the others, who would be blamed for his death? Her hands were clenched tightly round his notebook, willing him to survive, to come back to them with his dark eyes and quiet smile. But perhaps she would never talk to him again . . .

Quite soon, they hauled him up again. Helen's imagination retreated and reality took over. The cimmers cheered him as a hero as his head appeared. Kirby was smiling, but bruised from the sudden fall; he had a respectable haul of eggs, though some were broken. Helen watched as the sound eggs were carefully carried over to where several donkeys waited with wicker panniers, into which they were stowed.

'How did you do it?' He was far more heroic than she had given him credit for. Helen loved heroes and James Kirby she had hitherto classified as unheroic, for sitting by the fire in slippers. But there was obviously more to him than met the eye. She must guard against her susceptibility to handsome men, her lack of control over emotion.

Kirby laughed as he shed the harness and wiped off the bird lime. 'I've been climbing in Switzerland, so I'm quite used to ropes. I've always wanted to try this.'

With the sun the day had changed and the sea was now a sparkling blue. The men sat in a circle and invited the visitors to join them. 'Bait time,' they said. Delighted, Kirkby sat at ease on the grass and after some hesitation Helen did the same, glad to sit down after her fright, enjoying the warm sun on her face. She felt as though she had dangled on a rope herself.

The men each took an egg, cracked it and swallowed the contents whole. Then they offered eggs to Kirby and Helen. Should she try it? Helen looked at Kirby, who smiled at her. 'Very nutritious, you know.' Heroic again! He cracked his egg expertly in one hand, tipped his head back and swallowed it. She had never eaten a raw egg, but after a moment Helen followed his example. The cimmers smiled approvingly and offered them another egg. Some of the men lit pipes and leaned back on an elbow, relaxing after the tension.

The eggs tasted fishy, rather like those of hens fed on fish meal. One of the young men came to sit beside Helen. 'Dan won't introduce me, so I'll do it myself. How do you do, Miss Moore?' He was obviously trying to be polite. 'I'm Tom Fletcher. I'm in the fishing trade, like. And you're a maid at Seaview, then?'

Helen wriggled uncomfortably. 'Sort of, Tom. So—do you enjoy egg collecting?'

The lad grinned and ran his hands through crinkly hair. 'It's nice when it's over, lass, between you and me. But we do make a bob or two and that's always welcome.'

He looked sideways at Helen. 'I'd ask you to walk out one evening, but I don't think Mrs

Baker would like it. What do you think?'

Tom had spoken quietly, but he was overheard. 'Settle down, lad. Seaview's always busy in the evenings.' Dan leaned over and grinned at Helen. 'And I can't be having competition, now can I?'

'Mrs Baker has warned me against the lot of you,' Helen said severely, standing up to look out to sea.

As they trotted swiftly back to Bridlington, Helen moved restlessly on the bench. 'We could have walked here easily,' she said. 'I was used to walking a lot at home.'

'Of course we could. Perhaps you'd like to walk to Dane's Dyke with me one day?' James was smiling. 'If Miss Moore can get permission for another outing with James Kirby.'

'I might get permission if it's my half-day off. I'm a worker, sir, remember!' Helen had almost forgotten her kitchen duties in the excitement of the afternoon.

Kirby chuckled. 'It's workers I'm interested in, as I said. My book, Helen, is about the working lives of people on the coast. How they earn a living, all about their skills. Fishing is a skilled job, but on land it's not really appreciated. So most of the men can only work as labourers if they leave the sea. They have a hard life, you know. Those lads today—it's not just devilry. They need the money. Some of the eggs are sent by train to Hull or Leeds and they're used for all kinds of things. Did you

31

know that the patent-leather process uses eggs to get the shiny finish? There are egg collectors that buy them, too. And some of the lads sell them round the villages, Dan says.'

Dan might need the money to repair his boat. 'What about the birds, though? They might die out in time, if too many eggs are taken.'

'They leave enough, every year. In fact Dan tells me that if the cimmers were to stop raiding the nests there would be too many gulls. He reckons it's good that they keep the numbers down a bit.' They jogged on for a while, then Kirby said, 'There's a man at Whitby, Frank Sutcliffe. He takes marvellous photographs of the working folk, the harbours and the boats. But I want to get behind the pictures, to the life that goes on in those old cottages and in the little boats. I want to know how the people live.' It seemed that he was talking to her as an equal.

Helen was dubious. 'But won't they hate being questioned? A photograph is one thing, but to tell your life story to a stranger . . . well, some older men might like to tell you a tale, but I doubt whether the women would want to talk to you.'

'You're probably right, and I have thought of that. I've started with the old lads in the harbour, talking about the good old days.'

There was a lot to record in the diary, Helen was thinking as they got back to

Seaview. Those big pear-shaped eggs with the blotches were like nothing she had seen before, but her mind was still full of the danger, the enjoyment of risk that had shocked her at Bempton. What must it be like to hang in space, with the rock face zooming to meet you and the waves crashing on the beach so far below? In her mind's eye she sketched the man on the end of the rope, hanging over the enormous drop. She would try that sketch later.

The clock in the hall was chiming four as she went up the Seaview steps, but Helen could hardly hear it above the din. The hall was full of suitcases and two small children were shrieking as they ran up and down the stairs. The boy trailed a stick along the banisters and the girl bounced from step to step. The quiet boarding house was in uproar.

James vanished into the dining-room before Helen could thank him for the outing, merely grinning ruefully and closing the door firmly behind him. Mary came out of the kitchen looking grimmer than usual, wiping her hands on her apron. 'Visitors,' she said, with a world of meaning in the word. 'You'd best get changed and come to help me, Helen. Do you like children?'

The little girl bounced again with a shriek from the second step, launched herself outwards and knocked Helen down.

'I thought I did!' Helen panted, breathless.

'But now I'm not so sure!'

THREE

'But I thought they were due on Saturday?' This was evidently the end of Helen's afternoon off. She had thought that her summer at Seaview would be quiet, even a little boring, but it seemed that she had been wrong.

'So did I, but here they are and they need their rooms.' Mary went back to the kitchen and Helen ran upstairs to change. She was caught on her return by a large woman in a purple dress.

'Why are our rooms not ready?' she shrilled at Helen, as the only staff in sight. 'I demand to be shown to my room immediately! I have travelled from Leeds and I need to rest. Lancelot! Carlotta! Stop that noise at once!' Her words had no effect on the children, who merely changed their noise to a wail as soon as they saw her.

'Wanna go to the sea! Wanna go NOW!'

Helen tried to steady her nerves; she had fondly imagined that she liked children, until now. These brats were going to be hard to like. 'Yes, madam. We understood that you would be arriving on Saturday,' she said in what she hoped was a housekeeper's firm tone. 'We will do our best for you as soon as possible. Perhaps you would like to take the children for a walk until the rooms are ready?' The noise of the seabird colony had hardly been more raucous than the sounds made by two little children in a confined space. If only their mother would take them away.

'This is very poor service indeed. We were never treated so badly at Scarborough. I told Mr Ponsonby that we should go to Scarborough. Did I not, George?' A submissive-looking head of the family had now appeared, hiding, behind his beard, a defeated expression.

'Yes, dear.' If only they had gone to Scarborough, but no doubt it was more expensive than Bridlington. And Bridlington was supposed to be rather quieter, more genteel; at least it had been until the Ponsonby family erupted on to the scene. 'I will take the children out for a while,' he added with a faint smile at Helen. And the poor man wandered off with Lancelot in his sailor suit and Carlotta in her satin frills, both arguing furiously.

As Helen was arranging the table for dinner James got up from his writing-table, looking rather worried. 'How long are they staying, Helen? I do hope those children settle down. For yours and Mary's sake, as well as the rest of us. It was bedlam in here until they went out.' He ran a hand through his black hair. 'I'm trying to write up this afternoon's experience.'

'The Ponsonbys were booked in for a week, starting on Saturday, sir. But Mrs Ponsonby is not happy with the service here, so they may not stay.' Helen demurely set out the cruet.

'The service here is wonderful!' James said warmly. 'But I'm sure they will stay, moaners always do. Do you think Mary would let me eat in the kitchen? No? No, I don't, either. Oh Lord!' Kirby ran his fingers through his hair again.

Helen arranged the dining-chairs. As she left the room she looked back at the poor writer, his peace shattered. His hair was standing up on end where his hands had run through it. 'Thank you for the trip this afternoon, Mr Kirby. It was amazing . . so many birds! I shall never forget it. And the men hanging like spiders . . .' she shuddered. 'That was enough to give you bad dreams.'

'I hope not! Be sure to try some sketches, Helen. I think Mary was pleased with her eggs.' James seemed to be pleased with his expedition and his eyes looked a little less tragic, but just as appealing as he smiled at Helen.

Things seemed slightly tense even in the kitchen. A large leg of mutton was roasting in the oven, spiked and fragrant with rosemary. The roast potatoes were browning and the pies were perfect, but Mary was not happy. 'Stir that soup, lass, look sharp. You'll have to move a bit faster with all them folks to serve.' It was far from her usual calm temper, but there had been provocation. 'And take a cup of tea up to Mrs Ponsonby or there'll be more trouble.'

Dan came in from the back yard, cleaned of bird-droppings and with a big smile for his mother. 'Brought you a load of driftwood for the fire, Ma. I spent the day well.' The devious lad was accounting for his time without mentioning the egg-collecting, which was just as well. He winked at Helen as one conspirator to another, but she turned away.

'Good lad.' Mary's face softened a little as she looked at him. 'Lord knows we're going to need it, with all these meals to cook. You can have your dinner later, Daniel. We have to feed the guests first.'

Helen had changed back into her black dress and white cap. She felt like a model domestic and she carried the tea upstairs without mishap, but she did not find favour with the new guest. The lady was sitting at a small table in the window. You would think that the glorious view over the bay would have impressed her, but Mrs Ponsonby was glaring at the tea tray. 'I would have preferred the tea in a silver pot, with milk in a silver jug, not china. It is what I expect. And with a biscuit. Cream when I take coffee, of course.' Mrs Ponsonby sniffed. The service here is far inferior to Scarborough, as I mentioned before.' She sipped the despised cup of tea delicately.

'I will inform the kitchen, madam,' Helen said loftily as though they had a vast establishment. This woman would need firm handling. 'Will there be anything—' The sentence stopped abruptly as the children barged into the room, yelling.

'We saw a boat! Mama, Lancelot pulled my hair!' Carlotta was very much the worse for her walk. Her ringlets had dropped out of curl and the satin dress hung limply round her chubby frame, dark with seawater and sand.

Lancelot stood dripping on to the carpet and smirking. 'Carlotta is a stupid girl.' His collar was torn.

The doting mother closed her eyes. 'George, take them away immediately. At least there is a bathroom. They will need to be bathed before dinner.'

Mr Ponsonby's pale eyes met Helen's pathetically. 'I suppose you wouldn't be able to look after the children for us? But of course, I would need to ask Mrs Baker.' He disappeared.

'I believe that I will be required in the kitchen this evening,' Helen said as smoothly as she could, backing out of the room. She expected that Mary would think so too, but to her dismay her employer was siding with George when she got back to the kitchen. She evidently felt sorry for the poor downtrodden husband.

'Of course, Mr Ponsonby. Helen can bathe the bairns and give them supper in the sitting-room, while the guests have dinner. And then she can put them to bed.' Mary nodded firmly at Helen. George looked most relieved and went upstairs to give the good news to his wife.

'But . . . Mary!' This was appalling. 'You will need my help here, with the meal to serve!'

'Nay, Susie's here. She and me have done this many a time, never fear.' Susie, who was only five feet tall, looked across the table and smiled proudly. For all her youth she did seem to be a useful little person. 'You told me you're the eldest of three, you've looked after bairns afore, so don't make a fuss. It will be better for the other guests.' Mary had made up her mind.

As Helen went wearily upstairs Carlotta was screaming again, her face purple. How could they get through the evening? She was about to fail her first test as Mary's assistant. Mary had said it was no bed of roses; it had seemed at first that all the guests would be like Mr Kirby and the quiet Miss Burton, but there was no safe haven at Seaview.

'Lancelot, please sit here and read this book while Carlotta has her bath.' The assertive tone of voice would have quelled Helen's younger brother and sister when they were small, but it had no effect on Lancelot. It was a pity that there were no suitable children's books at Seaview; she had given him an old copy of the *Leisure Hour* magazine.

'Shan't. I want to play with the cat.' The small mouth was set in obstinate lines.

Helen sighed. The cat did not want to play with Lancelot and it had taken refuge in the kitchen. 'How old are you, Lancelot?'

'I'm seven and Carly's five. But what's it got to do with you?' demanded the little darling. 'Are you our new nursemaid?'

'I do hope not.' Helen smiled back. 'But why do you not have a nursemaid with you?' Your parents obviously can't cope, she added to herself, adjusting the set of her cap, and I'm not sure that I can.

'They don't stay long. Mama says they're un—ungrateful girls.' A loud splashing was heard from the bathroom and Helen hurried off to find Carlotta bouncing in the bath of water, fully clothed. It was going to be difficult to watch two of them at once. Her heart went out to the succession of nursemaids to the Ponsonby children. No wonder they didn't stay long in that household. No wage would compensate for the permanent loss of your reason.

Somehow, by means of guile and fast talking Helen managed to get the children clean and into their nightclothes. She took them to the sitting-room. A bright fire was burning and Lancelot immediately attacked it with the poker. 'Don't do that!' Helen said automatically. 'Sit still for a few minutes and you shall have your supper.'

'We want pirate food, we're pirates. And some rum, pirates have rum, don't they?' Lancelot's imagination was running away with him.

'Pirates eat whatever they can get, they have *big* appetites,' Helen said hopefully.

'I'm hungry,' Carlotta whined. 'What's for supper?'

'It's a surprise, I'll go and fetch it from the kitchen.' It would be a surprise to Helen too. She had no idea what Mary would give the children for supper, but it wouldn't be the roast meat. 'It's a waste to give bairns the same food as adults,' she had told Helen. 'They leave half of it and it's only fit for the pig.'

The kitchen was a haven of peace after the bathroom, even though it was busy and quite hot. Kipper the cat was lurking under the table, Susie was preparing the children's supper and Mary was carrying the roast into the dining-room. Wonder of wonders, young Daniel was up to his elbows in hot water in the sink, washing the soup dishes from the first course. He caught Helen's look of surprise and grinned. 'Keep everything shipshape, that's what we say.'

'I'm glad that Mary has extra help,' Helen said gravely, trying not to laugh at the sight of a tough fisherman doing housework. 'Do you often work in the kitchen?'

'I can help anywhere I'm needed. Working on boats teaches you to be quick and tidy and

41

to turn your hand to anything. When we go out on bigger boats I sometimes have to cook as well. I'm not ashamed of it, you know!' He turned his blue eyes on to her. 'How are you getting on with those bairns?' Helen shook her head and then brightened as an idea came to her, but as she opened her mouth Dan waved her away with a wet arm. 'No no, I draw the line at helping with children. I'll tackle anything except bairns.'

Susie was beaming again across the table; she always seemed to look happy and that must be an asset for a boarding house. 'Helen, I made little fishes for them, fish cakes.' The patties were in the shape of a fish, with peas for eyes and strips of carrot for fins and tails. 'Most bairns love them.'

Carrying the tray into the sitting-room Helen had her doubts, and the children were true to form. 'That's stupid!' Lancelot declared after one look at the fish cakes and Carlotta echoed him.

'Stoopid!' She turned her back on the table, angelic in her little white nightdress, apart from the petulant expression. 'Don't want any.'

'Don't eat peas,' was the boy's contribution.

'But of course, you are not to eat these. Please don't touch them. They are for some other, good children,' Helen told them sternly. 'You won't get any supper, Mrs Baker says. You made too much noise. That's the surprise.'

After digesting this information for a few moments the children eyed the table. 'Ha, we'll eat them first. The other children can go hungry,' Carlotta said with satisfaction and took up her fork. Soon the fish cakes were demolished, although Lancelot spat out the peas and they were squashed into the carpet.

'Good lass,' said Mary when Helen reported back to the kitchen that the children had eaten supper and were in bed. The food had slowed them down and it had not been too hard to get them settled. They had taken a bowl of walnuts and a nutcracker from the table in case they felt hungry in the night, but if it kept them quiet Helen was not going to argue. 'Take coffee into the dining-room, will you, and then you can tidy up the sitting-room after the bairns, before guests go in.'

The coffee was fragrant as Helen carried it in and she realized that she had not eaten or drunk anything since lunchtime except for a raw egg on the cliff top. In the dining-room smiling faces greeted her. Mr Kirby and Mr Ponsonby were deep in talk about business and the salesman was being fascinated by Mrs Ponsonby with an account of the glories of Scarborough.

The schoolteacher, Miss Burton, excused herself and took her coffee upstairs. On the first step she turned as Helen came out of the dining-room. 'Well done, Helen. Those children were over-excited and I was so glad you took them away.' Miss Burton would be going home on Friday after school; she would not have to endure life at Seaview again until Monday night. Lucky Miss Burton, although as a schoolteacher she must have had to deal with other children who were 'over-excited.' But at least she would have some authority over them.

Back in the kitchen, Helen felt suddenly tired. 'May I have a cup of tea and a bite of bread and butter?' she asked Mary.

'I thought you'd be fair clemmed by now. I saved you a plate of dinner yonder,' Mary said comfortably. Everything had gone to plan and the meal had evidently been a success; the mistress of Seaview was calm again.

The next morning the children were up early. They dressed themselves and were very quiet for a while. Kipper the cat was unwise enough to stalk through the house and she was seized and pulled into the broom cupboard with Lancelot and Carlotta.

Helen was busy lighting the fires and was unaware of the children until there was a crash and a howl from a cat in terror, followed by a sound like galloping horses. Kipper was careering wildly down the hall, her paws stuck in walnut shells, tapping on the floor tiles, slipping and sliding, vocalizing as only a cat can when she is seriously upset. The children chased her, shrieking encouragement. She headed for the kitchen, dodging round table

44

and chair legs, mewing loudly all the time. Mary dropped the teapot.

It was difficult to catch a hysterical cat, but in the end Dan cornered her and rescued Kipper from the walnut shells, getting scratched in the process. 'All in the morning's work,' he said ironically to Helen. 'Can't you control your bairns?' He stroked the trembling cat, trying to calm her.

'They are not my bairns, thank goodness,' Helen told him crossly, then realized that he was trying to provoke a reaction. 'One thing I've learned: never let children have walnuts. You might remember that when you grow up.' He laughed and made a face at her.

Mrs Ponsonby came downstairs in lurid lime green and cooed, 'Clever Lancelot! However did you think of it?'

'I did,' boasted Carlotta.

'No you didn't, stupid! I did!' Lancelot gave his sister a thump and she howled.

'Breakfast time, I think. Come this way.' Helen led them into the dining-room.

*   *   *

'Mr Watson's going out, you can clean his room,' Helen was told as Mary read the morning's post. 'You never know when it will be wanted again.'

Mr Watson the salesman gave Helen a tip as he left. 'Good luck with those youngsters, they're a right handful,' he said. He was still laughing about the cat.

'Thank you, Mr Watson. It's only for a week or so.' Helen was trying to convince herself as much as anything. She decided to save any tips in case she got the chance to go shopping. Trying to avoid the Ponsonbys, she stripped the bed in the salesman's room and opened the window to let in the fresh sea breeze.

Mary brought in bed linen. As she went out Mrs Ponsonby caught her on the landing. 'There you are, Mrs Baker. I assume you will allow your maid to take charge of my children today? Their father has business in the town and I really am in need of a rest. My poor nerves are quite shattered.'

Helen froze, waiting for Mary's reply. They all had shattered nerves, especially poor Kipper. A whole day with those two would be a very long day indeed. The children were always busy; Lancelot had discovered the piano in the sitting-room and was busy bashing the keys, while Carlotta had taken a pair of scissors to the carpet.

'Certainly not this morning, madam. We have work to do. Later in the day, about three, Helen may be free to take the bairns for a short while.' Mary did not wait to listen to the reply, but stumped off back to the kitchen. A few minutes later James smiled at Helen as he slid out of the door on an errand of his own. Obviously his heroism did not extend to children like these, but the smile was sympathetic and it made Helen feel a little less anxious.

All hands breathed a sigh of relief when Mrs Ponsonby bowed to the inevitable and sailed forth under a parasol with the children trailing unwillingly behind, arguing furiously about where they wanted to go. 'I want ice cream!' wailed Carlotta, although they had only just finished breakfast.

'Best I could do,' Mary commented. 'Helen can clean the rest of the rooms, Susie'll scrub the kitchen.'

Dan laughed at Helen as he went out. 'That was a lucky escape for you, lass. Did you tell the lady that tide's coming in?'

The day was warm and bright and Helen enjoyed her work. At mid-morning the women were having a cup of tea in the kitchen when there was a rap at the back door. 'Veggies, Mrs Baker!'

Mary went to the door. 'Come in Ruth, and have a cup.'

A young girl staggered in under the weight of a big box and lowered it with difficulty to the floor. 'There's taties and carrots, and a few leaves of spinach. But turnips are done . . . and beans aren't ready yet. Sorry, Mrs Baker.' She looked round the room. 'Is—is Daniel safe? I saw his boat, all smashed . . .'

'Daniel's come out of it better than I expected.' Mary poured a cup of tea from the big teapot and the girl sank gratefully into a chair. 'Nowt but a few bruises.' She looked at the box of vegetables. 'I suppose you won't have any salad stuff?'

Ruth coughed nervously and Helen wondered whether she was fond of the lad. The girl was painfully thin, with jutting cheekbones in a pale face surrounded by blonde hair. 'I can bring some lettuce round later, if you like.' She gulped the tea and then stood up. 'Must be off, got more calls to make and donkey's waiting. He doesn't like to be left standing too long.'

'Can I see your donkey? I love donkeys.' Helen picked up half a carrot from the sink and went out with Ruth to where the donkey stood in the lane outside.

'He's called Moses.' Ruth stroked his nose and looked shyly at Helen. 'He belongs to Mr Johnson the greengrocer. I work for him, but I pretend that Moses belongs to me.' The creature nuzzled her as if he agreed, then took the carrot daintily from Helen.

Ruth seemed so young, and so thin. 'How old are you, Ruth? If you don't mind my asking. I'm eighteen,' Helen offered, not wanting to offend the lass.

'Sixteen, but folks think I'm younger. Better go, there's a lot of calls to make.' The donkey had panniers on either side, loaded with vegetables; they looked a vulnerable pair as they trudged off down the street.

Mary Baker sighed when the girl had gone. 'She has a bad look, that one. Now Susie, you can put this stuff away.'

Some time later Helen was sweeping the hall and picking up stray walnut shells when the front door crashed open and Carlotta ran in, sobbing. She was closely followed by her mother in a great state of agitation. 'You must help us! Lancelot will drown! He's on a rock and he can't get back! He *would* go further out, I begged him to come back, but you know what Lancelot is like. So brave and independent!'

Helen's first, unworthy thought was to leave the little fellow on his rock until the tide turned, but she suppressed it. Mrs Ponsonby grasped her arm with surprising strength and dragged her to the door, but there Helen dug her toes in. 'I must tell Mrs Baker where we're going . . . and I'll ask her to mind Carlotta.'

Mary was calm. 'He'll be up towards Flamborough from here, that's where the rocks are. Won't be far, I should think, just wade out and talk him into coming back with you, lass. It'll be safe enough.' She had evidently seen visitors in trouble on the rocks before. 'You can do it, Helen?'

'Of course.' Helen ran out to join the boy's mother. The sea was a sparkling deep blue and there were little sails at intervals across the bay where the cobles were out; the fishermen were probably baiting their lobster pots. There were as yet few visitors in the town, but one or two figures in straw hats could be seen in the distance, strolling down towards the harbour. It was a peaceful scene with no hint of danger, but the tide was still racing in across the sand.

The family had walked a surprisingly long way from the boarding house, past the stretches of clean, smooth sand, up towards the rockier shore to the north of the town. 'He wanted to find fossils in the rocks,' Mrs Ponsonby sobbed. 'Mr Kirby told him where to find them.' There was nobody else at all on this stretch of beach and the houses had been left behind.

Lancelot was howling loudly, with no one to hear except the gulls wheeling above him and almost drowning his cries with their own laments. The group of rocks he was on seemed to be surrounded by shallow water.

'Don't worry—I'm coming!' Helen shouted to reassure him. She took off her shoes and stockings, tucked up her skirt and waded in. The sea was quite cold at first. She had to concentrate to avoid falling over submerged rocks and she took her eyes off the boy for a while.

There was another shriek from Mrs Ponsonby. Helen looked up to see that the tide had now covered Lancelot's rock and he was thrashing about in the water. 'Why can't they stay on the sands, why come up here?' she asked the seabirds savagely. She was now waist deep in water.

The main thing was to keep Lancelot calm. When she reached him Helen tried to laugh. 'This is a new game! Shall we try to get back now, if you've had enough?'

She grasped him and Lancelot clung to her so tightly that he nearly pulled her under the water. She put her arms round him and held him up. 'Look, you can float like this. Let's just float home, shall we?' Dry land seemed quite a long way off, when she looked back to where the anxious figure stood waiting. Why couldn't the woman have done this herself an hour ago, when the water was shallow? Some people had no sense at all.

The boy looked at Helen. 'Can we get home? We won't be drowned?'

'Don't be silly, pirates don't drown and you're a pirate, don't forget.' No, pirates usually hanged or died in a fight, according to the story books. 'Pirates are tough, they like being in the sea!' Helen wished she knew how much higher the water was likely to rise. She could swim a little, but to carry the boy back was going to be difficult if the water was too deep for wading. And if he panicked they could both drown. She looked round in despair. She had lost contact with the rock now that it had disappeared and she was floating, her feet no longer touching the sand, struggling to keep Lancelot's head above water.

51

What would Mother and Father think if they lost their elder daughter? The sea had no mercy. Helen was growing cold and she would soon be exhausted; her clothes were weighing her down. 'Keep your head up, Lancelot,' she said as firmly as she could. 'We're going to float back to the beach with the tide.' But the relentless sea was sucking them out again, out and into the cold waters of the bay. It might be the Bay of Safety for some, perhaps, but deep and dangerous for her; the shore was receding. Helen felt herself bumping against the rocks, but she had no control. 'Keep your head up, Lancelot,' she said again. 'Pirates always keep their heads high.' It would soon be over.

FOUR

The water was sucking them down, although Helen was resisting with all her strength. The tide and the waves seemed to be pulling different ways and Lancelot's rock was left behind. Although there were more rocks ahead, they looked jagged and dangerous. If only she hadn't rushed into this! Surely there would have been someone more experienced to rescue the lad? Surely someone would see them? Try to keep calm, the tide might turn soon. With an effort she raised her head once more and looked round. The wide bay seemed tranquil in the sunlight, deceptively serene.

One of the boats in the bay was a rowing boat with one man in it. Helen thought it might be drawing nearer. If only the boatman could see them. She shouted, but the oars kept up their steady rhythm. Was the man coming their way? Distances were hard to measure on the sea. Helen watched as the boat moved over the water. 'Yes, he's coming, Lancelot! The boat's coming for us!'

It seemed a very long time before the rowing boat pulled alongside and she heard it gently bump on a submerged rock. All the fishermen in their blue ganseys looked alike, but this one turned out to be Dan. 'Now, young feller! Nice pickle you're in!' He grinned cheerfully, as though he rescued people every day.

'Thank you, thank you, Daniel!' Her arms were aching and Helen knew she could not have held on to the boy much longer.

The young fisherman was unperturbed. 'Stand on this rock, Helen, it's right here beside the boat. Can you feel it? Right. Just hold boat while I get the lad in. There . . . now get in yourself . . . steady does it, don't rock the boat.' He turned to the shivering Lancelot. 'Before I take you home, lad, you've got to make a promise. One that you will keep for the rest of your life.'

'Yes, Mr Baker.' Lancelot's confidence had evaporated. He was shivering and looked so pathetic that it was almost possible to feel sorry for him, but Dan had no mercy. Helen sank down thankfully on the wooden seat; she had used the last of her strength.

'Say after me, "I solemnly swear that I will never be cruel to any animal again." If you don't, I'll leave you here.' Dan's voice had a savage note. 'You know what this is about, don't you? That poor cat. And others, I'll be bound.' He took up the oars again. 'You're the sort of horrible little brat who pulls the wings off butterflies.'

'I sol-solemnly swear. . . !' Lancelot quavered. 'No, I never touched a butterfly, Mr Baker.'

'Now I'd better get you both home before you catch your deaths of cold.' The breeze was blowing through Helen's wet dress and she too was trying to stop shivering. 'But you've a way to walk from the boat landing and that should warm you up.' Dan looked across at Helen as he rowed them briskly to shore. 'I can't think why somebody else didn't come to get him. Why did it have to be you, lass?'

'Well . . . his mother asked me; she probably thought I was local, used to the tides. There was no time to look for anybody else.'

'You did well, but come for me next time you go swimming.' The blue eyes glinted with mockery, the superiority of the young hero who had saved the day. Daniel was undoubtedly a hero. 'You look like a mermaid.

Very nice,' he added wickedly.

Helen glanced down in embarrassment and realized that the wet dress was clinging to her figure in a most immodest way. 'I suppose you meet mermaids quite often in your job?' His answer was a wink.

Mrs Ponsonby was effusive when her darling was returned to her, and for once she volunteered to look after him herself. She offered them a guinea each for the rescue and rather to Helen's surprise, Dan accepted for both of them. 'That'll buy staves to mend the coble. Thanks very much,' he said. 'We'll get back to sea the sooner.' Helen shook her head but Dan said quietly, 'You did more than me. You deserve it.'

She was, after all, a servant, so Helen said no more.

By the time that three o'clock came round, order was restored, the children were clean and dry and of course they were ready for the next adventure. 'Mrs Baker said you could take us out!'

Helen was firm. 'We will go for a walk on dry land, not on the beach.' She thought for a moment. 'We can go down to the harbour and look at the boats.'

Bridlington harbour was surrounded by stone walls; it was quite small and boats could only get in at high tide, which was now past. Several cobles with brown sails were tied up to the wall, their sides exposed as the water receded. One or two were damaged and Helen wondered which one belonged to Dan and his friends. There were also some bigger boats being repainted, presumably for the summer. Holding both children firmly by the hand, Helen walked slowly round to the quay where the fishing boats delivered their catch. Most had done so, but one coble was still unloading and there was Dan again, swinging baskets of fish up from the boat by winding a handle on a hoist. Lancelot looked the other way.

In a few minutes Dan joined them. 'Which is your boat, Mr Baker?' Carlotta asked politely and Helen nearly fell into the harbour with surprise. 'Is it the big one?'

Lancelot was still gazing steadily out to sea, but at this he turned.

'Mr Baker only has a little one, a rowing boat. I was in it this morning,' he added importantly.

Dan laughed at them both. 'Nay, I'd not get many fish in the rowing boat. I was putting out a few lobster pots. The big one belongs to my uncle Bob. See yon coble—the *Seabird*? That's ours, and we've been working on it. Dave's there now.' Dave heard his name and waved to them; Helen recognized the young man who had dragged Dan in from the sea. 'We got some planks right away with the money your ma gave us. *Seabird*'s clinker-built, the planks overlap. So you see, young feller, you getting caught by the tide turned out very well in the end. But don't go doing it again, lad.'

Helen looked at the coble, one of several being patched up after the storm. It had oars and a brown sail that was neatly tied up at the moment; there was just room for three men. 'But where do you sleep?' she asked. There was no cabin or decking.

'Well, we don't stay out above twelve hours or so, we come home to bed. But once we've shot the lines, one man can go to sleep on the sail if we're out at night.'

'But you said you were the cook? Not in this boat, I suppose.'

'On the herring they're the bigger boats, lass. We go for a few days at a time. That's later in the year. I'm just a hand then, of course. Can't afford to buy one o' those, not unless I rescue a whole school of youngsters!' Dan's smile was almost irresistible and the blue gansey was the same colour as his eyes. Helen had to remind herself that she was never going to fall in love again. Not for years, anyway. Her knees felt a little shaky, but that was probably with being in the sea for so long.

*　　*　　*

That night Helen wrote up the day in her journal with a sketch of the vegetable girl with the donkey, trudging down the street; there was an air of pathos about Ruth and somehow she managed to capture it in the downward curves, the bowed shoulders. She did a quick drawing of the sea rescue, with the gallant fisherman arriving in his boat. For the drawings Mr Kirby had given her some sheets of good drawing paper on condition that she showed him the results, so although Helen was tired she did her best. They were in soft pencil, so she could make corrections when needed.

Lancelot promises to be good, but we have no faith in his promises. Seaview will only settle down when that family leaves.

She added an account of their walk to the harbour.

The little fishing boats are beautiful in a way, nice curving lines when you see them out of the water. Dan says they are clinker-built. They look like pictures of Viking boats . . . perhaps he is a Viking? His eyes are very blue.

The following day Helen was approached by Mr Ponsonby as she cleared the breakfast table after everyone else had left the room. 'My dear, I have something important to ask you.' He coughed nervously and his pale eyes had a worried look. 'We were . . .wondering whether you would like to join our household, as nursemaid to the children. They seem to have taken to you, as a matter of fact. Oh yes, I know they can be difficult,' he waved his hand dismissively as Helen opened her mouth to decline the offer. 'We would give you a comfortable room, of course, and there would be some travel in the summer months.' He held out a hand persuasively. 'Excellent wages, too.'

'Thank you, Mr Ponsonby, but I'm not able to accept. I have just started work here for the summer, but it's only temporary and I will be going home to the farm at the end of the season —to my parents.' Thank goodness.

The children's father looked surprised. 'You don't look or speak like a farm girl. It's a pity, but at least you can help us with them while we are here in Bridlington. I will ask Mrs Baker for you.'

The traitorous Mrs Baker gave her consent for Helen to be appointed temporary nursemaid. Down in the kitchen Dan laughed at Helen's frown. 'Ma said it would be the best answer for everybody,' he said with a smirk. 'And you can do it, lass. You have a way with the little angels, haven't you?'

Fortunately the weather was fine for the next few days. Lancelot wanted to explore the beach and Carlotta had ambitious sandcastles in mind, but Helen managed to keep them both happy without actually drowning them. In one way she was glad of the assignment; it was so good to be out in the sunshine by the sparkling sea, barefoot on the sand with her skirt tucked up a little to keep it out of the water.

When Lancelot howled noisily to be taken to the lighthouse, Helen sat him down on a towel and sat beside him. 'It would be interesting, but it's too far to walk, Lancelot. You would be worn out before we got there and you're too big to carry. Now, what do you think we can do, if you really want to go there?'

Lancelot stopped howling and actually thought for a moment. 'We could ask Mr Baker to take us in his boat!'

'No!' Carlotta put in the veto. 'I'll be sick.' She made revolting noises. It was just as well because Dan would naturally not be available, having drawn the line at bairns except in an emergency. And it would be impossible to get up to the lighthouse from the sea in any case.

Lancelot was quiet for a whole two minutes before he spoke again. 'Well . . . I could ask Papa to get one of those horses with a carriage to take us there.'

'Good idea, Lancelot. It won't be today, but we can ask him tonight and he may be able to arrange it.'

Oddly enough they had a pleasant trip to the Flamborough lighthouse, with an old bored horse that hardly broke into a trot. They talked about the work of the lighthouse keeper and what an important job it was, and how every lighthouse had a different sequence of flashes, so you could tell where you were in a storm. 'It must be good to see the light, when you're out in the dark,' Lancelot volunteered. He was becoming almost human. Perhaps his fright had done him good.

Afterwards, Helen tried logic again. 'So you see, if you want to do something it's wise to ask politely, at the right time too! And to work out before you start whether what you want is possible. Some things are not possible, you know. That means they can't be done.'

Carlotta turned up her pretty nose. 'I don't care about possible,' she said.

Lancelot looked at her with pity. 'You're only five, you don't know anything. I'll have to tell you what's possible.' After that, everything they wanted to do was debated and put to the possibility test, which made for a much quieter life. Helen had the impression that the Ponsonbys had not explained very much to their children.

*　　　*　　　*

James Kirby strode along the road in the morning light, humming to himself. He had just said goodbye to the Ponsonby family and that was certainly a cause for rejoicing. Normally he enjoyed the ebb and flow of guests at Seaview, watching them come and go from his table in the window of the dining-room. But those children had been very trying,

61

although Helen had done her best. In fact there had been an improvement in their manners by the end of their stay. You had to admire the way Helen took on whatever task she was given.

'You should meet the herb woman, James,' Mary Baker had said. 'She would give you a story or two for your book.' As he was leaving she had added, 'If you do go to Ivy Cottage could you ask her for some cough medicine? That poor lass Ruth is in need; she's got bad lungs, I fear. And you could bring me some dried mint.' Mary had her own reasons for recommending the herb woman.

Seabirds swooped over the water and fishing boats dotted the bay; on such a morning it must be good to be out on that sparkling sea. James decided to ask one of the skippers to take him out on a fishing trip, to see at first hand how they worked.

He was walking south so far, looking down the curve of the bay where in the blue distance were the low-lying sands of Holderness. A road turned inland and Kirby followed it. The short turf of the seaside vegetation gave way gradually to shrubs and then trees, wherever there was shelter from the sea wind. Soon a line of hedges defined farmland and in the distance the green swell of the land rose to the skyline. Kirby was looking for a cottage on the outskirts of a village. Mary Baker had given him directions, but he saw no houses; there was nothing but a rioting mass of spring green. He went on, along a narrow lane between tall hedges white with may blossom. A woman with a large basket was gathering plants and he approached her. 'Good day, I'm looking for Ivy Cottage. Can you tell me where it is?'

The woman looked at him with inscrutable grey eyes in a deeply sunburned face. She had dark hair tied back in a long plait and she was tall, almost as tall as Kirby. 'And what would you want with Ivy Cottage?' The tone was not truculent, but it was very self-possessed. 'If you can't find Ivy Cottage for yourself, you won't be welcome there.' The woman went on with her task.

In spite of himself, Kirby felt vaguely uneasy. 'Perhaps it's very near?' Did it matter very much whether he found it or not? Only if he was ashamed to go back to Seaview empty-handed and admit that he had been lost. He looked round and saw what he had missed before. Behind the nearest hedge was a green mound of vegetation, nestling into a low green bank and surrounded on two sides by a garden. It was nearly invisible, but now he could just see the ivy-covered walls of a cottage, the outline of small windows and a roof covered with moss and lichen. 'I see what you mean, it certainly tests your powers of observation.' There was a silence.

Kirby moved a little nearer and looked carefully at the house; the idea of a dwelling

63

that blended with the earth was a good one. But was it practical? He glanced into the basket and saw that the woman had picked a variety of weeds, mainly nettles and sorrel; this was the herb woman he had come to see. 'Mary Baker sent me,' he said simply.

'You'd better come in.' There was a strange aura of power about the woman and he stepped across the threshold hesitantly. The cottage was dark, aromatic with the scent of herbs. Anything could be lurking in those dark corners. Kirby's head brushed against something soft and he flinched, but it was only a bunch of dried sage hanging from the rafters. 'Are the walls not very damp, all covered with ivy?' he asked, making an effort to be practical. It must be odd to live in a heap of vegetation, but it certainly looked picturesque.

'Nay, ivy takes all the water when it rains. Sucks it all up. It's very dry in here, needs to be, for drying the herbs.' The woman put down her basket and looked at him. 'What do you want of Ivy Cole? You're a writer.' She peered at him through the gloom. 'I suppose you've heard that I'm a witch.'

' "Fillet of a fenny snake in the cauldron boil and bake. . ." ' he said lightly but in spite of himself, James felt a slight cold shiver down his spine. He was not superstitious—was he?—but that was exactly the feeling he had in this house. There was an ancient mood here, but this was 1890, not the Middle Ages and James

Kirby was a modern man. However, Mary was right. Ivy Cole was potential book material, full of personality and no doubt with a history behind her. The cottage had an atmosphere you could almost touch. He could interview a so-called 'witch' for the book without losing credibility. But she was not a storybook character, a wrinkled crone; this was a vigorous woman in the prime of life. 'Please tell me what you do—how you do your witching. I've never interviewed a witch before. I thought they had all died out as science came in. Will you talk to me, Mrs Cole?' Kirby felt for his notebook.

'My name is Ivy,' the woman said slowly in her deep, musical voice.

'And yours, I think is . . . James Kirby. I suppose you've come about the book.' She took the weeds from the basket and swished them about in a bowl of water.

Was her name a coincidence, or did she cultivate ivy deliberately? 'Perhaps you are a witch, you seem to know a lot about me. But I have come on an errand. Mary Baker would like a bag of dried mint and also something for a young woman's cough.' Kirby felt in his pocket for some money, thinking that a business transaction might ease the conversation. How much would she charge?

'No need to pay, I'll see Mary.' The witch took down a jar of dried mint and shook some into a bag. Then she looked along her shelves

of jars and bottles, muttering. 'Cough, cough
. . . what shall I send? Nasturtium seeds . . .
none left. Horehound syrup, made last week
with fresh leaves, yes.' She put a bottle of dark-
looking liquid on the table. 'Will that be all,
young man? I have work to do and you have
seen the witch now, so you can go away and
put fear into your readers. Folks use my name
to frighten naughty bairns round here.'

Kirby looked round and yes, there was a
broomstick made of heather twigs in one dark
corner. Research was not always easy; she had
decided not to help him, but he would not be
dismissed just yet. 'What will you do with the
weeds you were picking just now? Nettle and
sorrel and . . . dandelion?'

The witch sighed. 'At least you know the
names of plants. You'd better sit down. I can
talk to you while I make the pudding.' Kirby
looked surprised. 'You've never heard of nettle
pudding? Sour dock pudding, to some. Best
thing for spring complaints. But you've never
gone short of greens in spring, I suppose.
Money can buy greens any time in the town.'
She sounded as though she lived a hundred
miles from Bridlington instead of three. It was
a different world up here, out of the sight of
the sea.

'Tell me more.' Kirby sat down at the table
and watched as Ivy chopped the washed greens
and put them in a bowl. She proceeded to slice
a small onion and added it to the bowl.

'Make yourself useful, pull that pan of water over the fire.' Ivy added a handful of rice and then salt, pepper and dried herbs and put the mixture into a muslin bag, which was lowered into the pan of water. 'There, a good mix; the sour dock gives it some bite.'

'You're saying that country people don't get enough vegetables?' Kirby was busily taking notes. He would ask Mary about the pudding.

The witch shook her head. 'The spring greens are slow to grow, up this way, and folks feel the lack. Like sailors on shipboard, you see, that get scurvy. There's no cabbages till June. There's plenty of greens growing wild, but folks are very wary. They reckon everybody will think they're starving if they eat weeds. So I make up this pudding—this and a boiled egg makes a grand dinner. The wives don't mind it and the men'll eat it if there's nothing else.' She laughed. 'I give the hens dried nettle as well, they lay the better for that and a few spells.'

Now that she had started the woman wanted to talk. Kirby settled into his chair; this was not magic spells, but it was worth recording and she seemed to expect to be consulted. 'The only wild green I've eaten is watercress. But don't nettle leaves sting the mouth? I noticed you didn't touch them when you made the pudding.'

The witch sat down opposite Kirby. 'The sting goes when they're boiled. I can give you pages of notes about how to use nettles. They used to treat the stems like flax and spin a yarn, to make sheets and such.'

'I am interested in people, their lives and work,' Kirby explained. 'Books are written about the rich and famous, but nobody notices the lives of ordinary folk. I look for the interest, the drama in that. So yes, I'd like to know more about a working witch.' He looked hard at her, but she was unperturbed. 'And of course, the fisherfolk. I would like a mixture of sea and country, of male and female workers. Traditional work, the sort that is disappearing as the twentieth century gets nearer.'

'I see,' she said drily. It was impossible to read the witch's expression.

'Herbs will disappear, no doubt, as the research goes on and the medical people use chemicals instead, it's started already. Then, too, I think that in a hundred years, most people will live in towns and work with machines. They will be out of touch with plants and the earth.' Kirby sat back in his chair to wait for her reaction.

'Cup of tea, Kirby?' The witch was thawing a little. 'I don't agree with you. Men will still have to catch fish and you can't make that into a town job, or an easy one. And farmers will still be needed to plough the land to grow food.' She moved a kettle over the other side of the fire to join the pudding, which was bubbling gently in the pan. The scent of herbs and onions was wafting into the room.

Kirby accepted the offer of tea and an oatcake. It was good practice for a researcher to eat and drink with people when they invited him to join them, but he was not sure what kind of a brew she would give him. Was it safe to drink tea with Ivy? Looking up into the dim recesses of the roof he saw that the cottage was of crock construction, built round stout timber beams made from two small tree trunks that gradually came together to meet in the middle of the roof. It must be centuries old. 'And so to witching, looking round I see no skulls or crystal balls. Do you tell fortunes? I think you are an herbalist, Ivy Cole—what a suitable name you have! But how did you become a witch?'

The woman looked over the table at him and her face seemed to change in the dim light. 'Do you really want to know?'

FIVE

The tea Ivy handed him was dark green and opaque, but it tasted quite pleasant. Kirby drank it and waited for her reply. This story would provide a contrast, even a note of mystery in his chronicle of working lives.

The woman looked at him with strange grey eyes. 'I don't set out to frighten folks, but it's

69

not hard to be named a witch. I live here in the ivy, with all the little birds nesting round me in spring and it seems unnatural to some. You'd be surprised how many little birds live in these walls, Kirby, flycatchers and finches and tits.' Her smile was loving. 'But that's not all. A few years ago Vicar stopped them decorating the pews with ivy in the church at Christmas. He said it was pagan.' Ivy threw another piece of driftwood on the fire. 'A few buildings round here have a Green Man carved somewhere in them, a face framed in ivy leaves that dates back to the old religion. Have you seen it?' She smiled again at the thought. 'Some still think that the Green Man has powers.'

'I'm an architect, Ivy. So yes, I do know about the symbol . . . it's been used by Christians as well as pagans, you know. There's even one in Bridlington Priory.' Kirby had the strange feeling that Ivy herself might date back to pagan times.

'And then, I don't go to church, you see. But even so, some of my cures actually work and that's a sign, of course. A pact with the Devil!' She had a clear, carefree laugh.

'So they think you can tame the birds and that you're a pagan. Not the first herbalist to be so labelled, I suppose.'

Ivy sat up in her chair. 'Aye. A lot of the fishermen are superstitious . . . did you know that?' She offered him more oatcake. 'And I'm a single woman, with no bairns. That counts against you. Lost my man when I was young, but folks round here don't remember.' She poured him more tea from the big earthenware pot.

'And worst of all, this cottage is by the Gypsey Race.' She paused and then went on, 'That's the stream you walked by. It's got an odd reputation.' Ivy stopped abruptly. 'This here tea is a mixture of mint and chamomile . . . I make all sorts of tea.'

'That's the stream that ends up in the harbour, isn't it? What's the problem with the Gypsey Race?'

'Well, it flows by those ancient pagan sites in the valley—you might try sage tea, it's supposed to be good for scholars.' Ivy took down another jar and shook out some grey powder. 'You can try this, if you like.'

'Thank you. Would you like to talk about your work? In more detail, I mean? I would like to hear of your cures—it must be good to be able to help people.' Kirby thought of the story he would write.

'Next time you come.' It was good that she expected to see him again. 'I'll bore you with it, how I pick herbs in summer and dry them, big bunches like those up there. I pick everything in season. Rub them into a powder. Autumn's the busiest time, saving things for the winter: elderberries, brambles, rose hips. And winter's a fell time for the folks at sea and the poor lasses on the rocks. It's hard, the

71

winter, folks need my remedies then.' Ivy got up and took his cup and plate.

'Do you ever . . . try a little witching, as it were? Magic? It could be tempting, given your reputation.'

The woman gave him a straight look. 'No mumbo jumbo . . . but I can sometimes tell folks things they didn't know about themselves. You can see what might happen; you can see where they're heading. Sometimes, a warning might do some good.'

'What do you think might happen to me?' Perhaps he should not have asked.

Ivy Cole looked at him carefully. 'Shall I prophesy? I think you are going to have a shock to your system. Pain, but then great gain. A new love, maybe, to take away the loneliness.'

Kirby was surprised. 'How do you know I am lonely?'

'You don't deny it; it's in your eyes, James Kirby. I study folks, you see, the way they are.' The witch paused and Kirby waited. 'Living here on my own, I likely have more time to think than folks in a cottage with five bairns and a man out in a boat. Thinking takes time, you'll know that. Writers must have to think. And'—she lowered her voice—'I can use the rods and the pendulum, I sometimes find things that are lost.' What did that mean? Ivy said no more but it was evidently important to her, the core of her craft.

As Kirby left, the witch offered a word of advice. 'You'd best find a handy lass to talk to the fisherwomen for you, for the book. The men might not take kindly to it if you go round asking questions while they're away at sea.'

'I will proceed with caution.' It would be uncomfortable to be assaulted by an angry fisherman. 'Maybe I should give you some advice, Ivy. Why don't you keep a cat?'

Kirby picked up the parcel for Mary.

The witch shook her head vigorously. 'Too obvious! And I like my birds about the place. A cat would hunt them.' She suddenly smiled at him. 'Why not write about your own work? You're an architect.'

How did she . . . of course, Kirby remembered he had told her that. 'I did write a book about the history of architecture, that's why I am interested in your cottage.'

On the walk back to Bridlington, Kirby realized that he had not thought of his own work for some time. He would need to go back to York soon, to check on progress. His firm of architects was quite capable of running itself for a while, but there was a big project coming up, a new hospital. Architecture and engineering had changed even in the few years since he had qualified, and last year had been an amazing one. A bridge over the Forth estuary had been opened and so had a dazzling new tower in Paris, and although it seemed to be less useful than the bridge, the Eiffel Tower was more spectacular.

Coming back into Bridlington Quay, it was hard to think of leaving. Kirby could have chosen to write a book about workers elsewhere, but this little town had the call of the unfamiliar, the sea and the fascinating life of the harbour. Down there were age old, traditional occupations that needed to be documented before it was too late.

Living in Bridlington had given him a change of scene, had done him good. It had taken him away from the empty house in York, the ache of memories and the thoughts of what might have been. He and Sarah had only been married for two years when she died of pneumonia, in a damp winter when freezing fog lapped the city for days on end. This was the third year since her death, but James Kirby still wondered whether she might have lived if he had taken her away from York, from the flat plain below sea level to some warmer place with drier air. The thought was hard to bear.

At Seaview there were letters waiting for him on the hall table. Helen was standing in the hall reading a letter of her own and she had tears in her eyes. Kirby smiled at her encouragingly and she put the letter in her pocket. 'From my mother . . . I just felt a bit homesick for a moment, that's all. No, no bad news or anything like that.'

'It's good to learn to be away from home, to

be independent,' Kirby told her gently. 'And you enjoy working with Mary, don't you? I think you're very good, Helen, especially with children!' They both laughed.

The doorbell rang and Helen went to answer it, straightening her cap as she went. Two women stood on the step, with several suitcases. 'Seaview? Yes, this is the place, Mother.' The younger woman smiled as she walked in and Kirby thought he had never before seen anyone so beautiful. 'I am Maud Spencer. I think Mrs Baker is expecting us.' She had a small hat perched on shining blonde hair, a perfect oval face and widely spaced eyes that swept past Helen without looking at her and locked with Kirby's own.

There was a flurry of activity and the Spencers were wafted upstairs with their bags while Kirby stood looking up the stairs after them. After a few minutes he went into the dining-room. Helen came downstairs again and started to lay the dining table with two more places. 'Do you think they'll be nice?' she whispered. Boarders who were classified as 'nice' by the hands were appreciative, quiet and paid their bills.

'Nice? I'm not sure, but isn't she beautiful?' Kirby stood up and looked out of the long windows to where the sea moved restlessly only a few yards away. 'I've heard from my business partner and it means I must go away, Helen, probably in a day or two. Just for a few weeks . . . the business in York needs attention.'

'Would you like me to tell Mrs Baker? Perhaps you can let us know the exact dates.' That would mean another room to let to short term guests. 'We'll be sorry to see you go, sir,' Helen added professionally and then gave him a friendly smile.

Kirby laughed. 'Will you? Yes, I expect you will if my room is taken by a family with noisy children.' He thought for a while and, as Helen was about to leave the room, he added, 'This is going to upset my plans for the seaside book. I was hoping to finish it soon, I have a publisher waiting. Now, Helen, you can help me if you will. Observe what goes on here, talk to the fisher girls if you can find the time and write it all up for me, in the way that you write your journal. Anything that strikes you about the lives of the people and the way they earn a living, especially the women. Sketch as much as you can. Would you like to do that?'

'Well, if you think what I can find out would interest you,' Helen said doubtfully.

'Of course, it would keep me in touch. I can always ask questions if your meaning isn't clear. Only if Mrs Baker doesn't mind, of course, and you have the time.' Of course Mrs Baker probably didn't know that when she sent her helper off to bed at half past nine, time was then spent on the journal and the sketches.

Dinner that night was rather late and Kirby, spruced up and in a clean shirt, felt younger than for some time as he chatted to the guests as they waited for the meal. The Spencer ladies were down early, but the mother was extremely deaf and went to sit by the fire with her crochet work. Three salesmen drifted towards each other and eventually Kirby was left with Miss Spencer. She wore a soft, drifting violet scarf that matched the colour of her eyes and her dress emphasized a beautiful figure. What was such a striking woman doing with her old mother in a place like this? 'Would you not have preferred to stay at Scarborough for the sea air? Bridlington is very quiet, you know.'

The young woman laughed musically and arranged her skirts around her as she sat. 'I could say the same to you, Mr Kirby. You must have some interest here.'

It was too soon to talk about the book. 'Unfortunately'—now why had he said that? 'Unfortunately I'm leaving soon, to go back to York.'

The beautiful violet eyes looked up at him and the long lashes fluttered. 'You sound sorry to leave. Is there some attachment, perhaps, a lady who keeps you here?'

Maybe so, now that you have arrived. Kirby felt an unaccustomed stir of excitement as he gazed into that lovely face. Dragging his eyes away from her, he looked up reluctantly as

Helen brought in the soup course. 'Here comes dinner.'

'I too regret that you are leaving,' the young woman said softly, as Kirby drew out a chair for her at the table. 'Could you not be persuaded to stay for a while?'

Kirby wondered whether he should stay in Bridlington for a day or two longer. Was this what they meant by love at first sight? 'I . . . might be able to stay for another day or so. Perhaps you would allow me to take you for a drive, to see the sights? Bridlington has some wonderful views. And your mother, of course.'

The fair head was graciously inclined. 'Thank you, Mr Kirby. That would be very pleasant. I am sure Mother will be thrilled.'

They chatted easily during dinner and Kirby felt a strange thrill himself, for the first time for several years. Life had been grey, but it was suddenly much more interesting. Should he grow a beard? Women seemed to find men with beards more manly, he had heard. Mrs Spencer nodded and smiled, unable to hear any of the conversations round the table. She would make a wonderful chaperon. Drinking his coffee, James suddenly wondered whether Ivy Cole's prediction for him might come true.

*   *   *

'Come out in the boat, love. I'm taking it out, want to be seen about the place to get more customers. It's a grand day, it's Saturday afternoon . . . and you never seem to get out of the house.' The kitchen doorway was blocked by a large man with a beard and a fisherman's cap and he was looking at Mary. Helen had seen him once before; he was Mary's brother Bob.

'There's a lot to do, but I might come. It's a while since I went round the bay.' Mary sighed.

'We've only two in for dinner tonight, the others are going out,' Helen reminded her, looking out of the window at the afternoon sunlight glowing on the garden. 'We'll manage, Mary.' It was indeed seldom that Mary Baker escaped from the ceaseless round of duties.

'You should all come, that was my idea. But hurry up, tide won't wait.' Bob folded his arms resignedly. 'Make your mind up.

It was decided that Helen should go, since she had never been out in the bay, and Susie would carry on with the work. As Mary and Helen walked down to the harbour together the older woman explained that Bob was planning to take visitors out fishing during the summer season, and on rides around the bay. On a fine Saturday afternoon with a calm sea and bright sunshine, he thought it was a good idea to be seen sailing along to Flamborough in full view, to the envy of land bound visitors. The sight would advertise the boat and reinforce his notice board on the quay.

The tide was in and the boat was riding high

in the harbour, so it was only a short walk along a plank to get on board. Just as Bob was casting off, a slim figure hopped nimbly aboard 'Need another hand, Uncle?' Dan asked cheerily. There was already a man in the bows, evidently to help to sail the vessel.

Bob grinned and slapped Dan on the back. 'Lazy lad, you've come for the ride.'

'What kind of a boat is this?' Helen asked Mary quietly. To report to Mr Kirby or even to write her journal about this was going to be difficult, given her ignorance of anything to do with the sea. But this was the sort of thing that might interest him.

'It's a yawl, the *Mary Jane* is, bigger than Dan's boat. Bob takes it herringing in the season. Later on, towards back end. For fishing they take about eight lads; of course, they net the herring.' Mary sat down and pulled the shawl around her. 't'u be breezy, out in the bay.'

Herringing, what an awkward word. Helen watched as the boat slid out of the narrow harbour entrance and the wind caught the creamy coloured sails. They flapped and cracked above her and she thought how beautiful and stately the *Mary Jane* would look from the shore. Seagulls swooped and screamed around them, skimming the deep blue dancing waves. 'It's lovely!' she said to Mary, looking up at the sails.

'It's getting to be old-fashioned, though,'

Dan chimed in. 'The big trawlers out for herring on the Dogger are steamers now and they can catch far more fish than we can. They can run us down, too, without even seeing us,' he finished bitterly.

'That's what worries me,' his mother said quietly. Helen decided to ask more about the steamboats later. There seemed to be none in Bridlington harbour.

For some time they sailed parallel with the shore. A thin strip of beach dotted with holidaymakers was all that was left of the sands, as the high tide had come nearly up to the sea wall. It was gradually left behind and they passed the place where Lancelot had been caught by the tide. Dan sat in the seat beside Helen and he pointed it out with a smile. 'The lad was nearly tame by the time he left. Offered to give me a fossil he'd found.'

'Did you take it?' For Lancelot to offer a gift to someone seemed out of character.

'Nay, I told him I'd plenty. But it was good on him, all the same.' Dan flashed the blue eyes at her. 'I reckon we did him good, the pair of us. Taught him a lesson.' He turned in his seat. 'Up ahead you can see Dane's Dyke,' and he pointed to a dark gash in the chalk cliffs that came down sheer to the sea. 'That village up on top is Sewerby; there's a grand house up there.'

Dane's Dyke was a steep-sided tangle of trees and bushes and Helen remembered she had seen it before, from the landward side. 'Mr Kirby says it's man made, an earthwork, it was dug to defend . . . but I'm not sure what it was they were defending. What a lot of people they must have needed to throw up so much earth!'

Mary was talking to Bob about his chances with the visitors and Dan looked over at his uncle. 'You could dress as a pirate, Uncle Bob. An eye patch and a band round your head would do the trick. The bairns would love it.' He turned to Helen. 'Just think how those youngsters last week would have liked to sail in a pirate ship.'

Bob laughed, but Helen shuddered. 'Just think how the pirates would enjoy fishing them out when they fell overboard! Of course, pirates don't exist any more, do they? Or at least, not in Bridlington Bay.' She clutched her bonnet in a sudden gust of wind.

Dan looked mysterious. 'No, but smugglers might.' They were drawing out to sea a little as the boat approached Flamborough Head. 'There's caves in the bottom of those cliffs, see, smugglers' caves. At the dark of the moon, they say, the boats come in to land the stuff from Holland and France.'

Helen laughed at him. 'And then?'

'And then,' Dan looked round, but no one else was listening. 'Then a cart comes down from the wild country at the top. A cart with rags round the horse's hoofs, and rags tied round the wheels, and all the gear oiled or muffled. No creaks, even. The men are all in dark clothes with blackened faces . . . they pass through the country like ghosts.' He paused to see the effect; Helen was all attention.

'Is this true?' Helen wondered whether Mr Kirby had heard of smugglers in this part of the world. 'How can they get away with it, with coastguards everywhere?'

'The smugglers have friends, plenty of friends and in unlikely places. And they say there's a tunnel, all the way from that cave to Rudston Church. Quite a long way inland, see. That there is called Smuggler's Cave.'

Helen looked at the caves, hollowed out of the limestone by the restless sea. 'Really, Dan?'

The lad chuckled. 'Well, that's the name and that's what they tell the visitors. It makes a good story. An old lad I went to sea with told me it was really Dovecote Cave they used, a bit further along.'

Helen looked across again to where the cliffs gleamed white, innocent in the sun. 'I think you're telling me history, Dan. Even at home we heard tales of smugglers, but they were oh, over a hundred years ago, when the duty was high and they brought in tobacco and such. But what would they bring in these days? I think you're planning to take holiday folks out yourself and you're practising your stories on me.'

'Now that's a grand idea, I could tell 'em a tale or two.' Dan dropped his voice. 'Ah, lass, do yourself a favour. I came today to sit beside a pretty girl and talk to her. No business ideas in my head.' He looked at the blushing Helen as the boat hit bigger waves and one broke over the side. The yawl slid into a trough and he steadied Helen with one arm around her. She was quite sorry when he let her go. What a rogue he was, but it was strange how much more exciting life seemed to be when Dan was there.

The *Mary Jane* was pitching by now and Dan went to help with the sails. Helen held on to the seat grimly, feeling as though she were riding a bucking horse and wondering how men managed to fish as well as sail a boat in these conditions.

Helen had hoped to see the seabird nesting sites from the sea, but Bob turned for home before the tip of the headland was reached, standing out to sea a little as he did so. Bridlington looked very small in the distance and now Helen could see the two distinct areas, the old town and the quay, with the newer boarding-houses strung along the sea front.

As the sea grew calmer Dan came back to his seat and Helen asked him, 'Do you ever sail with your uncle on fishing trips?'

The young man shook his head. 'I'd like to go with him, Bob knows where the best places are. But Ma won't allow it.' Helen looked incredulous. 'Stands to reason, a lot of folks feel the same.'

'But why?'

Dan's young face was grim. 'You know, lass, it's a risky game at times. You don't want to lose two men in your family at once, so you sort of spread the risk. We go to sea in different boats.'

Helen said quietly, 'And your mother has already lost your dad . . .' and Dan grew up without a father.

'Ay, so long ago I hardly remember him. But Ma never forgets that night.' Dan gave himself a shake to get rid of the spray that had fallen on him. 'Maybe that's why these folks go smuggling. They are well used to taking risks.'

Helen's shawl by now was dripping wet, but she noticed that the gansey Dan wore was dry. The oiled wool must be so tightly spun and knitted that the water could not penetrate; so that was why every fisherman seemed to wear a close-fitting gansey. 'So do you really think that it still happens—the smuggling, I mean?'

'Who knows, except the lads in the dark? But I tell you what, Helen, I found a spout lantern, not so long ago. That must mean something. It wasn't too old.'

Another new term. 'A lantern? What does that prove?' Surely anyone could use a lantern.

'Why, a spout lantern is used to signal the shore when the boat comes in. It's got a light inside and a narrow spout, so you can point the light, beam it to one place and it won't be seen by . . . by anybody else who might be watching.' He laughed. 'I found it on the beach at low tide. I'll show you when we get home.'

Helen wanted the trip to go on forever, but the beautiful boat with the breeze filling her sails was coming back in her stately way to Bridlington harbour. 'We've had an exciting afternoon!' Dan said mockingly, but with an admiring glance at his mother's helper. Mary was more relaxed than Helen had ever seen her and Uncle Bob was quietly satisfied with the *Mary Jane's* performance. Perhaps it was the hint of danger, but there was something exhilarating, exciting about the sea.

SIX

'Our Dan, I told you to leave Helen alone. You're not to go turning her head with your chatter.' Mary was talking to Dan in a furious whisper as Helen walked into the kitchen after the boat trip. Should she pretend she had not heard anything?

Helen decided to intervene and put down the tray of dishes on the table. 'Mary, it was my fault. I asked Dan a lot of questions. It was a lovely afternoon.'

Mary glared at her helper. 'Well, Helen,

your mother told me to look after you and I intend to do it. There's to be no flirting with young men while you're in my care. And I might as well tell you, lass, that unbeknown to you she said that you might be inclined to the lads too much. That there was a young man in the next village whom they were worried about . . . but you'll know all about that. Now, let's get on with serving dessert.'

This was embarrassing. Helen blushed as she realized that Mary had been told about Charlie. She had fallen in love with the lad and it had lasted a whole month, agony and ecstasy, before it fell apart. Her heart was still broken of course, but the agony was fading now. Working in Bridlington, and Dan's blue eyes, had helped her to forget Charlie for whole hours at a time. She bit her lip, but said nothing.

Dan made his way cautiously to the door and as he passed Helen he winked at her.

'Dinna fash yersel', lassie,' he croaked in a guttural Scottish accent as he went out.

After Dan had gone there was silence for a while. Helen picked up the tray, feeling ruffled. It was a pity if you couldn't have a pleasant conversation with someone just because he was of the opposite sex. But then it wouldn't have been quite so enjoyable with a girl, would it? She took the dessert into the dining-room and brought the empty dinner plates back for washing up. Eventually Mary came over and smiled ruefully at her helper. 'The truth is, as I've told you before Helen, you can do better than a local lad. Even if he is my own son. Have you any idea what sort of a life his wife will have? How they have to struggle with hard work, fishermen and their wives?' She shook her head. 'Besides, I don't want you to get too fond of the lad. He's fickle, our Daniel. That's the best word for it.'

It was a good time to change the subject and there was something that Helen had wanted to ask since she came to Seaview. 'You know about it, you were a fisherman's wife. But Mary . . . if it's not rude to ask . . . I don't want to offend you, but how did you end up at Seaview, with this lovely house?' A well-furnished boarding house with lofty ceilings and seven guest bedrooms did not seem to fit with the story of Mary's past life. Her husband had been skilled, he had owned his boat, but the profits from fishing would not have been large even in a good year.

To Helen's surprise, Mary gave her an approving look. 'Nay, no offence taken. You've got your head screwed on, all right. It's a good question lass, and many a one is envious of me, to this day. But I reckon I earned this place.' She folded her arms complacently. 'After Fred died I took work here as a maid, they let me bring Daniel. It was hard to find a place where they would take a bairn, and o' course I had to earn our living. After a few years I was made up to housekeeper. And then Mrs Brogden that owned Seaview stopped taking guests as she got older, but I stayed on. I looked after her until she died and the old girl was good to me. She had no relations living, so she left it all to me. Me and Daniel, she took a fancy to the lad. He was always good at talking to the ladies, even as a little chap.'

Helen smiled and said what a wonderful piece of luck, but she was thinking about the bleak picture Mary had painted of a poor fisherman. Daniel was an only child, so this house would be his one day. But if he was so committed to the sea, he would probably keep fishing and buy a bigger boat when he could get his hands on some money. His wife would still be married to a fisherman. Not that it interested Helen Moore, of course.

What sort of a man did she really wish to marry? As she dried the dishes Helen daydreamed; she would like a husband who had a large and prosperous farm, or at least a house in the country. She could imagine a slim, handsome man with blue eyes, who laughed and told stories like . . . Dan Baker. But that was ridiculous. As Mary had implied, her parents would be horrified. How about a dark-eyed architect with wide shoulders, a fearless climber like James? Mr Kirby was attractive after all and working with him would be interesting, but he would hardly look at a country girl. Helen sighed.

Mr Kirby looked disappointed at dinner and Helen smiled at him as she took the coffee in. He and a small salesman were the only guests dining, although more visitors were expected soon. Was he sorry that the beautiful Miss Spencer had gone out with her mother to see friends? He had seemed very enthusiastic at breakfast that morning, but now he was almost moping. 'You're off to York on Monday, then, Mr Kirby?' she asked brightly. They were still waiting for him to tell them exactly when he planned to leave and to return.

Mr Kirby was staring out of the window. 'Yes, yes,' he said absently. 'Did I tell you I'll be back in about three weeks?' He sighed. 'I'd better get some writing done tonight.'

Sunday morning dawned wet and windy. Old Mrs Spencer decided at breakfast that they should stay at Seaview for the day and get on with their needlework. As Helen poured the coffee the daughter looked annoyed, but there was nothing to be done. 'I am sorry, Mr Kirby, but my mother catches cold so easily, I don't like to take her out in bad weather. Perhaps we can take a drive with you some other time?' She leaned over the coffee pot to look at him and Miss Spencer's neckline was so low she might easily have caught cold herself. Helen lingered in the room, fiddling with dishes on the sideboard, to see what happened next.

'It depends on how long you can stay, Miss

Spencer. I must go to York on business and I won't be back for three weeks.' Mr Kirby's shoulders were hunched; he looked very unlike the strong confident man Helen knew.

The lady gazed into his eyes. 'That is a pity, Mr Kirby. Did you say York? As a matter of fact, we are to visit York next week. Perhaps you could advise me on the most interesting places to visit. I hear that York has some good museums.' She frowned at Helen as if to send her away, but said nothing to her.

Helen rearranged the silver on the sideboard once more and prepared to leave the dining-room. As she picked up the tray Mr Kirby said eagerly, 'Of course, Miss Spencer. If you like, I will find the time to show you York myself. Where will you be staying?'

A rather cunning look passed over the beautiful face and Helen wondered whether the Spencers' trip to York had just been invented. She decided that Miss Spencer was a fortune-hunter; she had read about such creatures, who preyed on men. They either married them, or relieved them of their wealth. Helen rarely thought about money, but she realized that Mr Kirby must have quite a lot. Perhaps with his bright intelligence he would see through the woman soon? Helen felt as though she would like to protect James; the poor soul was even more susceptible than Helen herself.

That Sunday Mr Kirby stayed in the sitting-room all day with the Spencers. The bell rang frequently for more firewood, or smelling-salts for dear Mama. During the afternoon Mrs Spencer retired for a nap and her daughter invited Mr Kirby to sit beside her on the sofa. Helen, coming in with a fresh pot of tea, caught a whiff of some delightful perfume.

Mr Kirby was bending over an album of his photographs, sitting close to the lady and Miss Spencer was pointing to them with a delicate fingertip. She wore the gauzy, low-cut blouse that Helen had noticed before, over a long, deep-purple skirt that was hitched up just enough to reveal an ankle. Helen had never really seen anyone set out to look seductive before, but Miss Spencer somehow made her blush. What sort of an effect would the woman have on a man, even a sensible man like Mr Kirby?

Helen thought back to her brief affair with Charlie. She hadn't in the least tried to encourage him, had not even realized the effect she was having until Charlie had become quite . . . enthusiastic. It was a good job her father had come into the stable at that point, just after Charlie had kissed her. The sad awakening had come later, when she discovered that the lad desperately wanted to get her into the hayloft, but he had no interest in marriage, or a future together. No interest in Helen as a person, it seemed. He was just out for some fun, and when she realized it her heart was broken. Soon after that, she had come to Bridlington. As she left the room Helen thought that Mr Kirby was bound to be enchanted. But was it fair of a woman to do that deliberately to a man?

Mrs Baker was not put out at the news. 'There's plenty of folks about wanting rooms just now, we'll not worry about James, although he is such a nice quiet gent.' She looked at Helen. 'He seems to like talking to you.'

Helen felt that an explanation was called for. 'He asked me to—well, to write down anything that I notice or find out about the working people . . . for his book. Only in my spare time, of course,' she added quickly.

Mary seemed quite happy with this idea. 'As long as you keep away from the young lads,' she warned.

*   *   *

Cream-topped waves curled invitingly over the streaming sand outside the dining-room window, but Helen had only time for a brief glance at the morning before she was called to order. 'Three for coffee and four for tea, the gentlemen would like kippers but the ladies want scrambled eggs for breakfast . . .' Helen sometimes needed to write down the orders; it would be easy to forget them before she reached the kitchen. Miss Burton was the only long-term guest and the house was full of holidaymakers. They brought quantities of shells, sand and seaweed into the house with them and created much more work than usual, but they were cheerful and determined to enjoy themselves and Helen laughed at their jokes, so everyone was happy.

The whole of the next week was extremely busy at Seaview and Helen had no time to think about anything but work. Dan was not about; his boat was mended. 'The lads are trying to make up for lost time and they'll spend every day that they can out in the bay, except for Sunday,' Mary explained. 'To the fishermen, it's either unlucky or against religion to go out on a Sunday, depending on your point of view.'

Helen nodded. 'It's the same on the farms.'

An older woman, Freda, was brought in for a few hours every day to help with the washing and cleaning. 'It's grand to have a bit of money in my pocket at my age,' she confided to Helen. 'And get away from the old man for a bit.' Freda was quiet and very thorough.

'Now Freda's here, you can still have a few hours off one afternoon,' Mary told Helen. 'I've an errand for you, if you fancy a walk. You can fetch me some more stuff from Ivy Cole.'

That morning, the girl Ruth delivered some vegetables. She looked so pale that Mary looked at her anxiously. 'Did the cough mixture do you no good, lass?'

Ruth nodded vigorously. 'Cough's gone, thanks, Mrs Baker. It was good of you.'

'If you're sure.' Mary didn't look at all sure. 'Helen's going up to Ivy Cottage soon, she can get some more if you need it.' When the girl had gone, Mary looked at Helen. 'That lass takes on too much, if you ask me. She's baiting lines as well as doing the delivery round for Mr Johnson the greengrocer. Ruth's an orphan, her folks are dead, so I suppose it's hard for her to make ends meet.'

Helen was not sure what baiting lines involved, but it sounded messy. 'She doesn't go fishing, does she?'

Mary looked at her with pity. 'Nay, Helen, women never go fishing. But they often work harder than the men.' She paused, then added, 'Matter of fact, Ruth baits lines for our Daniel. He pays her to do it, of course. It's mostly their wives and daughters that do the job, but Dan has no wife as yet.' So perhaps that was why Ruth looked so anxious after the storm; Dan was part of her livelihood.

It was not until Saturday that the apprentice housekeeper escaped into the sunshine. It was good to get out of the black dress with white lace at the neck and to take off the little white cap. The day was warm and Helen put on a cotton dress in a light blue material, and on Mary's advice took a straw hat and a small straw basket for the errand. Just for a few

95

hours she would forget about being a servant and feel more like a summer visitor at the seaside. The Seaview uniform made her feel older and more serious, but this was partly because she was being given more responsibility as Mary Baker trained her to be a 'proper housekeeper', as she described it.

Saturday was the time for day-trippers. Helen looked among the crowds eagerly, but saw no one she knew. It would be interesting to meet Ivy Cole. Mr Kirby had said the woman might be a witch, but he said it with a smile as though he didn't believe it. He had written about her for his book and this could be a chance to gather some more information for him.

As she walked along she met a reminder of home: several Wolds wagons, drawn by heavy horses and decked out with flowers and ribbons. Helen's family had several such large, high-sided wagons. Suddenly she remembered her first trip to Bridlington as a child, in one of Father's wagons that had been used for a different purpose that week. 'We've been leading muck all week and now boss expects us to turn out like a show wagon,' the carter had grumbled, but it was all done in time. There had been hardly a whiff of farmyard manure about the outfit by the time they slowly rumbled down to the sea.

Today in the old tradition the wagons had brought country people into the town to enjoy the sea air and also the amusements, which were fast becoming a new tradition. This year the favourite was the switchback miniature railway, which gave the visitors a wild swooping ride with momentary glimpses of the sea from on high. The child in Helen would have loved a ride on the switchback, but it would be no fun to go there alone. Would Dan enjoy it, or were the fishermen scornful about such frivolity? To them, the seaside was their workplace, and a grim one at times. Helen sighed and turned on the inland track, realizing that she missed her younger sister. Perhaps that was why she enjoyed the carefree Dan's company.

Ivy Cottage was not hard to find, with the sun shining on the glossy leaves. As Helen went up the flagged path between clumps of rosemary she heard voices. Out in the garden among the buzzing bees were two women. One was tall and dark; she must be the witch, although she was not all that old and was quite handsome. The other was smaller and about Helen's own age. She wore the strange cotton bonnet of a fishergirl, short skirts, leggings and stout boots.

'You must be Helen, I've been expecting you,' the older woman said pleasantly.

How did she know? 'This lass here is Jessie, and we're all going to have a cup of tea.' The statement was so firm that the girls followed her obediently into the cottage, where a kettle

97

was whistling on the fire. The warm smell of drying herbs was strong. 'Helen, you set out the cups, they're on the dresser there. Jessie, are your hands clean? You can slice the teacake. And how's Mary Baker, Helen? You'd better give me her list.'

The teacake was just as good as the one her mother made, a sweet bread cake with currants and sultanas in it. Young Jessie cut thick slices and was generous with the butter, working deftly with her red rough hands. She must have come to the cottage to buy salve for those hands, Helen thought as she looked at them.

'You working for Mrs Baker at Seaview?' Jessie looked slightly envious. 'That'll be a grand job.' She sighed. 'Better than mine, for sure.' She spoke with a broad accent.

To lighten the mood, Helen told the story of Lancelot, Carlotta and the walnut shells and the women laughed. 'So you see it's not always a grand job. That week was a bit of a struggle, and you do sometimes wonder why you have to work when nearly everybody else is on holiday.'

'That's a posh bonnet,' Jessie said sincerely. Helen had taken it off and it hung on her chair by the strings, a crisp new straw hat with a neat brim and small artificial flowers at the crown.

'It's not for working, of course, it's my best one,' Helen confessed. She looked at the other girl. 'Yours is different . . . we don't wear bonnets like that out Pocklington way.' She laughed. 'I just wear a white cap at Seaview, but Mary—Mrs Baker said that today I should keep the sun off my face.' At home in the summer she had often been nearly as brown as Jessie. Pale faces were a silly fashion and hard to achieve on a farm.

Mrs Cole poured them a second cup of tea. 'Take another piece of teacake, Helen. Now Jessie, show Helen your bonnet.'

'It's nowt to look at, just a working one.' Jessie grinned and took off her white cotton headgear. 'They do look funny, don't they? I never think about it, o' course, we all wear them. Widows wear a black one. This here is a double crown, a padding like, on top of your head. That's cos we carry the baskets of bait on our heads, it's the best way.' Jessie seemed quite proud of her work.

'Carry them on your head? Doesn't it hurt?' Helen had thought that only African women did that and she had always felt sorry for them.

'Nay, we have a ring, we call it a bun, to balance it on—mine's a sock, stuffed with sand. And this poke at front, that's to keep sun off. Not off my face, but out of my eyes so's I can see what I'm doing. There's a lot of glare off the sea.'

'And then you have a frill round the back.' Helen turned the bonnet over in her hands.

'That's to stop drips going down your neck, see? Cold water and slime from the basket of bait.' Jessie took a swig of tea. 'Every day but Saturday, we have to gather bait on the rocks. Today we don't! Tomorrow's Sunday and the men don't go to sea.' She laughed happily.

Mrs Cole looked across the table at Helen. 'There in that bonnet is the life of a fisherman's lass. It tells you a lot, that bonnet does. So if you ever feel hard done by, looking after visitors at Seaview when other folks are on holiday . . . just think about that bonnet and be thankful you don't need one.' Jessie nodded her agreement.

Jessie went off as soon as the teacake was finished, saying she had to clean the house. Mrs Cole got together the list of herbs that Mary had ordered, talking as she worked. 'What about the writer feller? Is he still there? Mary sent him up here one day to see me.'

'Mr Kirby's gone back to York for a few weeks.' At least now Helen had a story to tell about Jessie's hard life. 'He's collecting, you know, stories about the way people earn their living. He'll be interested in what Jessie said.' As she spoke, Helen was planning a sketch of Jessie, balancing a basket on her head, with the beach in the background.

Mrs Cole smiled. 'It's a different world, right enough, the fishermen's world. The visitors in town see the pretty little boats going out and they don't know the half of it. I've heard them say that it must be an easy life, going fishing every day, like being on holiday.'

'I've learned a little from Mary,' Helen admitted. 'Her son was nearly drowned, the first week I was here.' She looked round the cottage at the rows of jars on the shelves. 'Your own work must be interesting, Mrs Cole.'

'Well, I do a bit more than pick flowers in the sunshine . . . but it's easier than the fishing life.' Mrs Cole looked up to her bunches of drying herbs. 'Every season has its different jobs. I collect a lot of wild stuff, meadowsweet and agrimony, yarrow and dandelion, all for different uses. Garden herbs are growing, now weather's warming up. Now this here sage is good for more than stuffing for a roast rabbit. Did ever you hear of sage tea?'

This was surer ground for Helen. 'My mother makes it, she dries a lot of sage from the garden. She used to make a tea for my granny's indigestion.'

'Good lass. But there's more to it than that. It's a cure for sore throats and all sorts, and it even helps your memory, they say.' She wrapped the herbs in paper. 'Put these in your basket and be thankful you don't have to carry them on your head.'

At the gate Helen turned with a question. 'Why do the women carry loads on their heads?'

'Do you want the brutal truth? They'd be too heavy to carry far, otherwise.' The herb woman shook her head sadly. 'Poor Jessie's never known anything else. She's a fisherman's daughter, and her ma is dead. Her dad's Bert Hardy, he hails from Staithes. A good seaman is Bert, I suppose, but he works her hard.'

Helen was thinking about clothes as she strode along the track that would lead her back to Bridlington. That morning a departing guest had taken her aside. 'My dear, I've left two of my dresses in the wardrobe. You can have them . . . make dusters of them if they're no good to you. I'm tired of them.'

'Thank you, Mrs Morrison, you are very kind.' Helen had decided that the cotton dresses were far too good to cut up for dusters, but they were too small for her and there were other girls who needed a new dress more than she did. One had fitted Susie the kitchen helper, who was delighted. Now Helen was wondering whether Jessie would like the other, a serviceable green. But how would she react to such an offer from a stranger? Would she jib at the idea of charity?

Helen walked quickly. Soon she saw Jessie ahead, a small figure in the distance against the immensity of sea and sky. The girl waited for her to catch up and Helen noticed the straight back and graceful walk of the fishergirl as the two walked on together. It must be the result of carrying a basket on her head.

'I right enjoy going to see Mrs Cole.' Jessie smiled up at her and Helen thought that she would be quite pretty if she wasn't so work-worn. 'She helped a lot when Ma died, laid her out and everything. And afterwards she said I could go up to visit if I liked. So I do, just sometimes, and it's grand. I tell her what's going on in the harbour and that. Sometimes I take her messages and there's always a bite to eat.'

So Mrs Cole liked a bit of gossip. 'She must be a kind lady. 'Now, Jessie, I'm looking for a young woman just your size. Yes, and your colouring, that pretty dark hair.' Helen paused to create a little mystery.

Jessie looked down at her meagre self. 'Whatever for? Nay, there's nowt pretty about me.'

'Well, you know, the visitors at Seaview . . . we look after them well and sometimes they give us tips and things. This very morning, a lady gave me a dress that's too small for me. Would you like to try it on? You can have it, if we can make it fit.' It might even be too large for the little lass. Helen noticed a faint odour of fish, like a cloud round them as she walked beside Jessie. It must be hard to get rid of, but if you worked with fish all the time you probably wouldn't notice it, like the pigman on the farm at home. Everyone else could pick up the smell of pigs, but he was used to it.

Just for a moment Jessie's face had lit up, but now it fell again. 'Not if it's too posh. The other lasses would laugh at me in a fancy frock.'

103

Helen hid a smile. 'No, it's very plain and a quiet colour, a nice green. It would be fine for summer though, and maybe for going to see Mrs Cole.' She glanced at the sky; it was getting on for four. 'I'd better get back to Seaview, to serve the evening meal. I'll bring the dress to your house when I can, if you tell me where you live.'

'Oh . . . you couldn't do that . . . could you?' Jessie was tempted. 'I live on Beck Hill just above harbour there. It's not like what it is where you are . . . Helen.' She said the name shyly. 'Maybe Mrs Baker wouldn't like you to come up there.'

'Her own lad's a fisherman, so I can't see why she'd mind. That's settled then, next time I get a few hours off,' Helen finished briskly.

That night in her little bedroom Helen set out her paper on the wash stand she used as a desk, and continued the journal.

We went for a sail in Uncle Bob's boat, I think he is Captain Johnson but I'm not sure, it's a big boat and Mary says its a Yawl. The sea was a bit rough but not too bad. Dan came with us and he showed me the Smuggler's Caves. He said that there are still Smugglers here. That would be an interesting trade for the book. 'Please Mr Smuggler, can I ask you how you make a living?' But you might not live to write it down, they are supposed to be Dangerous

104

Men. I have met a fisher girl and will make notes for Mr Kirby.

It was good to work for Mr Kirby, Helen thought, as she blew out the candle and climbed into bed. She looked forward to showing him the journal and her drawings when he came back to Seaview. There was a cold feeling round her heart as she imagined him falling for Miss Spencer; he was going to show her round York. It would be wonderful to be beautiful, to have Mr Kirby leaning over and listening to your every word, to go round the ancient city with him and have dinner in a good hotel, looking over a candlelit table into those dark eyes . . . but this was daydreaming, which her mother said was a sin. Country girls did not fascinate young men like Mr Kirby.

SEVEN

'It's time you did some cooking, Helen,' Mary Baker announced one morning. 'I suppose you'll have learned some at home?'

Helen thought about the big kitchen at home. 'Yes, we have to cook dinners for the men at hay time and harvest and for the shearing gang, and that's often as many as the guests at Seaview. Not quite so fancy of course, but good solid dinners.' It might not be a good idea to say that she was a good cook, there was always something to learn.

Dan had walked in as his mother spoke. 'Here Ma, there's some young herring. Let the lass have a go at cooking fish.' The blue eyes gleamed at her.

Helen was less confident about fish. 'My mother used to make soused herrings in the season . . . I'm not sure how, though. But perhaps you'll show me.'

'That I will,' Mary said promptly. 'Bring them in, Dan, but clean them first, there's a good lad.'

'I will if Helen helps me, she needs to learn how to scale a fish.' Dan looked so demure that Mary let her go out into the yard with him, where the gleaming silver herring were lying on a stone bench.

Dan deftly scaled the first fish, slit it, cleaned it and somehow detached the head and the backbone so that all the bones came away cleanly. 'The more scales there are, the fresher the fish. There you are lass, now you have a go.' He stood close behind her and put his right hand over hers. 'Hold the knife this way.' He put the other arm round her waist very gently and grasped the fish. His breath tickled her cheek. 'The lasses down on the quay have to do this all day in herring season, gutting fish day in, day out. How would you like to do it for a living?' She could feel him laughing. 'My, Helen, I've never enjoyed cleaning fish so much before!'

Helen couldn't help laughing in her turn. 'Now Dan, keep your distance or the knife might slip,' she warned, moving away from him. The job was not easy and she tried to concentrate, but Dan's presence was distracting. It would not be wise to stay too long out in the yard. 'I'm sure you talk like that to other lasses. Well, with me it won't do. You'll get me into trouble with your mother.'

'No, Helen, not the other lasses, it's you I'm after. Haven't you noticed?' Dan's tone was light and she decided to ignore it. She was glad that he helped her by cleaning most of the fish himself. 'All you need is practice, Helen my love,' he said as he handled the knife expertly. 'I'll get you to help me the next time.' He grinned at her. 'I'll look forward to it, lass. It's a hard life, fishing. A man has to have something to look forward to.'

He was a rogue, but the feeling of Dan's warmth beside her lingered. As soon as she could, Helen took the tray of herrings back to the kitchen for the next lesson. Kipper the cat came out into the yard for her share of the feast, rubbing herself against Dan's legs.

Under Mary's watchful eye, Helen washed the herring fillets, added salt and pepper and rolled them up neatly with the skin inside. This much she remembered from home. Then they were put in a dish, covered with vinegar and water and sprinkled with spices. 'Simple, isn't it?' Dan grinned at her. Anybody would think he was a professional chef. 'Don't forget the onion rings.'

'Have you nowt better to do than to hang about the kitchen?' his mother demanded, but Daniel wheedled a cup of tea out of her before he went. He drank the tea with his eyes beamed on Helen and she was relieved when he disappeared, although the day was less bright without him.

'Now Helen, add a few onion rings and put the lid over the dish. They'll need over an hour in the oven . . . if we serve them for lunch, put them in at eleven. Yes, I'll leave them to you, don't let the fire get too hot. How many did you say want lunch today?'

Some of the guests opted for 'full board', which included a midday meal and it was Helen's job to ask at breakfast how many of the boarders would be back for lunch. The younger and more adventurous guests stayed out all day, but the middle-aged sometimes liked the security of a cooked lunch waiting for them at half past twelve. 'Only three, Mary, so there'll be plenty for us as well.' And enough for Dan, if he came back for lunch.

*   *   *

'You can have a couple of hours off before dinner,' Mary told Helen one Wednesday afternoon. It was a cloudy day and the North

Sea was a forbidding grey, a hostile colour merging indistinctly in the distance with the heavy sky. The waves had white caps, driven by a rising breeze but, in spite of the threatening rain, Helen decided to take the dress to Jessie as she had promised.

Shawled against the wind, Helen walked briskly towards the harbour and the huddle of cottages above it that was the centre of Bridlington's fishing industry.

This was an area where visitors to the town were seldom seen and she had never been here before. It was a separate world away from the ice creams and the sands.

Jessie's cottage was in a narrow street. The front of the houses was quiet, but when she strayed into an alley at the back Helen found that this was where the women worked. Children played in the alley and women were busy in the back yards. Big wicker baskets were everywhere and over it all hung the smell of fish.

As Helen looked round rather apprehensively, Jessie appeared from one of the yards. Her face broke into a big smile. 'You came! I never thought you would.'

'Here's the dress, try it, Jessie. I do hope you like it.' Helen handed over the bag. Jessie disappeared, the dress was tried on and found to fit perfectly; Jessie was in raptures, turning round and round in the kitchen and Helen was rather embarrassed. 'It was given to me, I told you so,' she protested.

'It's beautiful!' Jessie stroked the fabric with one rough finger. 'I'll wear it on Sundays to go to the mission.' In fact it did suit the girl very well and Helen was glad she'd thought of Jessie.

To change the subject, Helen ventured a question. 'What were you doing, Jessie, before I interrupted you?'

'You don't really want to know, do you? Just wait while I get changed.' Back in her working-clothes, Jessie led the way outside again into the yard. She pointed to a basket, then to a bath of water. 'This tide's bag of flithers, I have to skane them and put 'em in water, see.'

This was a foreign language to Helen. The smell was almost overpowering but she wanted to understand what was going on here. She looked at the basket. 'They're limpets, you get them from the rocks? And then what happens?'

'We skane 'em,' Jessie repeated. 'The fishing lines are baited, see. We used to use mussels to catch cod and such, but there isn't none left. Mussels were better.' Jessie went on with the work. Skaning was evidently the process of taking the soft body out of the shell to prepare the bait. 'We have to go at low tide to get flithers.' No wonder her hands were red and rough.

Helen looked at the lines, coiled in baskets with hundreds of hooks on them at intervals.

'You have to put bait on every hook?' She tried not to shudder at the thought of this cold, smelly and repetitive work going on every day, while only half a mile away holidaymakers strolled on the sea front. Cutting turnips in the rain on the farm was luxury by comparison. Would ordinary people want to read about such things? Mr Kirby's book might not appeal to what he called 'the general reader' if he went into such grim detail.

Jessie was deftly removing limpets from their shells. 'Got to keep going, Helen, I've nearly finished. Tide'll be in soon and I have to go down to meet boat.'

'Why, Jessie?' There was so much to learn about the daily routine. Jessie seemed to have enough work without meeting the fishing boats as they came in. 'You don't have to—haul the boat in, or anything?' A girl of about the same age as Jessie was listening to their talk and now she giggled.

Jessie laughed. 'Nay, they can get into harbour at high tide, not like some places where lasses have to pull them up. But we have to pick up lines and bring them home for cleaning—caving we call it. They're all fouled up with seaweed, old bait and such.' She saw Helen's expression of concern and laughed. 'We like working outside and we're used to it, you know. And then when the boats go on the herring they use nets and we don't need to bait lines. That'll be soon, summer's coming on.'

Another girl had come over and now she looked curiously at Helen. 'But then we have to gut herring all day and that's nearly as bad. You a maid in service? You're better off, then. Think on, don't wed a seaman if you wouldn't like to cut your hands on line bait!' Then, with a flick of a long plait, she was off again.

The yard was as clean and tidy as Jessie could manage, no doubt, but the smell from a bin of rotting bait was making Helen feel sick. She never wanted to eat fish again. She thought of the crowds of summer visitors who would happily buy their fish and chips, knowing nothing of the sordid back streets where this dirty work went on. Fighting nausea, Helen tried to remember all the new words she had learned. She would write down her findings for Mr Kirby as soon as she could, but meanwhile there might be even more information to glean.

After a few more minutes, Jessie wrapped herself in a black shawl and picked up a basket. 'I'll walk down to the harbour with you,' Helen offered. Jessie smiled uncertainly, but said nothing. A drizzling rain began to drift in from the sea.

The boats were coming in through the narrow harbour entrance one by one, patiently waiting their turn and Helen lingered to watch Jessie go to meet her father bringing in the coble *Seaspray.* Bert Hardy was a big, powerful man with a black beard and there were two

112

young lads with him in the boat, which was just like Dan's. They quickly disappeared and while he unloaded the day's catch onto the jetty, his daughter silently took the fishing lines out of the boat and coiled them into her basket.

Helen stood well back, trying to keep out of the way as three or four boats unloaded the day's catch of gleaming fish. Bert was talking to Jessie, then they both looked in her direction. He leapt on to the quay and suddenly there he was, standing over Helen. 'What you doing here?' he demanded. 'Giving my lass big ideas. Get back to where you belong, young woman.' He was large and menacing and in spite of herself, Helen felt almost afraid. But then she spoke up, for Jessie more than herself. 'Why? I'm doing no harm, Mr Hardy.'

'Get out,' the fisherman growled but Helen stood her ground, determined not to be intimidated.

'Please don't be offended, I was just interested in seeing the boats come in,' she said pleasantly. She realized that he was most agitated. 'What's wrong with that, Mr Hardy? Why shouldn't your Jessie talk to another lass, or have a nice dress for once?'

'Fishing's none of your business, miss. Keep your nose out of my affairs.' Hardy went back to his work and banged the last basket of fish hard on the dock. Jessie went on working without looking at Helen, her face scarlet with embarrassment. It had been a very public exchange of words.

Dan's coble, *Seabird,* newly repaired and looking smart, had now come nosing in. As soon as he tied up there was Ruth the vegetable girl, expertly taking out Dan's lines and coiling them in the shallow baskets. Two other women were collecting Robbie's and Dave's lines. *Seabird* had a good catch and Helen noticed that it was better than Bert Hardy's. 'I'll go and watch someone else, if you don't want me here.' It would be easier for Jessie if she moved away.

Dan had seen the exchange and now hopped on to the quay and lounged up in a casual way. 'What's this, Bert, taking over my best girl? Wait for me, lass, I'll walk you home.' He winked at Helen as he went back to his task and she felt reassured to see him. Hardy looked as though violence would come naturally to him; had the fishermen heard about Mr Kirby's book? Jessie knew of it from Ivy Cole, of course. Some of them might resent the idea.

The fish was soon sold, although Helen could not tell whether a deal was struck or whether a price had been agreed beforehand. With an apologetic look and a wave to Helen, Jessie went off with her father. Not wanting to wait for Dan, Helen decided to walk up the hill with Ruth. 'I didn't expect to be attacked like that,' she told the girl. 'Can I help you with the basket?' She was given the basket of lines to carry on her hip and although it seemed light at first, it got heavier as they went up the slope. 'What's wrong with Bert Hardy? Is he always so rude?'

The question was not answered directly. 'Jessie's a grand lass, she's a friend of mine,' Ruth said after a pause, pushing her fair hair out of her eyes and tucking it under the shawl. 'But her dad is a hard man.' She stopped as though she had said too much.

'What was Jessie's mother like?' Helen wondered.

'I don't remember her, she died when I was a bairn.' Ruth looked uncomfortable, so Helen said no more about Hardy.

Ruth's little cottage was in the same street as Jessie's. Helen put down the basket with relief; she noticed that Ruth was puffing as much as she was. Was the girl as ill as she looked? Perhaps a friendly word would help. 'The cough's all gone, Ruth?' she asked quietly. The rain was falling faster and the baskets had been taken into the kitchen, which was clean and neat. Ruth was uncoiling the lines and taking off the horrible debris. 'Thank you . . . yes. The mixture Mrs Baker gave me cured it in a week.' She staggered slightly and then sat down on a stool, where she continued the work. It's been a long day.'

Helen watched her anxiously. 'You're not

well, are you, Ruth?' She took a deep breath and went on. 'Do you get enough to eat?' The girl looked startled, so she added hastily, 'Sometimes folks that live alone don't cook, so they don't eat proper meals. That's all I meant.' There was no sign of a meal in the kitchen and the fire was not lit.

'I'm not very hungry, these days,' Ruth said faintly. 'But Mr Johnson the greengrocer, he often gives me veggies when I get back with the donkey. And Dan sometimes gives me fish. I do right well,' she finished with an attempt at a smile.

Ruth looked so forlorn that Helen didn't like to leave her, but she had to get back to work. 'I'm expected at Seaview,' she explained, moving to the door. She hardly knew the girl— what could she do to help her? On an impulse she said, 'Ruth, would you like to tell me what's wrong? Maybe we can help you.' Consumption was what everyone feared; would Mrs Cole be able to cure that, or even a doctor? Perhaps the lass couldn't afford a doctor.

Ruth burst into tears and sat on the stool, sobbing into her apron. Helen waited. After a few minutes she looked up with a tear-stained face. 'No—nobody can help me. I can't tell you what ails me, or even Mrs Baker. She's been so good to me since my mother died . . . everybody is so kind.' She struggled for composure and wiped her eyes. 'Dunnot worry about me, Helen. It can't be helped.'

A slow suspicion dawned upon Helen; she had seen this type of ailment before. This was so like the case of Maggie, a dairymaid on her parents' farm. Maggie was a plump, cheerful girl who was good at her job, but last summer she had developed mysterious ailments and was less able to work. Eventually Mrs Moore had diagnosed pregnancy, and Maggie had admitted that she'd been too friendly with the cowman. A hasty marriage had been arranged and all was well, but the incident had stuck in Helen's mind, an awful warning to single girls not to get into trouble. What if Maggie's lover had been unwilling or unable to marry her? That point was made by Helen's mother. Maggie would be a fallen woman.

Helen took a deep breath and grasped the doorknob. 'Ruth, forgive me if I'm wrong, but . . . might you be expecting a baby?' She spoke quietly in case anyone in the yard was listening.

Ruth looked at Helen with wide, startled grey eyes. 'How did you know? I haven't told anybody.' A sob escaped her. 'And I'm so sick . . . sick every morning.' She wrapped her arms round herself, looking frailer than ever.

Helen's own face was white with shock. How could a lass with no family survive, if she had a baby to look after? Would the fishing people here be as horrified as most of the community if an unwed girl had a baby? If

117

Helen had guessed, so would other people, very soon. 'Oh dear, Ruth. How—difficult for you! It seemed inadequate. There was another possibility. 'Have you a —will the father marry you, do you think?' She thought back to thevillage she came from and the gossip in the village shop. 'Quite a few young women have a baby soon after they're wed. It does happen, you know.' She was sixteen . . . rather young for marriage.

Ruth's face was still bleak. 'Nay, he left a while ago, went to sea on a long trip to Australia. I'll not see him again.' She looked at Helen's expression. 'Don't blame the lad, he never knew about the baby.'

So that avenue was closed. A young, irresponsible lad had sailed off and left his girl behind with the burden of responsibility. It was hard to work out what Ruth could do; she looked as though she was exhausted with worry. But at least something might be done to ease the sickness. After a few minutes' thought, Helen had a suggestion. 'I'll go to see the herb woman . . . she might help.'

Ruth interrupted fiercely. 'I'm not going to do away with it! Never!' Her fists were clenched. 'I couldn't kill a baby, I'd rather kill myself.' She looked so desperate that Helen was afraid for her. Sobs racked her frail body and Helen longed to put her arms round the girl. Instead, she put a gentle hand on her shoulder.

'I didn't mean that,' Helen said soothingly. 'Just that Mrs Cole might have something for morning sickness, I think that's what they call it.' Ruth looked dubious and so she added, 'I won't tell anyone else, promise. I'll be back to see you when I can. And—remember, it could happen to anybody, Ruth. It could have happened to me . . . I was—er, getting involved with the wrong man.'

Ruth managed a smile. 'Thank you, Helen. The shame will be hard to bear.'

Back at Seaview the kitchen was busy and Helen had no time for anything but work for several hours. 'When it rains we always get more in for dinner,' Mary explained. 'And they take longer over the meal when they're not going out again.'

When Helen began to attack the mountain of dirty dishes, Dan came in to help her. He was shiny with soap and Helen had noticed that there was never a smell of fish on Dan. He must change his clothes in the evenings and she suspected he took a bath in one of the guest bathrooms when the coast was clear. But of course, he had been brought up at Seaview—quite a privilege for a young man.

'What did you do to upset Bert Hardy?' Dan looked at her with one eyebrow raised as she stacked dishes in the sink. 'He was right mad, was Bert.'

'Nothing at all, Dan. I was talking to Jessie, that was all. Passed on to her a dress that was given to me, if you must know.' Should she tell Dan what else she was doing?

'And taking notes for James Kirby,' Dan said knowingly. 'James has talked to me and a few of the others about fishing and I thought he would rope you in to talk to the lasses.' He dried the plates expertly. 'The lads know about the book, they laugh about being famous. But Bert Hardy doesn't like it, he's very edgy these days. Says folks should mind their own business . . . he thought you were snooping. Maybe he's cross that we catch more fish than he does.'

'Well, I'll keep away from him. But I hope he doesn't take it out on poor Jessie, although I think she could look after herself. She's a bright girl.' Helen looked carefully at Dan, but he showed no reaction. Which one of the girls did he fancy?

'Yes, I admit I'm looking for a story for Sir, but I find it very interesting. Now Dan, tell me about your boat.'

Dan was very happy to talk about his work. 'There's three of us in *Seabird*; we shoot three lines each.' That was a lot of bait; Helen had seen that each line had hundreds of hooks. She was thinking from the women's point of view. 'Of course, we all take our own lines.' So Ruth would only have to look after Dan's lines. 'We shoot lines across the tide and then wait a few hours before hauling 'em up again.'

'Why do you do it? Why be a fisherman?'

Helen wanted to know.

'I like the independence, I suppose, and being out at sea, there's a bit of skill, a lot of luck—something about it, I can't explain. Heaven knows we don't do it to make a fortune, although sometimes we have a good catch. Not knowing what the next day will bring, a feast or a famine—that's surely better than a routine job.' He laughed as he stacked plates in the cupboard. 'I would hate to work to a fixed routine. Every day's different at sea and you never know how it'll turn out.' Dan grinned. 'And we're our own bosses out there, there's nobody nagging and telling us what to do.' The last remark was for the benefit of his mother, who had just come into the kitchen.

Mary had been keeping an eye on them both, Helen knew, but evidently she accepted that Dan was behaving properly. 'There's nowt wrong with lasses and lads talking good sense,' she admitted and her smile reminded Helen of Dan's.

That night Helen wrote down the day's adventures, although she said nothing about poor Ruth. That was private, however much it might have interested a researcher who wanted to know how the working people lived. She sketched the quay with a coble tied up and wondered what James Kirby would think of her drawings. Then, idly, she began to draw a pirate ship, flying the skull-and-crossbones flag, with swashbuckling figures on the deck.

She began a story about them, a story to read to children like Lancelot; it would need plenty of action to keep his interest. Just before she blew out the candle, the story was labelled JOLLY PIRATES. Working at the seaside did strange things to the imagination.

EIGHT

The next week, Helen suggested that Mary might like some more herbs from Mrs Cole. 'Well, if you want a walk, lass, you can get me some fresh mint. New potatoes are coming in this week and they're nowt without mint.'

On the walk to Ivy Cottage, Helen tried desperately to work out how she could get what she wanted from Mrs Cole without giving Ruth's secret away. By the time she arrived at the cottage she still had no plan, so she started with the mint. 'And if you don't mind, could I buy a root or two of mint from you? I could grow some in a pot in the yard for Mrs Baker. We always grow mint at home, it's so easy.'

Ivy Cole looked at Helen with approval. They were standing in her garden, having gathered a large bunch of mint and the herb woman took a trowel and dug up some mint roots as they were talking. 'You've been brought up right, I can tell. Everybody should have a few herbs at their back door. Nay, lass,

I'll give them to you. I'm not so poor that I can't give a few plants away. Now, do you know how many different types of mint there are?'

They went into the cottage for the ritual cup of tea and as the kettle was boiling Helen said quietly, 'Mrs Cole, I have a friend that's expecting a baby. Have you any herb that would help her?'

The change in the herb woman was immediate. 'I'll have no truck with abortion. Never have, never will. You've come to the wrong place for that, lass.' Ivy Cole glared at her. 'If that's what you want, you can go home right now. I don't want to see you again.'

Helen stood to face her. 'No no, Mrs Cole, that was not what I meant. It's just that she gets very bad morning sickness and she's hardly eating anything . . . and I think there was something my mother used for it. The sickness I mean.' It was the second time she had been misunderstood.

'That's different . . . there's a few.' Mrs Cole looked at her carefully. 'It's not for you, is it? No, sorry, I can see it's not.' She looked round the shelves. 'Chamomile . . . no, that's too strong. I'll give you some raspberry-leaf tea, and maybe dill for the digestion.' She gestured for Helen to sit down.

Looking round Ivy's kitchen, Helen thought what a comfortable place it was. Everything there had a use and most of the space was taken up with herbs. A clutch of wicker baskets hung from the ceiling. Leaning against the wall was a pair of hazel sticks and Helen remembered seeing something like them before. It had been a few years ago, when her father's farm was short of water in a dry summer. They had called in a dowser and the man had walked across a paddock with the sticks held in front of him, and told them where to dig for a hidden spring.

'You're looking very thoughtful, Helen,' Ivy commented.

'Your hazel rods—they reminded me of a man who found water for us on the farm one summer.'

The woman laughed. 'Those rods get me a bad reputation in the village. Folks think it's satanic, you see. Sometimes I can find lost things with them, or with a pendulum . . . but I don't know how I do it.'

'Well, it is strange, I suppose, but my father was very pleased that we found water for the sheep.' Helen then remembered that one or two of the farm men had looked uneasy about the dowser and said he was uncanny. She looked at Ivy Cole.

'No, love,' Ivy said then. 'I'm not a witch.'

*   *   *

'How very beautiful it is!' Maud Spencer gazed up at a great stained-glass window in York

Minster and the rosy light fell softly on her upturned face. She made a wonderful companion, James thought as he watched her. Maud was so interested in everything, so keen to learn its history.

'It's a pity that I have to work on most days at the office, but I've been away for a while. It would have been good to spend more time with you,' James said as they moved away from the window.

'But James, I do understand. Your work, your profession must come first. Mama and I are so grateful that you can spare us a little time. The new hospital plans must take up a great deal of your thoughts at the moment.' Maud was so considerate.

'That's true.' James had put in some very early mornings at the office and the plans were taking shape. He had slipped away most afternoons to escort the Spencers. 'But I do want to make sure that you see as much of York as possible, while you are here.' Maud had been most appreciative of the museums, the art gallery and the walks on the walls that surrounded the ancient city.

Mrs Spencer went with them as convention dictated and James was at first surprised that she could keep up so well, climbing steps and standing for hours. But then he realized that she was not as old as he had at first thought: barely fifty perhaps. Her deafness made her seem older, and the old-fashioned clothes she

125

wore.

James had always loved the theatre and he intended to take Maud to see at least one play. He said on the Friday, 'Can you come to the theatre tonight? I suppose Mrs Spencer might not enjoy the play—her poor hearing must be a burden.'

Maud glanced over to where her mother sat upright in a chair, gazing about her vaguely. 'Mama? She likes to see the people, the women's dresses—she would love to come.'

James managed to get three reasonable seats and there was time for a light meal before the performance began, although it took Maud so long to change her dress that James thought they would be late. Waiting for her at the small hotel where they were staying, it was hard to remember that the last time he had been in York he had felt lonely and miserable. James Kirby had a new lease of life; he felt vital, full of energy. He pulled his watch out to check the time and then stuffed it back hastily into his pocket as the ladies descended the stairs. 'No, Maud, you are not late, we have plenty of time.' How could anyone criticize when the finished product was so beautiful?

The play was a witty comedy and all three enjoyed it, even Mrs Spencer, who laughed with the rest. It was hard to see how someone so deaf could enjoy the evening, but the ear trumpet was in evidence and Maud said that her mother loved the theatre. 'She laughs when she sees the audience laughing,' she explained.

After the play, James was invited into the Spencers' hotel for a drink. After a short time Mama went to bed. Maud turned her beautiful eyes on James. 'Thank you for a wonderful week, James, I shall never forget it.' She was wearing a dark-red evening gown that showed off her creamy skin to perfection. The golden hair glistened in the lamplight. 'Next week we really must go to London, I have business there.' She drew a light shawl round her shoulders with a graceful movement. 'More's the pity.'

The shock was like a physical blow. Maud was leaving and James was not prepared for it, he had not thought ahead; for a moment he felt giddy, but then he recovered himself. 'That is a pity, but—please come to dinner with me at my house, before you go. Tomorrow evening? That's settled, then.' As he left, Maud reached up on tiptoe and kissed his cheek. Standing in the hotel foyer, he felt a thrill run through him. Gently he put an arm round her waist and returned her kiss.

How would he pass the time until he saw her again? But the real question was: what was James to do about Maud Spencer? He had known her for such a short time, but . . . he was obsessed. Was it enough, would it be rash to propose marriage so soon? Tomorrow night would be the ideal occasion. But perhaps he needed a little more time to think about it. He could arrange to see her on their return from London. It was not such a tragedy, after all. It was strange to think that he still had no idea where they had their home; he knew very little about them.

The next morning, in the cold light of day James realized that he needed to make preparations for his love feast. Mrs Appleby would have to be organized and that was never easy. The widow lived in a small cottage attached to James's house and it was her duty to keep his house clean and to cook for him when he was at home—which these days was not often. He attacked after breakfast, when Mrs Appleby was clearing the table.

'Two extra to dinner? Could've done with more notice,' she grunted. 'Gents from the office, I suppose? That'll be pies, Stilton cheese and plenty of port.' Mrs Appleby had no finesse.

James shook his head. 'Ladies, as a matter of fact, Mrs Appleby. Roast chicken I think, with a clear soup to start with. And a light dessert with a little whipped cream. That should not be too difficult, surely?' He looked round his dining-room. 'Open the windows and air the room. Would you like me to do anything?' Mary Baker at Bridlington would have taken it all in her stride.

'Nay, *you* can't do owt,' his helper said, with

heavy emphasis. Mrs Appleby's idea of duty did not extend to deference. 'Unless you can go and buy a chicken, and don't pick a boiling fowl, either.'

James looked at an empty silver vase on the sideboard. He would buy some flowers to cheer the room. For the first time he realized that it had a neglected look and some of his possessions were scattered about. He tidied the papers and books and noticed that his gold watch lay on a small side table where he had taken it out of his pocket the night before. Living alone had made him rather untidy. But it was getting late, he should be in the office by now. Even though it was Saturday there was urgent work to do. 'I'll bring it in about four . . . will that be soon enough?'

'You had better make it sooner. I'll have to pluck it and all, before it goes in the oven.' Mrs Appleby sighed. 'Nobody realizes how much work goes into a dinner party.'

James shrugged on his jacket and went to the door. 'Surely I can buy one ready plucked and dressed? You've had it very easy this summer so far, Mrs Appleby!' He ran down the steps lightly, whistling, and then realized that his treasured housekeeper was watching him with suspicion through the window.

Thinking about the engineer's report for the new hospital, working on the plans, James still had the image of Maud's beautiful, serene face in the back of his mind. Why did she have to go to London? He would try to find out what her 'business' might be. She had hinted that her father had left a great deal of money and that she and Mama were comfortably off, and liked to visit different parts of the country during the summer months. Perhaps she had to see to her investments.

That evening Maud arrived in a beautiful, shimmering grey gown and pearls. Even her mother looked brighter than usual. Mrs Appleby had risen to the occasion and the meal she produced was excellent. The conversation turned to architecture and James enjoyed explaining the various styles to be seen in York to Maud, who was so interested in everything he had to say and made intelligent comments.

There was only one sour note the whole evening. James went out to ask Mrs Appleby to make coffee. When he came back to the dining-room, mother and daughter seemed to be talking together very quietly. But how could they do that if Mrs Spencer was deaf? They broke off as he came in and Maud said in the usual loud voice she used for her mother, 'Will you take coffee, Mama?' But the incident made James feel slightly uneasy. Were things not quite as they had seemed?

'This house is Georgian, I believe?' Maud looked round the drawing-room with appreciation.

'Late Georgian . . . it belonged to my

parents, but when they retired I took it over.' James stood up. 'Would you like to look over the house, Maud?' He extended a hand to her and she rose gracefully to her feet. 'My father was a doctor and the room across here was his surgery...'

Mama stayed by the fire and James conducted Maud up the stairs. The rooms were lit by the evening sun and the lady exclaimed at their beautiful high ceilings and elaborate cornices. They spent some time looking round, and then James turned to lead the way back downstairs. Maud was standing close to him on the landing and acting on impulse, he slid his arms round her and pulled her into a close embrace. Had he gone too far? But no, her lovely face was raised for his kiss. It was a long, long kiss and it really seemed that Maud felt the same urgency. And then it was over and with a sigh, she pulled away and patted her hair into place. She sailed down the wide staircase in front of him, a beautiful vision in floating grey.

Soon after this the Spencers asked for a cab to be called and made their way home to their hotel. As he held open the door she gave him a long look and a mysterious, alluring smile. 'I will let you know when we come back from London,' Maud promised. 'Will you miss me, James?'

James was left wondering about Maud. When they were gone, the house seemed

131

empty and forlorn. But if she had deliberately tried to entice him, Maud could not have done a better job. She had given him encouragement, her kiss was warm and her body had clung to his . . . and then she disappeared, leaving him hungry for more of her company. Was it because he had been alone for so long, or was this to be the love of his life?

The next few days were busy at work, making up for lost time and to take his mind off the lady, James spent the evenings writing up chapters of his book. It was not until the next Wednesday that he noticed a scarf on a chair, evidently left behind by Maud. But he had no address for her. Of course, he could wait until she came back from London, but it would be rather pleasant to send her the scarf with a note, a good excuse to keep in touch. On his way home from work the next night, he went to the hotel where she had stayed. 'Could you give me a forwarding address for Mrs and Miss Spencer?' he asked at the reception desk.

The middle-aged woman picked up the guest register. 'Certainly, sir. They would have given an address when they signed in.' She ran a finger down several pages of names. 'Here it is . . . 21 Badger's Lane, York.'

'Are you sure?' But the Spencers were new to York, he had shown them round . . . James felt bewildered. By this time a new guest was signing in, so he thanked the woman and wandered out into the street. Perhaps Badger's Lane was another hotel or guest house, a place where they had stayed before . . .

James knew York well, having lived there most of his life. He soon found the house in Badger's Lane; it was a tall building, divided into three apartments, each with its own bell. The second bell was clearly labelled 'Spencer.'

The warm summer evening felt almost cold to James as he walked home. For some reason, Maud had pretended that she was new to York, while all the time she and her mother had a house here. They must live here. Why would she want to deceive him?

A further shock was waiting for him at home. Mrs Appleby brought his dinner into the dining-room with a long face. 'Lamb chops, new potatoes and peas, boss, and have you moved that there vase?' She pointed to the sideboard. There was a space where the antique silver vase had been.

'That reminds me . . . have you seen my gold watch? I can't remember when I had it last. It was on that table last week.' James and Mrs Appleby looked at each other. 'Perhaps we've been robbed. Are any locks forced, or any windows broken?'

Mrs Appleby shook her head and shuffled off. James decided to inspect the whole house as soon as he finished dinner. He ate his meal sombrely. James had another watch that he used for work, so he had not missed the gold one. Where had he put it? How could he be so careless? His parents had given him that watch.

Later, a tour of the house yielded no suspicious signs. Mrs Appleby swore that the doors were kept locked. There seemed to be nothing else missing, but the watch and the vase were not found.

At the end of the evening, James went to the kitchen. Mrs Appleby had been with his family for twenty years and he sometimes dreaded her forthright remarks, but tonight she cut him to the heart. 'If you ask me, the only folks that've been in here was them two ladies. How well did you know them, boss? They were left on their own in there once or twice, when you came to the kitchen.'

There was nothing to say, and her employer turned on his heel. He could not believe he was so bad a judge of character. There must be another explanation.

*   *   *

For the next few days James exercised his imagination, trying to work out a reason for Maud Spencer's strange behaviour. Why would a citizen of York pretend that it was all new to her when he proudly showed off his city? But perhaps they didn't know York, after all. They might have recently moved and not yet started to live in the apartment. That might be it.

With relief, he discovered that the coal-cellar door in the basement had been left unlocked. James found it when he made a last despairing tour of the house, trying to find evidence of burglary. 'So you see, somebody could have crept in from the street and stolen my watch quite easily. The door must have been unlocked since the last coal delivery. We will have to be more careful in future.' James looked severely at his housekeeper. She had blamed his guests too readily, whereas the problem was her own carelessness. 'You are in the cottage most of the time when I'm at work—a thief would have all day to look round the house.'

In spite of the slight doubt still associated with the thought of Maud, or perhaps even because of it, she seemed even more desirable to him. But life flowed on; plans were drawn, birds sang in the leafy trees outside James's office window. The fine weather was a reminder of Bridlington, the quiet little port where there was always the swing of the sea, the mysteries of boats and fishing. It would be good to get back to the sparkling air, so different from the flat, stale air of York. He would go out for a day's fishing with Dan. With this thought, James applied himself to the work with even more energy and finished off a number of smaller projects. The hospital plans were sent off for approval and eventually the senior partner said to his colleague, George, 'I'll be off to Brid again tomorrow for a few weeks. I think you'll manage?'

'Of course, James.' George sounded almost pleased. 'We've made good progress, we can both take it easy for a bit.' He grinned. 'You should get a commission to design a lighthouse or something, set up an office down by the sea.'

'Now that's a good idea, you can come and join me there.' James had thought of that before, but York was far too central for them to give up the office there.

NINE

'Bad news.' Mary Baker came in from the hall with the morning's letters on her tray. She looked at the assembled hands having breakfast at the kitchen table, Helen and Susie at one end and Dan at the other, all cheerfully eating scrambled eggs washed down with large cups of tea. It was eight o'clock on a sunny morning, hardly the time for bad news.

Helen's heart sank a little at the sight of the grim face, but Dan laughed at her. 'What's up, Ma? Some gouty old gent decided to go to Scarborough instead?'

'Well, it is a cancellation, but it's for six folks. Three bedrooms for a week! A family with four bairns and they've all come down with the measles.' Mary shook her head and looked at the letter again. 'Worst of all, I've turned other folks away, telling them we're full up—no vacancies, and now rooms will be empty.'

'But only for a day or two, Mary,' Helen pointed out. 'We're getting more enquiries as the weather warms up.' She poured Mary a cup of tea. Helen had been working since six and the rooms were all clean and ready, with fresh, lavender-scented sheets on the beds and the shine of beeswax on the furniture.

It was not long before the bad news worked in Helen's favour. The day unfolded as usual; Dan went out to check his crab pots and Susie started on the preparations for lunch. When Ruth came in at mid-morning to deliver the vegetable order, Mary lamented that they might be wasted if more folks didn't turn up, but she took them and put the box away in the larder.

Ruth turned to Helen with a faint smile. 'That stuff you gave me was grand,' she said quietly. She still had a pinched look. Her bunched skirts and an enormous shawl concealed her shape, but Helen guessed that underneath it all the baby was showing. It was only a matter of time now before it was common knowledge.

'I'd like to come out with you one day, gathering bait, just to see how you work,'

Helen was saying when Mary came back.

'Well, we won't be on flithers for much longer, thank goodness.' Ruth accepted a cup of tea and sat with them at the big table. 'In May they give up long-lining, and then it's overing before herring season. But I suppose you'll not know what I mean,' she finished, looking with big eyes over the rim of her cup. Helen shook her head.

'Spring fishing's mainly cod and skate—they use over-lines and they're baited at sea,' Mary explained. 'But tell you what, lass, if you spend a day with young Ruth you'll really appreciate working here!'

'I do, I love working here,' Helen protested. 'Especially when we're busy!' The bustle of a full house was invigorating and most of the guests were happy with the service at Seaview. Unlike some seaside landladies, Mary never begrudged large helpings of food and was generous with fires and hot water. 'And I work on the farm at home, I'm used to outdoor work.'

'Ay, lass, but looking round sheep on a fine day isn't quite like Ruth's work. However . . . are you baiting today, Ruth?' Mary asked as the girl finished her tea and stood up. 'Because if you are, I can spare Helen for a few hours, as it happens. We've had a cancellation.'

An hour later Helen, wearing an assortment of clothes including a black shawl and an old pair of boots belonging to Mary, walked over to the rocky part of the shore where she could see several women with the large wicker baskets they used for collecting bait. Ruth was among them and so was Jessie, who waved to her cheerfully. 'Weather's breaking,' Ruth said, glancing at the sky. The bright morning sun was fast disappearing and black clouds were coming in over the sea. Helen put down the basket she was given and looked at the changing sky; already the wind blew cold.

'We'll go over yonder away from the others,' Ruth suggested. 'Flithers might be better over there.' Helen suspected she wanted to keep her secret from the other girls as long as she could. Ruth was even more bundled up than before and she wore thick knitted socks under a short skirt.

The tide was ebbing and there were pools of water among the rocks. 'You pull them off by sliding a knife under them, like this,' and Ruth expertly detached a limpet from its rock. 'We used to use mussels, they're better, but they've all gone, used up. And now flithers are getting harder to find. Here, Helen, I brought a knife for you.'

The work was more difficult than it looked. Limpets stuck to their rocks like—like limpets; Helen cut her hand when the knife slipped as she was leaning over a big rock. Her skirt was soon wet and trailing in the water, although she tried to hitch it up. The rain started to drift in from the sea on the wind, trickling down the back of her neck in spite of the shawl.

The minutes lengthened into hours and still they picked on. Stumbling on a slippery 'scam.' of smooth wet rock, Helen twisted her ankle. She was wet and cold, her shawl was dragging with the weight of rain, but worst of all her back began to ache from the continual stooping over the rocks to collect the flithers. The 'swill' as the basket was called seemed agonizingly slow to fill, but it became heavier as time went on and it was difficult to lug it over the rocks without falling. The swoop of gulls and the curl of the breakers went unheeded as Helen concentrated grimly on getting through the day. There was no seaside joy for the flither pickers. What must it be like in the winter? This was merely a cool summer's day.

When Ruth had filled her own basket and covered the bait with seaweed, she came to help Helen and they were able to talk a little, although Ruth kept on doggedly with the work. Stopping to straighten her back and wipe the rain from her face, Helen looked over at her. 'How can you do this every day? Especially in your condition. . .'

'Hush!' Ruth looked round quickly, but there was no one within earshot. 'Couldn't keep going much longer, but I reckon I'm lucky. They'll stop long-lining after this week, Dan's going out tomorrow and maybe the day after and that'll be the end for the season.' She sighed. 'And after that, I dunno. I really don't.'

Helen's hands were sore and the cuts were stinging in the sea water, she felt as if she could hardly go on, but Ruth was in trouble far worse. The work had evidently wearied her; she was paler than ever and her breathing ragged and fast. 'You sit here while I finish my basket, I know I'm slow,' Helen offered.

'Nay, you've done right well, Helen. We'll finish it together. Your basket'll keep me going for the last day.' The rain was now falling steadily from a leaden sky and the other pickers went home with full baskets, but Ruth and Helen worked on. The pain in Helen's back was now intense, but she would have to summon the strength to carry the basket up to Ruth's house.

It was certainly good experience if she wanted to deliver a full account of the fisherwomen's lives. 'But what about the men? It's easier for them, sitting in a boat, isn't it?' Helen began to think that the carefree Dan should have to do some of this backbreaking work.

Ruth did not agree. 'Men have a hard life, very hard,' she panted. 'It takes a lot of muscle to heave lines in when they're full, and nets the same. How would you like to row a coble in high seas and haul in fish? Most lasses couldn't do it. Yes, there's a sail, but it's not used when they're fishing. There's usually three men, or two men and a lad . . . it's hard, and risky. You have to know what you're doing, six mile out to sea in a high wind.'

At long last the swill was full and Helen thankfully gathered seaweed to keep the limpets moist. Did this hardship actually build character in the fisherwomen? Added to this work, many of them had children to raise and they all had the normal household chores to get through. They were remarkable people, but few outside the fishing community knew anything about their lives.

'Done at last!' Helen straightened slowly and looked about her, but the little town of Bridlington had vanished, although she could still hear insistent hammering from the carpenter's shop. Hiding the town was a dense white fog; she and Ruth were isolated, in a world of their own. 'We won't get lost, will we?' she said cheerfully to Ruth. 'We'll soon be home, and . . .' The sentence was never finished; Ruth had slowly collapsed into a shallow pool of water and lay there, groaning.

'Ruth! Get up, love, we can't stay here!' Helen's heart was beating wildly. The girl was slipping away, not really conscious of her surroundings. 'Ruth! What shall we do? Is it the baby?' Where was Dan when he was needed? But this time, there was no boat in sight and the fog would hide them from the town.

Ruth made a heroic effort. 'Fetch donkey.' Her head dropped sideways and her lips were blue. Donkey . . . where was the donkey? Helen had known where she was relative to the town when the fog came down . . . think, where was the donkey kept?

With a gasp of relief she realized that the donkey shed was not far away. Moses lived close to the beach, in a shed at the back of the greengrocer's shop and that was directly opposite where she was standing. 'Right, but I've got to get you out of the water first.' She dragged Ruth onto a clear patch of sand above the line of the tide, covered her with Mary's old shawl, then ran into the fog in the direction of Moses the donkey.

The shop loomed out of the fog just where she expected it to be, but Helen hesitated before going in. She was panting and she looked totally bedraggled in her present state, just like a beggar woman. And then, Ruth would probably not want Mr Johnson to know of her condition. She looked through the window past the piles of potatoes and onions. There were customers in the shop and Mr Johnson was fully occupied. Like a burglar she crept round to the back, intent on theft. She would steal the donkey for an hour or so.

Moses seemed to be pleased to see her; he was a good natured animal. With shaking fingers Helen put on his bridle, slung the panniers and a saddle on the donkey's back and led him out without being seen. 'It's the first time I've stolen anything, Moses,' she told him. 'But it's in a good cause.'

Sometimes farming experience comes in useful she thought, as Moses picked his way daintily over the beach, following her willingly. Full of energy now and warmer from walking fast, she remembered how exhausted and aching she had been before the crisis. Looking down at her hands Helen saw that they were raw and bleeding, but now she felt nothing. It was strange how an emergency changed everything.

Ruth was easy to find because the baskets of limpets marked the spot where the pathetic little heap of clothing lay on the sand; thank goodness the tide was still going out. 'Now, lass, can you move? Can you try to stand up?' Helen put her arm under the girl's shoulders and raised her up to a sitting position. 'Here's the donkey, we just have to get you up into the saddle.'

Ruth was very cold, but she was conscious and trying to stand; somehow she was heaved onto the donkey's back and the baskets were stowed in the panniers. Helen was thankful that the donkey was so strong, although he was small. Walking alongside she was able to support Ruth in the saddle. Slowly they made their way, on the sands as far as possible to avoid the town, and then when they reached the harbour the fog hid them from curious eyes.

Ruth's street was deserted. 'The women

must be working indoors because of the rain,' Helen said, but the only answer was a groan. First Ruth was half-carried into her house and then the precious baskets were unloaded in the yard. 'I'll light the fire before I take the donkey back,' Helen said firmly. There were kindling sticks and driftwood laid ready in the spotless hearth; Ruth's fireplace was a shining blackleaded cooking range.

'Put kettle on,' Ruth said faintly.

'What do you think ails you, love?' Helen asked gently.

'Pain here . . . I think baby's coming.' Ruth lifted her eyes and there was fear in them. 'Too soon . . . I fell over a rock, twisted myself and I think that did it.'

'Tell me where to find dry clothes and you can put them on while I go for help. Now, who's your doctor?'

'Don't have a doctor . . .' Ruth doubled up as another wave of pain hit her.

Out in the fog again, Helen thought of riding Moses, but she was much bigger than Ruth and it was probably quicker to lead him. It was also warmer if she walked beside him. Amazingly, the little donkey slipped back into his stable as if nothing had happened and Helen replaced the harness on the hooks as she had found it. 'Don't tell anybody,' she warned him and rubbed him down quickly before she left. He was damp from the rain, but would soon dry out.

As she left Moses' stable Helen knew what she should do. She retraced her steps then hitched up her skirt and took the uphill road to Ivy Cole's cottage, praying that the herb woman would be at home. To cover the ground more quickly she ran and walked alternately. By the time she reached Ivy Cottage a pale sun had come out and she could see the sea of fog below her, still hiding the town from view.

Ivy Cole had just finished baking loaves of bread and the fragrance reminded Helen that she was very hungry, but there was no time to lose. 'I think the baby's on the way, but Ruth says it's too soon. . . .' She explained the situation as Ivy put on stout walking boots and took down a basket from a hook in the ceiling. 'I've helped ewes to lamb, but this is different . . . I mean, it's not straightforward. So I came for you, Mrs Cole. I hope you don't mind.'

'Nay lass, you're over young to handle a birthing by yourself. You did right to come for me . . . here, have a slice of bread and honey, you can eat it while I pack the basket.' The herb woman sliced the bread deftly.

Eating the crusty white bread with the golden honey running down her chin, Helen thought that she had never tasted anything so good before. A drink of spring water, and she felt ready to take the road again. 'Thank you, Mrs Cole,' she said with great relief. Somehow the situation was not so frightening now that

146

Ivy Cole was in charge. There was a calmness spreading out from the woman, a feeling that you could almost touch. But underneath she felt a desperate fear for Ruth. She was so young, so undeveloped, not ready for motherhood.

They set off immediately and Ivy set such a pace that Helen had to struggle to keep up with her as they descended into the foggy town. As they went, Ivy asked questions but Helen had little information for her. 'She hasn't seen a doctor by the sound of it, and no one knows she's pregnant. Her sweetheart went off to Australia and he didn't know about the baby, so there's no one to support her.'

Ivy said grimly, 'It's always the same story. A lad has his fun and a lass suffers.'

Ruth's yard was busy when they reached her house. Jessie and two other girls were busy putting the bait on the lines that lay ready waiting. Jessie shook her head when she saw Helen. 'It's a bad job, but we're doing what we can. Poor lass would worry about lines, so we came to help.' She looked at Ivy and nodded. 'Glad you're here, Mrs Cole. We guessed a long while back what's up with Ruth.'

Helen went in with Ivy and they found Ruth curled up on the floor, still in her wet clothes. She offered no resistance and hardly seemed to be aware of their presence as they gently took off the sodden, sandy clothes and put on a dry dress and shawl.

147

Ivy stooped over the girl and then straightened when all was done. 'She's bleeding, of course.' She looked at Helen. 'Do you want to go and help the lasses in the yard? I can manage here for now.' She walked Helen to the door and when they were outside she added, 'I don't like the look of the lass. She'd be better off in the hospital, to my mind.'

'Is there . . . a hospital close by?' Helen was surprised.

'Ay, lass, there's the Lloyd Hospital in town, they do a good job, especially for fisherfolk.' Ivy turned back into the house and Helen went to join the girls in the yard.

It was late afternoon and Mary would wonder what had kept her so long. Helen felt torn between her duty at Seaview and worry about Ruth. She felt awkward in the yard; her fingers were still raw and it was hard to put the bait on the hooks. A cold wind was blowing fog between the houses, blowing through her damp clothes. What hope was there for Ruth, for any of these women, trapped in this life?

After a while, Jessie took pity on Helen. 'Don't worry, Helen, we'll soon be finished here. Hadn't you better go back to your place?'

Not knowing what to do, Helen went back to Ivy and found that nothing had changed. 'Put some more wood on fire for us, and then go back home,' Ivy told her, firmly but kindly. 'You've done your bit. Lasses here can fetch a horse and trap to take her to hospital, I think that's what we'll do. It's my belief that this baby won't come without a lot of help.'

Guiltily, Helen said goodbye to the girls and walked back through the harbour. There were few people about. As she passed the little tourist shop by the harbour, a big man came out and scowled at her. It was Bert Hardy, Jessie's father. 'Still hanging about round here? Why don't you stick with your own kind?' He was carrying two large boxes and grunted with the effort.

Helen said nothing but stared after him as he walked away, purely to annoy him. He carried the boxes along the quay to where his boat was moored and jumped aboard, then lifted them in after him.

Once at Seaview Helen hoped to creep upstairs unnoticed and change into clean dry clothes before going down to the kitchen, but as she slipped in through the back door she ran into Daniel. His eyes widened at the sight of her. 'Hey lass, where've you been? You look like a drowned rat!' He laughed in his usual carefree way, but his eyes were worried.

'Oh, Dan . . .' The strain had been too much and Helen stood looking at him with tears on her face. She could not forget the poor girl lying on the floor in a pool of water and blood. Having a baby must be a terrible ordeal, but for Ruth. . . . She tried to hide a sob.

Dan turned quickly and led her into the

washhouse in the yard. 'Don't go in yet, there's a guest in the kitchen giving Ma a piece of her mind. No, nothing to worry about, it happens sometimes. Mother will say yes and no, and let it all go by. But you, Helen, what's up, lass? I've never seen you in such a mess before.' He sat on the deal table and swung his legs. 'But yes, I know . . . there was talk of your going with the lasses, fither picking. It would be too much for you.'

Should she tell him what had happened? Helen hesitated and Dan took her hand gently, then turned it over in his own. 'I thought so, it's too hard for a lass like you. But it's over, Helen, you needn't cry, lass.' He looked at her keenly. 'What else has happened?'

'I—I was with Ruth, and she—collapsed, out on the rocks. I took her home on the donkey.' That part at least Helen felt she could be proud of. 'And then I fetched Mrs Cole.'

Dan looked serious. 'What's wrong with Ruth, then? Did she fall or summat?'

There was no point in hiding the truth; it would be all over the harbour by tomorrow. 'Ruth's in trouble, Dan. She's all alone, she's expecting a baby . . . and her lad has gone off to Australia.' Dan would have known the lad, he employed Ruth to bait his lines. 'Did you know him? He's been thoughtless, if nothing worse.'

Helen realized that Dan had slipped off the table and was standing in front of her, his face white with shock. 'A bairn? Oh, hell. I'd no idea . . . what on earth can we do? Oh Helen, what will she do?' He looked so stricken that Helen reached out and put a hand on his shoulder. 'There was a young lad, Eddie; he stayed with her a while ago . . . lodged in her spare room because he had nowhere to go, so she took him in. Kind like that, Ruth is. Folks might blame Eddie.' He turned away. 'It's a bad job, Helen.'

'But is it fair to blame the other lad, if the baby's not his?' Helen was still not quite sure about Dan. After all, he must have spent time with Ruth. Could he . . .? It was easy to imagine a girl falling for Dan, letting him love her if that was what he wanted. He would be hard to resist.

Dan looked at her and his young face was grim; all his lightness was gone. 'Eddie's gone, Helen. He was drowned at sea in the winter. They found him in the end . . . knew him by his Brid gansey, the pattern on it. A grand young lad, was Eddie. He came out with Robbie and me once or twice. Ay, it might have been Eddie, but he can't help her now.'

Helen looked at Dan thoughtfully; he seemed very young for his age and now she felt older than Dan. 'Do you love her?' she asked abruptly.

The young man looked startled. 'Well . . . I

151

fancied her, you know, sometimes. I like the lass. But—I don't want to marry Ruth, just like that, if that's what you mean. It's not my baby, Helen.' But he still had not mentioned the lad who went to Australia.

TEN

'Well, Ruth, and how are you?' Helen's words sounded hollow in her own ears. She could see how Ruth was, quite clearly. What could anyone find to say to her? The girl lay quite still in the hospital bed, her face nearly as white as the sheets, her eyes blank and hopeless.

A thin little voice came up from the bed. 'Helen. Thank you for everything . . . you were grand. And Moses.'

It was some days after Ruth's collapse and Mary had suggested that Helen walk up to the Lloyd Hospital to see her. 'Then you'll settle down and stop moithering,' she suggested. Helen had been working all morning, but was preoccupied and had to be spoken to at least twice before she answered. 'She'll be in good hands up there.'

Mary knew some of the story, but no one knew the whole truth. Although Dan might be suspected, Ruth was obviously never going to tell and the other girls had apparently gossiped about poor Eddie when he stayed with Ruth, so Dan might escape the blame. Ruth was so shy that her real feelings would have been well hidden. But how could such a shy little thing get into such trouble? It was usually the bold girls like their dairymaid . . . Helen's thoughts went round and round. The next dilemma for Ruth would be how to support herself and the baby.

'You'll find she's very low,' the nurse had whispered when Helen asked about Ruth Rawson. 'She lost too much blood, she's very weak. And she lost the baby, of course. It was born dead, poor mite. There was nothing we could do.'

Helen stood by the bed holding a bunch of flowers and trying to find something to say. It must be terrible to lose a baby, however much trouble it would have brought and Ruth had been quite determined that she wanted to keep it. 'You'll soon be up and about.' But what had Ruth to look forward to? A hard life and not even a chance of marriage, now her reputation was gone. Ruth would be labelled as a fallen woman. 'You'll soon get better, Ruth.'

'I don't want to get better. I want to die.' It was only a whisper, but the bleakness in it was horrifying. Helen felt as though she were looking into a black pit. In her own sheltered life she had never imagined such misery. 'Don't try to hold me . . . I want to go.' Helen sat down in a chair by the bed and thought furiously. Was there any hope that she could hold out, to comfort Ruth? 'He was a boy,' the little voice whispered. 'My baby boy.' Tears rolled out from under her eyelids and down Ruth's pale face. 'I wanted to keep him . . . somebody of my own.'

Helen swallowed her own tears and said as calmly as she could, 'Have you no relations, Ruth? No brother or sister?' She knew that the girl's parents were both dead.

'No . . . nobody will worry when I go. It won't matter.' Ruth was obviously not playing for sympathy. It was the unvarnished truth.

The next day and the next week were just the same. Helen went to see Ruth for a few minutes and came away feeling more depressed each time she visited. Mary went with her on one visit and the doctor told Mrs Baker, whom he evidently knew, that they felt that Ruth was slipping away. 'She has no will to live, we're powerless to help her,' he said sadly. She still had curtains round the bed to shield her from the rest of the ward.

One day Dan was with Ruth when Helen visited. She had guessed that he had to face his worker at some time. After all, Dan was Ruth's employer in the line-fishing season; he had probably told the nurse that he was her boss. He sat by the bed opposite Helen, straight and slim, the picture of health and vitality except for his worried frown. Ruth was weaker than ever, Helen thought as she took the girl's almost transparent hand. 'I want to say something to Dan,' Ruth whispered. Helen stood up to leave, but Ruth held on to her. 'Please stay, Helen.'

Helen put her arm round the girl and raised her up a little on the pillows. Ruth was a little more animated than she had been. 'Dan, when I've gone, don't you blame yourself. You couldn't look after me . . . nobody could help what happened.' Her eyes closed and they thought she had fallen asleep. Then with an obvious effort she roused herself again. 'You're not to worry, Dan. Just . . . take care. You too, Helen.'

Helen turned the words over and over in her mind. Dan looked most concerned, if not guilty. It seemed to point to some kind of bond; had Dan been the lover who caused her problems, or was it just that he employed her? Was his interest kindly, or did he prey on young girls? It was a chilling thought.

'Come on, lass, get well. We'll all help you, honest.' Dan stretched out and gently took Ruth's hand.

The next day the nurses said that Ruth was very ill and should not be disturbed. It was Wednesday; Helen had a few hours to spare before the evening meal at Seaview.

Ruth needed help desperately and her time was running out. There was only one thing for it. She would have to see Ivy Cole, to see

155

whether something could be done before it was too late. If anyone could pull Ruth back from the brink it was Mrs Cole, but how it could be done, Helen had no clue.

The lovely June afternoon was fragrant with roses as Helen walked through the town. The summer season was getting under way and crowds of people were strolling at leisure, laughing and talking. The pretty dresses of the women were a world away from the drab working clothes of the fishergirls. When she was only halfway to the herb woman's cottage, Helen looked over a hedge and saw her walking slowly across a grass field. Helen stopped by the gate to watch; at first she thought that Ivy must be looking for herbs, but this time she had no basket. She carried two thin sticks in front of her as she walked. A man who was obviously a farmer was watching Ivy from a distance. Seeing Helen, he strolled over to the gate to speak to her. 'Good day. You looking for Mrs Cole? She's got her hands full, just at present.'

'Yes, I can see that she's busy . . . is she dowsing?' It was important to see Ivy and she would be worth waiting for.

'Looking for water. There used to be a spring round here, and I want to make a water trough for cattle. Ay, Ivy's dowsing for water, lass. Ever seen it before?'

Helen nodded and looked over at Ivy again, who was now a little nearer to the gate. The process went on for some time but eventually, the sticks twitched and jerked. The farmer hurried over to her and stuck a pole in the ground. 'I think you've got it. Just try a few other spots, in case.' Ivy obediently went round in a circle but when she came back to the pole, the sticks jerked more violently than ever.

'This is it, John. I reckon we've found your spring.' Ivy Cole looked up and saw Helen at the gate. 'Come in, lass, you can try with the rods.'

This was like witchcraft, a weird sort of a skill. Helen tentatively took the rods in her hands and walked across the uneven grass. They were just hazel twigs, nothing more. She tried holding them tightly and then slackened her grip, but it made no difference. Nothing happened, even when she approached the marker.

The farmer laughed. 'That's why we get Ivy in. It's a gift, seemingly. Some folks don't hold with it, they think it's a bit heathen like. But I knew Ivy would find the water if it was still there. I've seen her work before.' As they watched he took a spade and dug a deep hole in the pasture. Water soon began to trickle into it.

Ivy Cole watched the water rising with the mysterious sticks under her arm. And how's the patient? I've been to see her once, but she was asleep.'

'Well . . .' Helen did not like to discuss poor

Ruth in front of a stranger. 'She needs—encouraging. I came to ask you to see her, she's very down.'

They were walking up to the farmhouse and Helen looked round the yard. You could tell a lot about people from their yard. Contented hens clucked and scratched in straw under the barn and a huge carthorse looked out over the stable door onto a yard swept clean of dirt. A range of farm tools hung from hooks on the cart-house wall. The farmer led them through the yard and opened a gate into the garden. 'Come up and have a cup of tea, both of you,' he suggested. 'Martha has kettle on, I'll be bound.' Helen looked around her with delight at the pretty flower garden, sheltered by a well-kept hedge, where roses were just coming into bloom. They passed a neat vegetable plot with rows of potatoes in flower, beans climbing up a trellis and quantities of cabbages. These were people after her own heart; they liked order and growing plants, they took care to live in pleasant surroundings. Some farmers said there was no time for gardens in their lives.

'Now, this here sponge cake was made specially for Ivy's visit. So you both have to have a piece,' Martha said firmly as soon as they appeared. The farmer's wife was rather bent, with a pleasant, placid face and she wore a clean white apron.

Helen was introduced to the farmer and his

158

wife. 'Helen Moore's a farmer's daughter. John and Martha Beck have a nice little farm here,' Ivy explained.

'Ay, but we're fast getting too old to get through the work,' John Beck lamented.

'Inside and out, it fair keeps us going.' He turned to Helen. 'I suppose this young lady wouldn't be looking for a place, would she? We could just do with a nice lass, to live in and give us a hand with the work. We'd treat her like our own.'

Martha looked up eagerly from pouring the tea. 'How about it, lass? We nobbut have one son and he's gone off to the university. Would you like a job with us, Helen? I'm sure Ivy will give you a character.'

Helen was shaking her head when an idea occurred to her. Ivy's eyes met hers; they had the same thought. 'No, I'm afraid I have a job for the summer and after that I have to go back to our family farm. But I do know a nice, hard-working lass who might be looking for just such a place.' She paused to think. 'In a week or two, when she's—free. But we'll have to talk to her first.'

When the tea had been drunk, Martha asked Helen if she would like to see the room that was reserved for this 'hard-working lass' if she ever appeared. 'We'd try to make her happy, to settle down with us,' the older woman said. 'And of course we could try it out for a few weeks first, to see if it suits.' She looked at Helen. 'I do hope we can find a lass soon.'

Helen was enchanted; the room was sunny and bright, with a cheerful patchwork quilt on the bed, pretty flowered curtains and a warm rag rug on the floor. She would have been quite happy to be given that room herself. 'It's lovely, Mrs Beck,' she said sincerely. It was considerably bigger than her little attic room at Seaview. 'What work would the lass be doing?'

'Housework, and gardening . . . she could feed poultry and cats and dogs, milk the cow— we don't have a dairy, there's only one cow and I make a bit of butter.' Martha smiled and smoothed her apron. 'I pride myself on our butter. But washing day's a trial to me now, I could do with a hand for the washing and ironing.' It sounded easier than picking flithers on the rocks, but so did almost anything a woman might be asked to do. 'Then there's pet lambs to feed, an' all. . . . It would suit a lass who likes animals and doesn't mind getting her hands dirty.'

'I came for you today to ask you to talk to Ruth,' Helen explained as she and Ivy walked down the farm track after the visit. 'She seems determined to die. There's nothing they can do to make her better, if she doesn't want to live.'

And yet . . . if she could meet the Becks . . . I think she'd love them, and the farm too. It's a nice mixture, a few pigs and ducks and chickens, they breed beef cattle as well. I can imagine she'd love feeding orphan lambs with a bottle. It would be easier than what she's used to and a sight cleaner too, and she'd get good food.' Ivy was thoughtful. 'How can we get her interested?'

Helen thought back to when she had first met Ruth, in the kitchen at Seaview. Even then she had been subdued. 'I think she's been miserable for a long time, and weighed down with work beyond her strength . . .' And probably hopelessly in love with Dan, although that would never be mentioned. Knowing the lad, Helen could imagine how the shy girl could easily be dazzled by those blue eyes and that merry laugh. Dan was a charmer, there was no doubt about it. 'I wonder if she'd like country life? She did love the donkey.'

Ivy laughed. 'Country life is no rest cure as we both know, but it has a soothing effect sometimes for folks who like plants and animals. And summer's here. We'll have to think of a way to reach Ruth.'

The next day Helen asked for an hour off in mid-afternoon, to visit the hospital. She could hardly say that they were trying to save Ruth's life, but Mary seemed to understand. 'Just make sure you get back for serving up dinner,' she warned, but with a smile. 'Two more guests in tonight, we'll be busy enough.'

Helen and Ivy met outside the hospital.

'What will we do if they say she's to have no visitors? And what will we say if we do get in?' Helen was doubtful about their mission. It was true that the Becks's farm would be a perfect place for Ruth; she would be away from whatever caused her downfall, and out of reach of the whispering fishergirls. But how could she be made to see it?

They did not make a promising start. The nurse on duty, rustling in a starched uniform, let them in after a little persuasion by Ivy. But Ruth had her face turned away and there was no movement in the bed. The rescuers both sat down by the bed and looked at each other. Then Ivy said, speaking very clearly, 'We'll talk a bit before Ruth wakes up. What did you think of those folks we met the other day?'

Was this going to do any good? Ruth did not move. Then Helen saw a possible line of attack, and took it. 'I was so sorry for the poor thing, that old lady, Martha Beck. Crying out for somebody to help her, all that work to do and she's got rheumatism. Did you see her twisted hands? I felt so sad that I couldn't help them, Ivy, when she asked if I'd like the job.'

'Ay. It's a grand little farm and only a mile or two from here, but they can't last much longer on their own. John Beck said as much to me. They need looking after, Helen. Some lass with a kind heart who wants to live in and help with the work. But lasses these days have their own lives to live, and most of 'em don't

162

know what hard work is.'

Helen took up the story. 'Fishermen's wives and daughters work hard enough, don't they? But they can't get away. Poor Martha, she has such a kind heart, but she'll never find a lass to repay all that kindness, and it'll break their hearts to leave the farms, sell all the animals.'

There was a movement in the bed and Ruth turned to face them. 'I was listening to what you said. Who are the folks you're talking about?'

Ivy turned to her as if surprised. 'We thought you were asleep, lass. It was just a place the other day . . . it so happened that Helen and me were visiting Fernhill Farm at the same time. We said we'd try to find them a young woman who wouldn't mind a quiet life in the country and who could help with the animals and such, a lass who likes animals. Trouble is, that job needs somebody who really wants to help.'

'Somebody quite unselfish, that's the need.' Helen looked at Ruth.

The girl met her eyes with a question in her own. 'Do you think I'm selfish? Too wrapped up in my own troubles?'

Ivy spoke for them both. 'We think you've had a load of trouble, enough to bring you down. It's natural to grieve. But there's so much to do in the world and so many folks needing help . . . folks like the ones we were speaking of, John and Martha Beck. There's always a reason for getting up again, Ruth.'

She struck her head theatrically and Helen almost laughed: Ivy was overacting. 'Now why didn't I think of it? That place would suit you. There's a nice little place for you to do some good, Ruth, if you're so minded. If you have the courage to get up and start again.'

A small amount of colour appeared in the pale face. 'You've got no right to organize my life. Go away, leave me in peace!' Her voice was stronger now as it rose in anger. 'You don't know what it's like, what I've been through!'

Ivy looked at her peacefully. 'Very good Ruth, we'll go now. But I've lost a bairn myself, as it happens, and a man. And Helen's lost sight of a lad she loved. It's hard we know, but it happens Ruth and we can't blame you for wanting to give up.' She paused and then added, 'We'll come back in a day or two, see how you're going.'

As they left the nurse appeared. 'You got a reaction out of her, anyway. It might do some good.'

As they left the hospital Helen asked, 'How did you know about Charlie? I'm recovering, of course, but it hurts.'

Ivy's grey eyes were bright with amusement. 'I'm supposed to be a witch, remember? At your age you're bound to have had your heart broken at least once. To me it was obvious why you were sent to Seaview for the summer. Now, I'm not sure whether we'll get anywhere with Ruth. But it's worth a try.'

164

ELEVEN

Seaview was ticking over busily when Helen got back from the hospital. There was a buzz of conversation from the drawing-room as the guests mingled before dinner, vegetables were cooking on the stove and trifles stood in a row on the kitchen table, waiting for their cream topping. She went quickly into the dining-room to lay out the cutlery and there was Mr Kirby, in his old place by the window. The evening sun was behind the house, but its light was reflected by the sea into the dining-room. Helen felt a rush of affection as she looked at him working away at the table, bathed in the evening light. It was so good that he was back.

'Helen!' He seemed genuinely pleased to see her. Mr Kirby looked thinner than she remembered him, and rather too pale. 'Have you got some stories for me? I've been working on the book, but there are some gaps and it must be finished soon.'

'Good evening, sir. Mary didn't mention you were coming back.' To her surprise, Helen found herself blushing slightly.

'That's because she didn't know until I walked in at three o'clock. I had to apologize of course, and I said I'd go out for dinner if it was easier for her. But she said there was plenty of dinner and I am to stay. Thank goodness my room was free.'

But of course, he was a favourite with Mary Baker. 'Your room's always the last to go, Mr Kirby, just in case you appear.' Helen gave him a smile across the table.

'I must go, I've been out this afternoon and Mary needs my help. But I do have some facts for you. I went out with the lasses, gathering bait.'

Kirby nodded. 'Excellent. I'll talk to you when you have a spare moment, Helen.'

After a hesitation at the door, she asked him, 'Did you meet Miss Spencer in York, Mr Kirby?' It sounded impertinent, once it came out.

Kirby's face changed for a moment and Helen thought he looked sad. 'I did. I showed them round the city, and of course they were impressed. I think—I hope that they will be coming back to Seaview before the end of the month.' That was less welcome news.

Helen thought she might be in trouble for being away so long, but Mary Baker was surprisingly calm. 'You can take in the soup when you're ready, Helen,' was all she said when Susie reported that everything was ready. Helen whipped cream for the trifles and she added a small spoonful of vanilla essence before the finish. Mary raised her eyebrows at this and Helen explained that this was the way her mother served whipped cream. 'Ay, well, right enough.'

A mixed group of guests looked up in anticipation as Helen carried in the plates of pea-and-ham soup. Demure in her black dress and white cap, she ignored one or two facetious remarks from a young man who was probably a commercial traveller. 'My, are all the girls in this town as bonny as you, honey? What a lovely bottom!' he began, ignoring Helen's frown and the icy looks from other guests. But when she brought in the dessert this young idiot pinched her as she passed his chair. Helen felt like hitting him with her tray, but business was business. 'Please do not do that, Mr Simpson,' she said severely, moving away.

'What's the matter, don't you like a bit of fun?' the youth enquired. He was a Geordie from up north, dark and good-looking in a flashy way; he obviously thought that any female would be sure to fall for his charm. Mr Simpson, who was flushed and might have had a glass or two of something strong before the meal, persisted. 'Come on, bonny lass. Give us a smile, do, don't be so miserable.' He managed to squeeze her round the waist as she distributed the trifles and she nearly dropped a dish. The temptation to pour a trifle over his head was great, but it would never do. Helen suddenly realized how helpless you were as a servant; thank goodness, few men she had met took advantage of that fact.

Mr Kirby left his place and stood over

Simpson, who grinned up at him. 'If you do anything like that again I will knock your head off,' he growled savagely. Helen was amazed at the change in the normally mild James Kirby. 'Let me know if he annoys you again, Miss Moore,' he said formally and went to sit down again. To the table at large he said, 'Miss Moore is the assistant housekeeper at Seaview. She and all the staff are entitled to respect.' The other guests nodded and smiled at Helen. Miss Burton looked repressively at the offender. 'Such behaviour is not tolerated here,' she said.

'Thank you, Mr Kirby, Miss Burton.' Helen left the room wondering whether the writer had over-dramatized the situation. Some of the salesmen thought they could flirt with a maid, but she was usually quite able to put them in their place, having had plenty of practice with seasonal workers at home. Her normal method was to step sharply on a man's foot if he came too near her, but it was not possible here; it was not wise to make a scene in the dining-room. Helen was sure that Roy Simpson posed no threat. He was just tiresome.

Later that night, she realized her error. It was eleven and the house was quiet. Helen had written her journal and was putting it away, dressed in her nightgown when the bedroom door opened and in walked Simpson with a grin on his face. 'Glad I found the right room.

Now, miss, I've come to apologize if I upset you down in the dining-room. But it's not my fault if you're so bonny, is it? Say you'll forgive me.' The idiot went down on his knees in front of her.

'Get out of my room at once!' Helen spoke quietly so as not to disturb the whole house. What should she do? This had never happened before. At first she had kept her door locked at night, but after a few weeks she had decided that it was not necessary. Dan, the only possible source of trouble as she had seen it, was safely down in the basement. She picked up a hairbrush, the only weapon to hand.

Simpson stood up and made a lunge, taking Helen off balance. They both fell on the bed and his arms were round her, surprisingly powerful. She could smell whisky on his breath. 'Now then, don't pretend you don't like it! Come on, lass, and don't struggle, you'll only make me worse.' The lout started to take off her nightdress and fondled her. 'You're leading me on, you naughty girl.' He kissed her roughly on the mouth.

It was so unfair; she was trying to get away from him. Black anger gave way to fear as she realized her predicament. Helen was struggling unsuccessfully to get free when James Kirby rushed in, waving a walking-stick. 'Get out of the house!' he shouted and beat the man about the head with his stick. 'If you

169

don't leave within ten minutes I will call the police.'

'She led me on, the bitch! What's a bloke to do?' Simpson dodged the worst of the blows and took off down the corridor.

Kirby watched him go, tactfully turning his back on Helen's undress. She wrapped herself quickly in the bedspread. 'Thank you so much, Mr Kirby. How did you know what was going on?'

Kirby still looked grim. 'I stayed up to keep an eye on things. I rather thought that Simpson might try something like this. He's dangerous.'

Helen was trembling. 'I feel dreadful. I didn't encourage him, honestly, Mr Kirby.' She put a hand to her bruised mouth.

Kirby smiled. 'I am sure you didn't. Get dressed and come down to the kitchen, girl. I think you need a hot drink before you go to sleep.'

Helen was trembling; she wrapped herself in a shawl and they crept down the stairs like burglars. Kirby stirred the fire to boil the kettle, he smiled reassuringly at Helen, then he went off to make sure that Simpson had departed with his belongings. 'I will report him to the police if I see him in the town again,' he promised when he came back. 'What a lout! He's the kind that thinks every young servant girl is his for the taking. It makes you realize what some women have to deal with. I'm afraid there are some very arrogant men about.' The dark eyes were concerned as Kirby looked over at her.

There were, too, some very kind and thoughtful men, thank goodness. 'Oh Mr Kirby . . . it would have gone badly for me if you hadn't come up,' Helen shuddered. Was this the kind of thing that had happened to Ruth? She sipped the hot tea, gradually feeling calmer. It was over, and no real damage had been done.

When the drinks were finished Kirby looked at Helen across the table. 'We'd better go, you have to get up early in the mornings. But Helen . . . will you call me James? You can drop the sir, you know. Mary and Dan both call me James, I'm almost like family here.'

'Very good, sir . . . James.' The rule at Seaview was to address the guests in the way that they preferred, but Helen felt oddly embarrassed. 'And thank you so much for tonight. I don't know how I could have got away from him, if you hadn't . . .'

'I saw him creep up the stairs to the attics, but it took me a minute or two to find the walking-stick. Have you a lock on the door? Good, I advise you to use it from now on.'

*   *   *

The episode with the guest haunted Helen for a day or two and her chief feeling was one of embarrassment. How could she have been so careless as to leave her door unlocked? The world was a dangerous place, she could see that now. Mary Baker was horrified when she heard the story. 'You should have let me know,' she said grimly to Kirby. 'He won't be staying here again. Now Helen, would you like to report him to the police? It must have affected your nerves.'

Helen thought for a moment. 'I'd rather forget about it. He's not local and he probably won't show up here again. He was only there for a few minutes before Mr Kirby came. It was unpleasant, but no harm was done.' Thank goodness; if James had not appeared she could have been raped. Simpson had been drunk enough not to care about consequences, but sober enough to be dangerous.

There was a strict rule at Seaview: no guests in the kitchen. But the next evening, Mary relaxed her rule and James was invited into the kitchen after the dinner had been served and cleared. Conscious of the honour, he sat at the corner of the table with paper and pencil in front of him and waited patiently for Helen and Dan to finish washing the dishes. Mary gave him another cup of coffee. 'I hope you realize the trouble young Helen was at, finding out stuff for your book,' she said severely, but with a small smile.

Dan had been invited to the conference because of his local knowledge; James had rarely managed to sit the lad down to talk to him. Mary hovered in the background until James brought her into the discussion. 'You can tell us whether it was the same in your day,' he said persuasively.

Outside was a chilly blue evening with a cool wind, but the kitchen was cosy and the kitchen fire was still red from being built up for cooking. When the work was done they assembled at the table and Helen looked round with satisfaction. This was a good place; she was enjoying her time at Seaview. She looked into the future; could she do what Mary was doing? What would it be like to run a good boarding house? She came from a farm, but farming was not really where she wanted to spend the rest of her life. Her parents would line up some suitable young farmer, but it would be good to make her own way in life. A bold idea for a female, but why not?

'Are you with us, Helen?' Dan was calling the meeting to order. Surprisingly, he took the lead. 'James, we know you want to—er— record the lives of working folks. Helen has a story to tell, and Ma and I can back her up. So we'll start with Helen, won't we?'

Mary smiled at Helen. 'I sent him to a good school, although you wouldn't often notice.'

Dan flashed her a smile with the blue eyes and applied himself to his task. 'So let's start with Helen. Your day out with the lasses.'

'Ay.' Helen did not usually speak in dialect, but Dan provoked her. 'Right lad, we was out there for hours pickin' flithers off rocks . . .' She settled down and gave them a clear account of what she had learned. Kirby took notes and Mary listened attentively.

Will you make us famous?' Dan asked with a wink at Helen and she frowned at him. This was a serious business.

Helen told him of the work of Jessie, Ruth and the rest. Of course Mary would know much more about the whole thing, but James said it was good to look with fresh eyes. 'We went for a trip round the bay, too, with Mary's brother,' she added. 'Over on the headland there are smugglers' caves, Dan says.'

Mary laughed scornfully, but Dan was serious. 'You remember I told you about finding the lantern? I really think there's something going on out there in the bay.'

James Kirby looked up from his notebook. 'Of course there was smuggling in the eighteenth century, but I thought the coastguards had put a stop to all that by now. And the taxes on imported goods are not so high—one would think it's not worth the risk.'

'And also, there are so many visitors about. How could criminals avoid being seen?' Helen put in.

'That can work two ways. When I was a lass, strangers down at the quay end of town were very rare,' Mary reminded them. And there were very few pleasure boats. I reckon it would be easier now to come and go without being spotted in the summer, just mix in with the holiday crowd. These days, folks like to watch the boats come in, but they don't really know what they're looking at, do they? Not that I agree with Dan,' she finished. 'But I think you have to keep an open mind.'

Dan sat back with his hands behind his head. 'Well, I can't prove anything, but I think there's more happening at night than line-fishing.' Mary looked glum as he proceeded, 'You remember the lantern, Helen? The other night there were lights in the bay. Rockets went up and when Robbie went to see about it, he was told that the lads were firing them off for the visitors. It was the Terry gang, some of the trawler lads who are a bit rough.' He grinned at his mother. 'Not like me, Ma. I'm a respectable boat owner.'

'So where is this leading?' James wanted to know.

Dan grinned and flashed a look over at Helen. 'I was watching the bay. I saw a glimmer of light, no more, but I reckoned that a boat was sitting out there while everybody's attention was on the flares. So . . .' he paused and looked round the table; every eye was on Dan, but he said no more.

'The rockets might have been a diversion,' James agreed.

'That's what I thought, James. There was

something—it was the dark of the moon, remember—something else going on, out from the harbour.' He glanced at his mother. 'We need to find out.'

Helen knew what Mary thought, and she agreed. 'Dan, you should report this to the coastguard or the police. It's not for you to go finding out.' She glared at him, but the silly lad just laughed.

'James and I will do a wee investigation.' Dan was imitating the Scottish fishermen again. 'Nothing dangerous, ye ken, but James might get some good stories maybe, liven up the book a bit—' He was interrupted by a loud knocking on the front door and everybody jumped.

Helen put her cap straight and went to answer it. In the last of the twilight she could just see two figures on the step, a man and woman, well-dressed and probably in their fifties. 'Could you possibly give us a room for two nights? We are sorry it's so late, but we've been dining with friends.'

Helen was about to open the door wide and let them in, but a new caution had taken over and she went to fetch Mary. Was it not suspicious that they appeared so late at night, with no booking? Mary's glance swept over the couple and past them to where an elegant trap and well-groomed horse stood waiting in the road. 'We've no stables, sir,' she said quietly.

The man glanced round and then smiled.

'My friends sent us here, with their trap and groom,' he explained. 'Our luggage is in the vehicle, we travelled by train.'

'Very well, sir, madam, come in. We have one room left, you shall have it. But I'm afraid it's at the back of the house, with no view of the sea.' People had complained in the past that, in a house called Seaview, all the rooms should front the sea.

The woman looked relieved. 'Thank you so much, we are very tired.' Her earrings caught the light as she moved her head and Helen thought how elegant they both looked. Was she wearing real diamonds? Her necklace and rings all seemed to match the earrings. She smiled a tired smile at Helen as she came in. Her husband motioned to the groom and the bags were brought in. Helen studied the newcomers, but she could see nothing suspicious about them. The man took off his hat as he stepped inside and his silver hair gleamed in the lamplight. He was the picture of respectability, stockily built and with an air of authority.

The room was ready, as the rooms always were. Helen took them up the stairs, followed by Dan with the bags. 'Our name is Bartlett. This is a pleasant room, thank you. No, we don't need anything else except perhaps a jug of water. Don't trouble to light the gas, the candle will do very well. What time do you serve breakfast?' The wife was now doing the talking.

'Well, well,' Dan said when they got back to the kitchen. 'Bartletts staying here! Bigger places must be full. If that's the bloke I think he is, he owns half Hull and a lot of steamboats. Must be him, I reckon.' He frowned and Helen remembered that Dan didn't like steamboats.

By the time the Bartletts had been settled in it was late and soon all hands went to bed. It was some time before Helen felt sleepy. Had the episode of Mr Simpson affected her more than she knew? A week ago she would never have looked for a reason when visitors appeared late at night. Some people booked weeks in advance, but others left it until the last minute, gambling on the fact that there were so many boarding houses and hotels in Bridlington. There was no reason not to trust them. If you ran a boarding house, you had to take strangers on trust.

The next morning the Bartletts came down to breakfast in good time. They were dressed quietly but expensively; Mrs Bartlett's only jewellery was a small diamond brooch. Helen was kept busy serving the meal but she watched the couple and decided that they were harmless. But were they just too good to be true? Pleasant and courteous, apologizing for troubling her for another piece of toast. Some guests enjoyed ordering Helen about, but not the Bartletts.

The morning post brought another surprise. 'The Spencers are coming back,' Mary announced. 'You'll remember them, Helen, the lady and her deaf mother. She asked me to tell Mr Kirby they're coming.' There was the hint of a smile. 'But we can't fit them in, not this week. They can have dinner, of course, but they'll have to sleep elsewhere. Maybe Mrs White will have room.'

Remember them? For weeks, Helen had been thinking about Miss Spencer and her unfortunate effect on James. Were the Spencers trailing James Kirby? They were not Helen's favourite guests. James was too good for her, Helen decided gloomily, too decent and honest to see through her. The thought of his possible future unhappiness was hard to bear.

As soon as breakfast was cleared, Helen was sent off to ask Mrs White for rooms for the Spencers. Her house in Church Street, in the old part of town, was smaller than Seaview and not so well known, and she was grateful for some more customers. 'Ay, lass, but I don't do dinner as you know, just bed and breakfast. So Mrs Baker might have to feed them.'

James had gone out to the library and Mary forgot to tell him about the Spencers' arrival when he came back. It was not until just before dinner, as Helen was putting fresh flowers on the table, that he walked into the sitting-room and saw the mother and daughter on the sofa,

179

Maud with a green dress arranged bewitchingly around her. He looked shocked and stammered something. Helen tactfully left the room, but not before she saw Maud sway gracefully to her feet and glide across the room to greet her old friend. 'James, where have you been all day? I was sure you would be here to greet us! And did you know we've been banished to another house? You will need to escort us there, after dinner.'

TWELVE

Dinner at Seaview was taken with all the guests assembled round the big mahogany dining table; fifteen people could be seated easily. That night the Spencers joined the other guests and Helen detected a coolness in Maud's manner, probably due to the fact that the Bartletts were talking to James. Miss Burton was in her usual place, quiet as ever, but taking a keen interest in the general conversation. She gave Helen a pleasant smile as the girl presented the basket of bread rolls.

The Bartletts dressed formally for dinner and Helen caught Maud Spencer looking enviously at Mrs Bartlett's gown, which was a quiet dark-blue but looked expensive and contrasted well with the sparkle of her earrings. They were an elegant pair, Helen thought as she served the meal, more suited to one of the top hotels than to the more modest Seaview. They were what she thought of as 'Scarborough types'. But it was good to know that Seaview had been recommended to people like them.

'Yes, we are actually from Hull. I'm in the fishing industry,' Bartlett was saying to James when Helen cleared the soup plates. He had a gravelly voice and a flat Yorkshire accent. 'I don't go out on the boats myself these days, thank goodness. That's a young man's job.'

When another guest politely admired her earrings, Mrs Bartlett said that they were a gift from her husband on her fiftieth birthday. 'So you see there are some good things about growing old.' She smiled. Helen, passing the tureens of vegetables, realized that Dan had been right. This was the fleet owner from Hull, enjoying his money and success.

The conversation round the table became general and James was called upon to give an account of the history of the area. He described the unusual self-government of the town, which had no lord of the manor but had been run by the citizens since a group of them bought the manor in the seventeenth century. Miss Burton agreed and James added a few details. 'They are rather like a town council, but they're called the Lords Feoffees,' he explained.

Maud had obviously been hanging on

181

James's words with great interest. 'You know so much, James—does he not?' She appealed to the other diners. James looked embarrassed, Helen thought as she served the coffee. The woman was very beautiful; any lonely man would feel the attraction. But when you listened to her, Miss Spencer was irritating. Surely James could see how insincere she was?

The Bartletts were staying for two more nights. Mr Bartlett explained, 'We're having a short holiday, and also my wife has promised to visit the hospital. She is to donate towards its upkeep, you see.'

The next day Helen had to point out where they would find the hospital, and was asked for her opinion. 'I've visited a young woman there recently, it's very clean and neat. The local people are only asked to pay what they can afford, so the hospital needs donations.' The sun was shining, the sea was sparkling, so Helen added, 'You could walk there in about half an hour. You would enjoy the walk.'

The Bartletts decided to take Helen's advice. They changed into walking shoes and set out, with an umbrella in case of showers. Helen hurried back to the kitchen to help with lunch; seven guests were expected to lunch, including Mr Kirby and the two Spencers. Why didn't they go out on such a lovely day?

The Spencers went for a short stroll along the sea front, accompanied by James. Helen wondered again about James; he seemed to be fascinated by the lady, but perhaps it was an unwilling fascination.

Dan had not been about the day before, but now he lounged into the kitchen while Helen was peeling potatoes and leaned on the table. 'Now we're into July, things are going to get busy. I'm off on the herring tonight. Will you miss me, Miss Moore?'

'Not at all, Mr Baker,' Helen said tersely, in case Mary was listening. 'But who will spy on the smugglers while you are gone?' She would miss Dan if he were away for a long time. He lightened the kitchen and was a good hand at washing dishes.

Dan laughed. 'Nay, lass, all the boats will be on the herring soon, I reckon there'll be no fancy business for a while. Lads that have been up north say shoals are good this year. Some from Staithes have been up to Aberdeen— they come down with the shoals and finish up at Yarmouth by the end of summer. Did you see those Scotchmen in harbour last week? There'll be more of that soon.' He beamed the blue eyes over the table. 'But dinna worry, I'll only be gone for a few days. We wait until the shoals are off Yorkshire and then go out. Our boats aren't big enough to stay out for too long, and the market here's good enough.'

'I suppose you'll net the herring—so there'll be no more of that dirty business of collecting bait. And that reminds me . . . is Ruth out of

183

hospital, do you know?' There had been no spare time to visit Ruth for the past few days.

'Jessie told me she's gone to stay with the herb woman up on the Gypsey Race. Poor lass is very down. I don't know how she got into that pickle. I suppose we'll never know.' Dan looked at her, the picture of innocence, his brow untroubled by guilt, it seemed. 'But yes, she's out of hospital. I don't know what she'll do next, but of course I've no work for her, now line-fishing's finished.'

Was Dan innocent? Helen would dearly like to know, but Ruth would never tell.

It was possible to imagine that the blue eyes could be hard and that he could selfishly take what he wanted, but he was usually so genial that one would think seduction would be more in his line, rather than cold-blooded rape. But in that case, why was she so unhappy and why could they not make a match of it, as the workers had done on her father's farm? Ruth was very young, but she was not coarse and, with a better life, she would probably be pretty.

It was good to know that Ruth was being cared for, but it would be a while before Helen could visit Ivy Cole to see how she was faring. Seaview was full and with Dan away there would be even more work to get through. It was their elderly maid's job to make the beds and tidy the rooms after the guests had gone out in the morning, but old Freda had been away for a week with a violent hay fever, so the job had fallen to Helen. With Freda missing, Helen had to move very quickly to keep up with the work in the time allotted, but she was becoming more experienced and enjoyed the challenge . . . until the day when the Bartletts were to leave.

That morning, Helen was amazed to meet Roy Simpson on the stairs, making his way down while the guests were at breakfast. 'What are you doing here?' she asked fiercely. 'You were told never to come here again.'

Simpson grinned and waved a razor in his hand. 'Left this in the bathroom, hinny. My property, entitled to get it back, see?' He disappeared with a bang of the front door.

Mary was indignant about Simpson's appearance. 'Yes, I saw the razor,' Helen felt bound to apologise, 'but I thought it must belong to James, so I left it on the shelf.'

Mr Bartlett went out straight after breakfast to look round the harbour, while his wife packed up their belongings. Flora Bartlett came downstairs at mid-morning with a worried look on her face. 'Helen, you came in to make up the bed while we were at breakfast?'

'Yes, Mrs Bartlett. Is anything wrong?'

'I seem to have mislaid my diamonds—they were in a leather jewel case, wrapped separately to prevent scratching. You didn't see them, did you?' She passed a hand over her eyes. 'They must be there somewhere, but I can't find them.'

A cold feeling crept over Helen as she realized that if anything went missing, the chambermaid would be the first to be blamed. 'No, madam. I didn't see a jewel case. Would you like me to help you to look for it?'

They both went up to the bedroom and searched through all the drawers and wardrobes. Mrs Bartlett emptied their suitcases and heaped up all the clothes on the bed, but the jewel case was nowhere to be found. The poor woman was distraught. 'My husband will be so very upset, there was a necklace, the earrings, a brooch . . . gifts from him. They're irreplaceable.' A tear rolled down her cheek. 'And, of course, worth a great deal of money.'

When Mr Bartlett came back and heard the news he was grim. He spoke very quietly to his wife, but there was a savage note in his voice as he said, 'You have been very careless, Flora. This is all your fault. Thieves watch out for people like you.' The poor woman broke down in tears.

Another search was made with no result, then Mary insisted that the police were called. She said they had to do the right thing. Mary, Helen and Susie were taken into the sitting-room and questioned separately. Then the police came back to Helen and asked her all sorts of questions. 'How can you tell real diamonds from fake?' the police sergeant asked abruptly.

Helen was bewildered. 'I've no idea.' Then she remembered reading about them. 'Diamonds can only be cut by another diamond . . . they're harder than anything else.'

The police exchanged significant glances. 'Well, miss, you do know a lot. Who took them, then?'

'You might ask Mr Simpson, a travelling salesman. He came in this morning to collect a razor he'd left behind. I met him on the stairs.' Suppose he'd stolen them? It was quite possible, Helen thought.

'Really.' The sergeant made a note. 'Do you remember what jewellery Mrs Bartlett wore?'

Helen thought for a moment. 'I noticed a necklace and earrings on the night she arrived, and the next day she wore a brooch. I couldn't describe them very well, though; I was serving meals.' She felt unreal, as though she were in a nightmare.

'We'll have to search your room.' The constable went off to conduct the search while the sergeant continued with questions. 'Mrs Baker says she's sure you are honest. But she hasn't known you very long, has she? Now, you can tell me about it.' The policeman leaned nearer and Helen backed off a little. His thick red neck bulged over the tightly buttoned uniform. 'Stands to reason, a lass on a

187

servant's wages might be tempted. One necklace like that would set you up for life, buy you a place of your own . . . is that how it was?' He suddenly shouted. 'Tell me, and quick, or it'll be the worse for you. Where are they?'

Silence. Helen sat still, stony faced and numb with shock.

He lowered his rough voice to a whisper. 'Hard labour you'll get, but sentence might be lighter if you tell me now. Save the force a lot of time and money. It's so obvious, you have to be the one that did it.'

Tears were not far away, but Helen was not going to let him break her. 'You know nothing about me. I'm here for the summer to learn housekeeping and I did not steal Mrs Bartlett's jewels!'

The constable, a younger man who looked a little scared, came back. 'Nowt, Sarge.' He put Helen's journal on the table. 'But there might be summat, a clue, in this.'

The sergeant flicked through Helen's precious papers and that was the last straw. Before they could stop her she stormed out of the room. In the hall she ran straight into Kirby. 'James, you must help me! Those men are bullying me! And they've got the journal and all my notes and drawings!'

James put his hands on Helen's shoulders. 'Steady, lass! Yes, Mary has just told me.' He walked with her to the sitting-room. 'Look here, officers, I have just heard what's going on. You are mistaken, and no doubt time will show that Miss Moore is innocent. I suggest you look elsewhere for the thief. I shall speak to the chief constable if you persist in harassing this young woman.' The men muttered, but James got his way. Helen was cautioned and told not to leave the area, but at last they went off to question the Bartletts again.

Back in the kitchen, Mary was wringing her hands. 'Nothing like this has ever happened here before. Never.'

Helen sat down, feeling very shaky, and Mary handed her a cup of tea. 'The best way to clear this up is to find the real thief,' James said firmly. But nobody could think of where to look. Dan would have had a theory by now, but Dan was away at sea. Would Dan suspect Miss Spencer? The wicked thought nagged at Helen. That would upset James, but it was possible. Maud had slipped out of the dining-room at one point while they were all at breakfast; Helen had met her on her way back.

'I never noticed the diamonds, but then, we've been busy,' Mary admitted. 'Were they real, do you think? I'd have offered to put them in the safe, if I'd known. We sometimes lock up valuables for guests.'

James smiled. 'If they were real, they're worth a fortune. I noticed, actually, that all the light seemed to come out of the top of the

189

stones, like a pinpoint of light it was. And there were several big diamonds in that necklace, as well as blue stones, sapphires, I think. It is hard to remember what you've seen. I don't make a practice of staring at ladies' bosoms, but the jewellery was unusual, I thought.'

As the day dragged on Helen wondered whether anything would ever be the same again. The other guests had been questioned, so everybody knew about the theft. The Bartletts eventually left, Mr Bartlett extremely displeased. He said he had important engagements in Hull and his wife was too tearful to speak to anyone; they were taken to the railway station to catch the Hull train. It was to be hoped that she would not be punished for the loss.

The Spencers went out to dinner with friends and the meal was a sombre affair at Seaview that evening. Afterwards, Helen could hardly eat her own meal; she was isolated, the object of suspicion. Miss Burton had been questioned when she came in after school and, like James, she told the police that she was sure Helen was innocent. But character references were not going to be enough to clear her of the theft.

'Freda's back tomorrow,' Mary said suddenly. 'That will be a help.'

'Then if you can spare me for a while I'd like to see Ivy Cole.' The thought of Ivy's calm presence was comforting.

*   *   *

'I don't know what to do, Helen.' Ruth's voice was as bleak as her white face as she looked across the beds of rosemary and lavender. They were sitting in the sun in Ivy's garden, but the herb woman was out in the lanes, gathering whatever herbs were ready in July; Ruth was not sure what they were. After a pause she continued, 'I can't stay here. Ivy is very kind, but I've got to earn my living. But then, I can't face the thought of my house . . . living there again. It has been so good to get away!'

Bees were buzzing among the bushes, making the most of the fine weather. The crowded fishermens' houses seemed a world away. Of course Ruth would shrink from facing the other girls who lived in the street. 'But you'd soon get over it, and folks would soon forget,' Helen tried to tell her, but the girl shook her head. Perhaps it was time to talk about something else, to take Ruth's mind off her troubles. 'I've had a few problems,' Helen confessed, and told Ruth about the jewellery theft.

'That's terrible,' Ruth wailed. 'I'd die if anybody accused me. It would be grand to find out what really happened, wouldn't it?'

'And before that. . . .' Helen had not

191

mentioned Mr Simpson to anyone, but she had to face the memory some time. 'A guest at Seaview came up to my room and tried to rape me. He nearly did; he'd have succeeded if Mr Kirby hadn't come along. It was frightening, but I was lucky.' She breathed deeply, closing her eyes. It was over, it would not happen again. 'It's the first time I've told anyone, but I can't forget it. I feel . . . different, and more suspicious.'

To Helen's surprise, when she opened her eyes Ruth was weeping helplessly. Soon she was sobbing; hard, heart-rending sobs. When they had subsided a little Ruth said with a catch in her breath, 'That's the worst thing that can happen, the very worst. It makes you feel dirty . . . shameful yourself. I know, Helen! I know all about it!' Then she looked at Helen, appalled. 'I never meant to say that.'

Helen put a hand on Ruth's. 'It was time you did, Ruth. There's a lot bottled up inside you, isn't there? I have wondered whether— something like that was the cause of your problems.'

'For years,' Ruth said wearily. 'He found me on my own one afternoon and . . . forced me, just after my ma had died. I was about thirteen then. After that, he used to . . . force me . . . every week or so. Sometimes in the night. I tried locking the door, but it was no use. He was clever, so nobody knew. It was easier to give in, then it was over sooner.' She stopped and Helen waited. 'He's a fisherman, used to creeping about at all hours and folks are used to seeing them go about in the night. The lads go off at odd hours, depending on tide.' She looked at Helen and shuddered. 'I can't tell you more, lass. He'll kill me if it gets out. But that's why I can't go home . . . to face that. It would start all over again.'

That bleak statement made Helen cry: the thought of unimaginable suffering. At thirteen, she herself had enjoyed life. To think that Ruth had no means of escape; until being taken to the hospital and then coming to Ivy's she had been living in that little house in fear, waiting for the next attack. Men like that did not deserve to live. It couldn't possibly be Dan . . . could it? He seemed so pleasant, but his mother had warned her against him and he did seem to have a selfish streak, although that was quite normal for an only child, Helen thought. But she had the feeling that she knew the man, and that was why Ruth wouldn't tell her.

The tears stood in Helen's eyes as she watched a bee foraging for nectar. She could never laugh and joke with Dan again. He was the lad with easy access to Ruth; he went to her house every day in the season for the bait. He could slip about the town in the night and, because he lived in the basement, even Mary never knew what time he came in. Yes, it could be Dan. Perhaps it was true, as a cynical older woman had once told Helen, that all men were beasts and not to be trusted. 'Trust no man,' she had said, an awful warning. Let it be anyone else . . . not Dan!

When Ivy Cole came back with her fragrant basket of summer flowers, she found both girls very quiet. She looked at them both, then said, 'Can you hear? Gypsey Race is running again.' Helen had been conscious for some time of the gurgle of water, like quiet laughter at the bottom of Ivy's garden. 'It comes and goes . . . it stops and starts in different places and that's why folks used to think it had something strange about it.'

Helen walked down the flagged garden path bordered with lavender to the edge of the stream. The Gypsey Race was shallow and clear, chuckling over pebbles and fringed with water-mint and long grasses. Standing there, Helen felt herself grow calmer. She would go back to Seaview with renewed strength and she would not despair, either for herself or for Ruth, but hope for better times. Was there in truth something special about this erratic stream? She walked back to the others with a lighter heart.

Ruth went inside to put the kettle on to boil and Ivy sat down on a garden chair.

'We'll have rosemary tea today, it's good for nerves and low spirits. Ruth still needs a lot of help. So, how are things at Seaview?' Her grey eyes were concerned when she heard Helen's story of the jewellery theft. 'I wonder . . . it might be worth trying to find them.'

'That would solve it all, but how?' Helen had been turning it over in her mind ever since. How could anyone know where to look? The rosemary tea might help her, too.

'I haven't done it for years, but—do you remember when you tried dowsing for water? Well, some folks can find other things— minerals, especially.'

'And diamonds and such are minerals, they come from the earth.' Helen sat up straight. This was weird stuff, but Ivy had certainly found the spring of water, that day in the field. 'Do you—do it with the hazel rods?'

'As I said, lass, I haven't done it much at all and not for many years. But it can be done with a pendulum. There's a piece of quartz on the shelf yonder. I've no idea how it works—it frightens some folks.' Ivy looked over at Helen with a gleam in her eyes. 'The witch at work . . . don't tell anyone! We'll have a cup of herb tea first. Can you draw a plan of Seaview, do you think?'

Rather mystified, Helen sketched out a plan of the layout at Seaview on the inside of a paper bag that Ivy gave her. When the teacups had been cleared away the herb woman took out a triangular piece of quartz on a very thin chain. Ruth looked frightened and went off to shell peas. Helen almost held her breath as she watched Ivy hold the pendulum over the plan.

It moved slightly on its chain, swung in a wide circle, but then was still. 'Nothing there.' Ivy looked up, still frowning with concentration. 'If it still works, that means the diamonds are not at Seaview. But I can't be sure.'

'And we have no idea where else to look,' Helen said quietly. 'Well, thank you for trying, Ivy.'

As she was putting away the pendulum in its bag, Ivy turned to Helen 'Find me a map. That might work . . . cast the net a little wider.' She stood up. 'And now, let's go in and try to persuade Ruth to take the farm job. Just for a week or two, at any rate.'

Helen shook her head. 'That's just as hopeless, if you ask me.'

*   *   *

Dan always looked forward to the summer, and this summer promised to be a good one. Richard Mason, the skipper of the yawl he sailed on, was a decent man, known for being lucky when fishing. Of course that was just superstition, but it was strange how some of the old sayings turned out to be true. It was unlucky to go out on a Sunday, and only months ago some lads from Flamborough had been caught in a storm one Sunday: one of them drowned.

Armed with their gear and some food from Ma, Dan and Robbie scrambled on board the yawl *Invincible* with good expectations of profit. It was a cloudy evening with light winds. About four hours east of Bridlington, they were among the herring. Down came the sail and the skipper turned *Invincible*'s head into the wind.

It was natural to start to calculate your profit, especially after a lean winter and spring. Dan was thinking with half his mind about how much the catch would be worth, while the other half concentrated on the job in hand. He was tying barrels to keep the warp afloat, the long, thick rope that held the nets, while Robbie tied on the nets and shot them over the side. Three other men and the skipper were below, having a bite to eat.

Clouds hid the stars and it was black out there on the water; there was a long, smooth swell. They had nearly finished and most of the nets were shot when out of the darkness they heard the sound of engines. Big engines; a steamboat was bearing down on them fast.

Robbie jumped up on the hatch with a lantern, waving frantically, but the boat came on. They could soon see its lights, but it was so big that the deck was high above them. Unless the trawler men were keeping a sharp watch they would not know that the Bridlington boat was there. Mason scrambled on deck, but it was too late to hoist the sails and, with the nets out, they could do nothing to avoid a collision.

'You've had it this time, lad,' Dan muttered

to himself. 'Too far out to get help, unless those buggers turn round and fish us out.' His mother would never recover if her son, like his father, was lost at sea. 'Sorry, Ma,' he whispered. Helen might comfort her. The yawl rocked violently in the trawler's bow wave; their huge nets were probably under her. If she was hit amidships and broke up, she would go down in a matter of minutes.

The *Invincible*'s crew watched helplessly as the steam trawler came on, so close they could pick out peeling paint on her side in the light of their lantern. Mason was shouting hoarsely, but his voice was lost in the inexorable thump of the engines. Dan shut his eyes as the steamer scraped by; it grazed their bows and then bit deeper; there was a splintering crash. The warp was tangled in the trawler's gear and was swept away, along with their barrels and nets. Their boat was listing badly and taking in water.

Was this the end? What a way to go, not fighting the elements like his ancestors, but pushed into eternity by a hulking great monster from the future. Men invented engines and then they took over; the world was finished. The beauty of sailing ships and the skill of their crews would soon be a thing of the past. Instead of fear Dan felt a mounting wave of anger, futile rage against the modern world and the greed that insisted on bigger ships and bigger profits. But it was too late now to worry about anything. There was confusion and shouting and there was water round his feet.

THIRTEEN

Dan was braced for the end, eyes shut, but minutes passed and he was still alive, after all. When he opened his eyes there was just time to see a large B and a number on the trawler's side, and her port of origin, Hull. Then with the sound of tearing timber she was gone, steaming heedlessly through the night. Had she seen the *Invincible*?

All hands turned to the pumps; the yawl was taking in water. Richard Mason cut free the remains of their gear, hoisted the sails and tried to rally the devastated crew. 'We'll get home, never fear,' he told them. 'It will take time, but we'll get there.'

'Do you believe him?' Robbie muttered. 'I doubt it, meself. She'll never last the trip back to Brid. Oh Dan, why did we come to sea?'

'Only the good die young, remember.' Dan looked up briefly from pumping and Robbie managed a grin. The lad was only fourteen, you had to encourage the youngsters, but it was going to be a long, dark night. They were all very weary when, rather to Dan's surprise, they made it into port at last.

'Here I am, Ma. Late again.' Dan limped into the kitchen the next evening and Helen caught her breath as she looked at him. It was going to be hard to forget her suspicions, to treat him as before and to laugh at his jokes. Ruth's story had affected her deeply. She could imagine the pain, both mental and physical and the shame that prevented her from seeking help. If only Ruth would tell the whole truth.

Dan was often scruffy when he came in from fishing, but tonight he looked battered and bruised, totally exhausted. 'Give us a bowl of soup and I'm off to bed.'

Gone was the charm, the beguiling look. This Dan was older and grimmer than before; it was possible to imagine him capable of anything.

Mary shook her head at her son and went out to find him some clean clothes. Helen heated up some leftover soup. 'What happened?' she asked quietly as she passed him a hunk of bread.

'Disaster.' Mary came back and sat down quietly at the table, listening. 'We were run down by a bloody big steam trawler,' Dan said briefly, slurping his soup. 'Ruined the gear . . . stove the hull. We've come back without any fish. Bartlett's boys just went steaming on, never even noticed us, I should think, or if they saw us, didn't care. We could all have been killed, of course. We were lucky to get back,

200

pumping water all the way.'

'Maybe you need more lights,' Mary suggested. 'It should mend?'

'Our boat? Well, it's a yawl, if you know what that means, Helen. Boat will mend, but Skipper hasn't got much heart for it, not at the moment anyway. Probably not much cash, either, we're only at the start of the season. That leaves me high and dry.' He looked ready to murder the trawler men. 'Robbie and me, we think this is going to get worse. Steam trawlers are going to wipe us out, given time.'

Helen thought about their farm, where similar things had happened. 'Well, I suppose that's progress. My father hires a steam engine to do the threshing. Steam is powerful, you know. Old folks don't like it and you don't need so many labourers, but it's quicker. So, maybe you'll go to sea with the steamboat owners, in a year or two.' It was easy to see why he was upset, but Dan was young enough to learn about steamboats. She poured him a mug of strong coffee to brace him.

'Well, thank goodness it's not your loss, Daniel,' Mary said philosophically. Not your boat, this time. And as Helen says, you might join a steam trawler crew one day.'

'Never!' The blue eyes flashed angrily. 'You've no idea, Ma, there were no steam trawlers in Dad's day. It's a labourer's job, you're just a stoker, there's no skill about it. It's as bad as working in the alum quarry like

Grandfather did . . . nasty, dirty work. It's nowt like sailing. And it's bad for the fish stocks.'

This must be serious; Dan was not easily upset. 'What does that mean? I suppose if they are big boats, they can catch more fish?' Helen could hardly believe that herring in the North Sea could be fished out.

Dan took a drink of coffee and set down the mug, as Kipper the cat came out from her place under the table and jumped up on his knee. Stroking the cat, Dan considered his answer; he looked too tired to think fast. 'Bigger boats, more hands on the job, that's true. But that's not all. When we go on the herring, we throw the small ones back. Anything caught in those big nets will die, so they only throw dead fish back.' He leaned back in his chair. 'And they stir up the bottom, disturb the plants and such that fish feed on.' After a heavy silence he added, 'We don't mind the Scotch and the Cornishmen coming in, don't think we do. There's plenty of fish for all when the shoals come down, but, these steam trawlers will take the living off us all.' He looked round. 'Where's James? He should know about this. He should write to the papers about it.'

Mary smiled thinly. 'James is taken up in the drawing-room. Miss Spencer is here.' So Mary had noticed his preoccupation with the beautiful guest.

'Oh well, I'll see him soon.' Dan seemed

indifferent to James's fate. He looked over at Helen. 'And how's Miss Moore? What's been going on?'

Mary looked at him carefully. 'I think we'll talk to you in the morning, my lad. Go to your bed.'

Dan staggered as he got to his feet and Helen thought how wise Mary was not to burden him with their problems just now. 'Goodnight, Dan,' she said neutrally. Only yesterday she had been longing for his help with finding the diamonds but after talking to Ruth she was not so sure.

Miss Spencer and Mr Kirby were sitting close together on the sofa when Helen went through to make up the fire. Unlike other boarding houses, Seaview always offered a fire in the evenings, even on summer nights. Kirby moved away from her slightly when Helen appeared. 'We were talking about the diamonds, Helen,' he said.

The lady looked at him disapprovingly. 'The less said the better, I should think, especially to the servants. One never knows. Dear James, you are so good, but you should not become involved.' Helen was treated to a cold look.

'Surely—' James began, but he was overruled. 'Mama says, and I agree, that the modern habit of treating servants as equals is deplorable. It leads to all kinds of liberties being taken, and then to jealousy and envy. And we all know what that means.' The lovely face looked as serene as ever, turned appealingly to Mr Kirby.

'You can bring us another pot of coffee, Moore.'

'Well, that puts me in my place,' Helen said cheerfully. She put some coal on the fire and departed, externally serene. James was looking uncomfortable. Outside the door she quaked; she had just been rude to a guest. But how dared Miss Spencer be so patronizing? The implication, too, had been there that Helen was responsible for the theft. Surely James wouldn't believe it?

Later that evening when the Spencers had gone to their rooms, James came into the kitchen. 'A word with you, Helen, if I may.' Helen was alone in the room and she nodded. 'I hate to say this, but Miss Spencer says she saw you coming out of the Bartletts' room while they were at breakfast. She went upstairs for something, that's when she saw you, looking very flushed and guilty and carrying a cloth bag. That's why she . . . said she thought you stole the jewels. I told her it couldn't be true. I told her not to mention it to anyone else.' Kirby's dark eyes were worried. 'Miss Spencer said she had thought about it, but her conscience would not allow her to keep silent.'

One could imagine just how adorable she would have looked when she said that. Miss Spencer should be on the stage. 'I suppose she told that to the police,' Helen said bitterly. She took a deep breath; it was an effort to keep calm. 'It's my job to make up the beds, as you know, James. And of course I changed the towels, that's all I was carrying—the laundry bag. As for looking flushed, I was trying to do two peoples' work that day. Freda was away . . .' She would not cry, but she felt like screaming.

Mary came into the kitchen. 'Time you were in bed, lass. Don't keep her up talking, James.'

James went off, with an apologetic look at Helen. 'Very well, Mary. Goodnight. Try not to worry, Helen. I'm sure it will all turn out all right.'

It was time for bed, but sleep was out of the question. Helen sat on her bed, shoulders slumped, too dejected to write the journal. Things could not be worse. She was accused of theft and Dan—bright, amusing Dan—might have a hidden side. He could be a cynical rapist. Dear James would have supported her but for Miss Spencer; he was heavily under her influence and might eventually believe, as she apparently did, that Helen was guilty. Come to think of it, why had Miss Spencer been upstairs at that time? She could have gone into the Bartletts' room at some point.

Helen sighed; suspicion was poisoning the whole atmosphere at Seaview. For a moment or two she thought of asking her father for help, but there were good reasons for keeping quiet. One was the devastating effect it would

205

have on her respectable family, and the other was a sense of independence. It was the first black time she had known since leaving home, and she would deal with it as an adult. Before she left, the family had agreed that Helen would not go home until the end of the summer.

The next morning Dan seemed to have recovered his normal cheerfulness. He ate a late breakfast with gusto and then announced, 'I can't go to sea, Ma, until the boat's mended. There's no pots out, crabs are over now, shells are soft.' He made a face.

'Why don't you walk over to Ivy Cole's and see how young Ruth's getting on?' Mary suggested. 'She was your worker, after all.'

A flicker passed over Dan's face. 'Well, I could borrow a trap and take you over there if you like, Mother dear.' Was his conscience bothering him? How would Ruth feel if he visited, assuming that he was her tormentor? And yet . . . when she thought she was dying, she had apparently forgiven him.

Mary was reading a recipe book at the table and she looked severely over her glasses at Dan. 'And how do you think I can leave the house, with all these guests? You can go on your own and I'll give you a list of stuff to get from Ivy.'

'You look worried, Ma.' Dan's cheerful face fell a little.

Helen turned from the sink to face him.

'Dan, you don't know what's happened while you were at sea. A guest lost some valuable jewels—and some people think that I stole them.' Helen's voice quavered in spite of herself.

There was a silence and the two women looked at Dan. The blue eyes took on a cold and steely look. 'What people? This could ruin the business, Seaview can't stand any hint of trouble. Now, tell me all about it. This needs sorting out. Whose were the jewels?'

Together they told him the story, and Dan whistled. 'The Bartletts' jewels? I told you that Bartlett owns half a dozen trawlers fishing out of Hull. It's ironic—it was one of their boats that ran us down. His crews are mostly jailbirds,' he finished contemptuously.

'But it's charitable to give men who've been in prison a job,' Helen said reasonably. 'There won't be much temptation out at sea and they can make a new start.' She had heard a talk once in Pocklington about the good work being done by charities to help unfortunate souls who had fallen by the wayside. Now she went cold to think that she could be among their number, if the theft were to be blamed on her. It could happen if the police couldn't find the real thief, because Helen Moore was the only person known to have been into the Bartletts' room. It was like looking into hell.

Dan's mind was evidently racing. 'That might be it! One of their workers knew about the diamonds, had a grudge against the Bartletts and crept in and stole them.' He sat back in the kitchen chair with the air of a man who had solved the mystery. 'They employ hundreds of men. Some of them might live hereabouts.'

'You could be under suspicion, if it's known you don't like the steam trawlers,' Helen told him bluntly. 'You've got a big enough grudge, after the accident.'

Dan shook his head. 'Not my boat. Skipper's the one who's suffered most.'

'Do you think we go about with our eyes shut?' Mary scoffed. 'I can't believe that a suspicious character could get in here without being seen.'

It was Dan's turn to scoff. 'They don't all creep about with a cudgel and an eyepatch. Have any tradesmen been here? Have you let any strangers in, for any reason? Who else was staying in the house as a guest? I should think it would be easier to get into Seaview than into the Bartletts' mansion; they'll have a lot of staff looking out for trouble. Rich people always do. By golly, Ma, we can't let the business go to rack and ruin. We'll have to do something. And increase security, as well.' He was obviously thinking of his inheritance.

'Mr Simpson came in for his razor,' Helen said. 'Could he have been the thief?'

'Maybe. We should find out where he went. Who does he work for?' But nobody knew and there was a thoughtful silence in the kitchen. After a moment or two Dan added, 'Don't worry, lass, you're ruled out as a suspect. You wouldn't have the nerve for it.' He gave Helen a flash of the old grin, but now it looked wolfish to her, predatory. 'I will stay in Brid today and see what I can find out.'

'Thank you very much!' She managed a laugh.

Mary sighed. 'I thought you were off to see Ruth. Very well, Helen can go. We need to help Ruth if we can.'

It was a fine day and it would be good to get out of Seaview for an hour or two. Helen went off after lunch had been served, in a slightly happier frame of mind, a basket over her arm and the bonnet on her head. Dan was on the case for his own reasons, and it would have been more comforting if he had ruled her out because of her good character. But at least he did not think that she could have stolen the jewels.

*　　*　　*

'Did you bring a map?' Ivy sounded unusually anxious. She and Ruth were crumbling dried herbs for storage when Helen arrived and the pungent aroma of sage and mint filled the room. Helen produced the map from her basket and the witch spread it out on the table. 'Now, we'll see.' She produced the quartz pendant and held it over the map, concentrating. 'Where—are—the—diamonds?' It was a strange procedure; how could it possibly work?

Sitting in the quiet kitchen and listening to the ticking of the old clock, Helen gradually relaxed and only then did she realize how tense she had been. She was innocent, she should have nothing to fear, but the cloud hung over her head. Of course, the jewels could be anywhere by now; they might have been whisked off to London.

Ruth looked over apprehensively, but went on with her work. Helen thought she was looking calmer and a little healthier for her stay at Ivy Cottage. Evidently Ivy had not liked to mention the Becks and their farm again, but the patient was now capable of walking . . . why not persuade her to come out? 'Ruth, I wonder if you'd like to come with me for a walk?' she said as casually as she could. The pendulum circled above the map . . . it was hard to drag your eyes away from it. 'Just for an hour or so.'

Just at that moment Ivy drew in her breath sharply, then looked across the table at Helen. 'I think they're still in the town.' The quartz appeared to be pointing to Bridlington. The map covered a large section of the east coast and the stone swung over towards Bridlington. 'Somebody must have hidden them there.' She laughed. 'That is, if we believe the stone.' She peered closely at the map. 'It's hard to say where . . . but it keeps swinging back to the old town, not the sands where the visitors go. Not Seaview, in other words. More like Church Street, that area. Or even the harbour.' She looked tired, as if it had been an effort. 'I wonder . . . Don't get your hopes up yet, lass. I am not sure, although I could feel a strong pull.'

'Thank you.' What else could she say? Helen was not sure how this helped; you could hardly search all the houses in the old town, or offer the pendulum as evidence to the police. 'Dan is trying to find out what happened, I'll let him know.' But Church Street . . . that could be Mrs White's, the boarding house that took the overflow from Seaview. The Spencers were staying there! Maud could have stolen the jewels and hidden them among her belongings. And then, Simpson had gone there when James threw him out. He'd had dinner at Seaview the night before the Bartletts arrived, but he may have intended to stay longer; he could have been there for the diamonds if he had known that the Bartletts were coming. But would a professional thief draw attention to himself by getting drunk and assaulting a woman? 'We had guests who later went to Church Street . . .' she would tell the police, but omit any mention of the pendulum. She paused and then added, 'Ivy, I've asked Ruth to come for a walk.'

Ivy's eyes lit up with understanding. 'Ay, we'll all go, it will do us good.' The witch looked drained, as though the pendulum had taken her energy. When Ruth went off to get her walking-shoes she said to Helen, 'We can walk past the farm, maybe see John and Martha.' Ivy had guessed what she was thinking. If Ruth could meet the couple, it could turn out well.

The afternoon was warm and they were all glad to reach the shade of the trees in the lane leading to the Becks' farm. Ivy carried a basket and now she said innocently, 'I'd like to call in here, Martha wants some dandelion coffee. She's trying it for the rheumatism.' So they all turned up the drive between well-trimmed hedges. There was no one in the house, but across a field they could see a horse and cart and the green fragrance of new-made hay came to them on the light breeze. 'Hay time,' Ivy said happily. 'I used to love it when I was a lass.'

It was enough to make a farm girl homesick. In a large bonnet and faded blue dress, Martha was turning the hay over with a two-pronged fork, letting it fall lightly to the ground. John was at the other side of the meadow, loading hay onto a farm wagon. In the next field a labourer was mowing more grass with long, rhythmical sweeps of the scythe. Birds sang in the trees and wreaths of sweet-scented honeysuckle trailed down round the old hawthorn hedges that marked the field boundaries. The sunshine, of course, made all the difference to life on the farm. It was like a picture in a story book of life in the country; even the horse posed picturesquely, swishing his tail at the flies. Helen breathed deeply, savouring the scents that reminded her of summer at home, now evocative because she was living with the sharp tang of sea breezes and the hard pavements of the town.

Ruth looked about her happily. 'What a lovely place! But I suppose it's very hard work if you live here.'

Martha was in trouble, Helen could see that as they came up to her. The kindly face was flushed and she moved stiffly. 'You should let younger folks do the job!' Ivy chided her, but Martha shook her head.

'There's only John and me, and it might rain by end of the week. We've got to make hay while we can.' She continued with the work. 'Excuse us for not stopping.'

Ivy looked round and then said firmly, 'Martha, you must have more forks somewhere. We can all help for an hour or so, it should make a difference.'

Martha nodded in the direction of the farmyard. 'There's two or three in barn yonder, but I don't like . . .' But by then Ivy was striding back to the barn.

'If the hay gets rain on it, it's spoiled, of course, or at least, not so good,' Helen explained to Ruth. She introduced Ruth to the farmer's wife.

'I'm sorry you find us like this, but it's hay time. We'll have a drink when field is finished,' Martha said apologetically, looking at Ruth. 'Nice to meet you, lass. You'll not be used to farm life, if you come from Brid.'

'My uncle has a farm out Sewerby way, he's always worried about hay. I'd like to try that,' Ruth said, watching Martha's movements.

When Ivy came back with three hay forks, the work went on much more quickly and soon the whole area was turned. Helen had often helped with the hay at home and Ivy was an expert. John came up with his wagon of hay and touched his cap to the visitors. 'My, it's not often we get help like this!'

'I've not done much, but I'm learning,' Ruth said earnestly. Her hands were only just turning pink from handling the fork, but already Helen's were sore.

'You're tougher than I am! It must be with working on the bait,' Helen told her.

Ruth smiled, a real smile for the first time. 'I can turn my hand to most things,' she said.

When the shadows were lengthening and they were beginning to feel weary, Martha brought out a big wicker basket from under a hedge and they sat under a tree to drink cold tea and eat currant scones spread lavishly with butter. Helen sat back contentedly. If this did not help Ruth nothing would, and it might also

214

help Martha. Come to think of it, she felt better herself for the change of scene. Seaview was an uneasy place at the moment.

John took his cap off to reveal a pleasant, open face, lined and brown from the sun. He looked at Martha and she nodded. 'Well, lass,' he said to Ruth, 'if you're looking for a place, you've just earned one. Would you like to work for us and help Martha for a bit?'

Ruth looked back at him over the rim of her mug and Helen thought she must be weighing him up as a potential rapist. It was sad, but that would be the way Ruth assessed men after her terrible experiences. Then she looked at Martha, considering. There was a long silence, then eventually she nodded. 'I'll come and help you out for hay time, and see how I manage the work. I can see that Mrs Beck needs a hand.'

'That I do, lass,' said Martha, who was still flushed. She held up her twisted hands. 'I don't want sympathy, but we're finding it hard to get through the hay.'

'We'll try the dandelion for a few weeks,' Ivy suggested. 'If there's no improvement we'll move on to comfrey. Rheumatism's a tough one to cure.'

'My word, Ivy, if anybody can help Martha, it's you,' John said as he passed his mug for a refill. Ruth nodded, as though she agreed.

*   *   *

The police sergeant was filling the hall when Helen arrived back at Seaview and her heart sank. All the problems came crowding back again. 'A word with you, miss,' he said heavily. 'Constable Smith is searching your room again. We've been advised that something may be hidden there.'

Helen was speechless with indignation and a cold, growing fear. What did he mean? A shiver went down her back. This must mean they had new evidence from someone. But they had searched her room before, and turned over all her belongings—the contents of her underwear drawer had been spread out over the bed, the last time. How could they expect to find anything now?

Mary came through from the kitchen and looked sternly at the sergeant. 'Don't be too long, we have to serve dinner soon.' Helen blushed; this was not good for Seaview. What would the guests think?

PC Smith ran down the stairs, holding something. He had soot on his hands. 'Found this up chimney,' he said triumphantly. It was a diamond ring.

'Let me see!' Helen demanded, but the policeman snatched it away from her. 'I've never seen this before! Who told you to look up the chimney?'

'They all say that,' the sergeant said wearily. 'This here is evidence, we will have to get Mrs

216

Bartlett to identify it of course, and then you're for it good and proper, my girl. Do you want to tell us your story now, or save it till later?'

FOURTEEN

Helen fought back her anger and clenched her fists at her sides. With a great effort she said clearly, 'I know nothing about this ring. Who told you to look in the chimney? That person must have put it there, to—to blame me.' She shivered to think that someone wished her ill.

The sergeant shook his heavy head. 'Nay, the person said they were watching you through the open door.' He marched her upstairs to the attics and stopped at her door. 'And see, if you stand at the fireplace you can be seen from the doorway, by anyone in the passage. But the passage is dark, so you might not see them.' He beamed, pleased to have proved his point. 'So it's the station for you, lass, you can tell us more about it there. You might as well tell the truth now.' He was very cheerful; the case was all but over. But it was getting late in the day and the sergeant was due to go off duty. 'We'll come for you in the morning,' he said heavily. 'And think on, it will be the worse for you if you're not here.'

The next morning Mary looked on in

sorrow as Helen went off with the police walking one on either side of her. Perhaps the older woman was now wondering whether her trust had been misplaced. Helen knew she had to stay rational and think clearly; emotion would not help. She had asked James about getting in touch with her father's solicitor and James had said he would do it, but it would take a few days. He was probably torn between Miss Spencer's account and Helen's; still sympathetic, but somehow detached.

There followed one of the worst mornings Helen had ever spent. She was left for an hour by herself in a bare room, with a hard bench to sit on. Her mind went churning in circles; she was cold with apprehension and sick with fear. To calm herself she thought about the Gypsey Race, the stream making its way between the low chalk hills, through the Great Wolds Valley to the North Sea. She could see it in her mind's eye, hear it gurgling peacefully. For many generations it had fascinated the wolds folk with its unpredictability, just like life. They too had experienced ups and downs, joy and sorrow; it happened to everybody. She was innocent of crime and eventually, if there was such a thing as justice, she would be set free. You were innocent until you were proved guilty; James had reminded her of that. But the ring might be taken as proof of guilt, especially in a servant girl. She was now for the first time without the protection of the Moore family name, their standing in the community. It was a lonely feeling.

At last the sergeant came in with another, apparently senior, policeman and they both questioned her with loud, hard voices, flinty faces and questions that tried to lead her into admitting guilt. They were doing their job, she reminded herself. It was probably the biggest robbery for years in this part of the world and there would be a big fuss in the newspapers. But how could she be proved guilty if she were innocent?

After what seemed hours, a junior constable looked in and called them away. Just before the door closed and the lock turned, Helen heard the senior man say, 'She sticks to her story. She must be used to being questioned.'

'Hardened criminal, most likely,' the sergeant rasped. 'Unless, of course, she's telling the truth?' The voice sounded dubious.

'Nah! She must ha' done it. Nobody else for it. We'll just have to . . .' the door closed on this interesting conversation.

The hours dragged by; what little sunshine struggled through the grimy window high in the wall told Helen that it was afternoon. She was given a drink of water and a small piece of bread and cheese. Time passed. A fly, a prisoner like herself, buzzed frantically against the window and she felt sorry for it. Neither of them deserved to be shut up in that dingy room. What would it be like in prison, deprived of your freedom for months or years? Once, the constable who had found the ring looked in and said gloomily that she would probably be there all night, unless she wanted to tell them the truth. Had Mrs Bartlett worn a diamond ring? It was likely, of course.

Fortunately for Helen there was a trawler in the bay that day with a good catch of herring, and several seamen celebrated their success with great thoroughness and quantities of drink. They became rowdy and were dragged to the police station to sober up. Helen was escorted back to Seaview in the evening light, since they now had no room for her. She was ordered to stay on the premises.

Back in the familiar kitchen, Helen felt some of the tension leave her. Mary gave her some dinner, cold meat and potato, and looked at her with sympathy. 'You don't believe I stole them, do you, Mary?' Some reassurance was needed; her hands were shaking as she tried to eat.

'I don't, lass. And I can tell you something else. But just a minute, I'll get James if he hasn't gone out.' Mary went off and Helen finished the food slowly. Until now she had felt too nervous to be hungry.

James came in looking worried and Mary gestured to him to sit at the table. 'Susie's gone home now, of course. But before she went she told me that she'd seen, actually seen Miss Spencer coming out of Helen's room, the day before the ring was found. Now, I think the lady must be asked to explain herself.' She smiled grimly.

'I can't believe that Maud would—there must be some explanation . . .' James was white; obviously any criticism of the Spencers would be hard for him to take. 'Perhaps she was looking for Helen? To give her something, maybe?'

Helen glared at him. James, her support, was deserting her. 'You know she dislikes me, James. She's hardly likely to give me anything.'

Daniel came in, fresh from a bath, and when he heard the story he whistled. 'The old lass has just gone up to bed, but Miss Spencer's in the sitting-room. Let's talk to her.' And to Helen's amazement Dan shepherded his mother, James and herself into the room and stood in front of Maud Spencer, who sat reading a book.

Dan didn't ask for explanations. 'We now know that you planted a ring in Helen's room, to discredit her. You were seen leaving the room and it was you who informed the police it was there.' The blue eyes were hard and Dan had dropped his Yorkshire tones; there was a steely edge to his voice as he rapped out the words.

Maud looked up at Dan with her large violet eyes. 'Do you really believe a tale like this?' She closed the book languidly and then stood up. 'Moore must be clutching at straws by now and you are foolish enough to believe her. I am surprised at you.'

'There are two possibilities,' Dan went on relentlessly. 'The first and most likely is that you stole the jewels. Your mother isn't really deaf, is she? It's just a front. You are probably a pair of thieves, taking opportunities wherever you can. You stole those diamonds, didn't you?'

Miss Spencer looked away. 'James, can you say nothing to support me? You know that I am an honest woman . . . and that Moore is obviously the thief.' Her hands were clenched and she was flushed as she looked round at them all.

James looked from Helen to Maud and back again. He sighed. 'Please clear yourself, Maud. I don't want to believe you are guilty. But my housekeeper said . . .' He stopped. 'I won't say more, except that I'm afraid I will have to tell the police about . . . something that happened in my house at York.' He passed a hand over his eyes. 'This is a great shock to me.'

'I'm going to fetch the police right away,' Dan said firmly and marched to the door.

'Stop!' Maud's voice was strangled and she began to weep. 'Are you going to tell us something?' Helen asked fiercely. The tears were no doubt another play for sympathy.

Dan looked at Maud, stony-faced. 'The police would love another suspect to grill, I am sure. Unless you tell us right now, I'll call them in.'

'Yes,' Maud gulped. She clasped her hands to her bosom, still theatrical. 'I am guilty . . . but not of the theft. I put the ring in her room to . . . get her into trouble. To discredit her with . . . James.' She drooped the lovely head. 'I was afraid he preferred Helen to me, and so . . . but I did not steal the jewels.'

There was silence apart from sobs from Maud and a long sigh from James.

Mary spoke for the first time. 'I don't know whether to believe her. It's a lame explanation, to my mind. Let's leave it until the morning; Miss Spencer can tell her own story to the police, just so long as she clears Helen of blame.' Her employer gave Helen an encouraging smile.

Dan laughed. 'I agree, after she's written and signed a statement of what she's just told us.' Mary brought paper and a pen and, shakily, Maud wrote a brief statement, which Dan then pocketed.

Helen managed a little sleep that night. It was a relief in a way when, in the morning, it was discovered that both the Spencers had gone. 'Bet they didn't pay the bill, neither,' Dan guessed, and he was right. James was utterly silent at breakfast and went out soon afterwards; Helen carried on with her work in a lighter frame of mind. Whether Maud had stolen the diamonds or not, at least her friends

223

knew that Helen had not stolen a ring.

*   *   *

The police station visit did not take Dan long. The sergeant made it clear that Helen was still suspected, but at least not now of stealing the ring. That had been their trump card, but it had turned out to be a cheap glass imitation, they admitted when pushed by Dan, and had never belonged to Mrs Bartlett. The Spencers would be followed up, in due course.

What should be done next? Go down to Green's and order new nets, of course. Dan had lost his own herring nets when the steam trawler tangled with them, along with all the bits of gear that you needed on the herring: ropes and cork and barrels to keep the nets afloat. The lads would all be doing the same thing in the next few days.

The chandler's shop was dark and musty, one of the old harbour buildings down by the water, crammed with canvas and fishing gear as well as souvenirs for tourists. Mixed up with lobster pots and floats were strings of Whitby jet and cheap brass ornaments, old ships' clocks and dusty paintings of sailing ships. It looked as though nobody cared about the goods or what they could be worth, but perhaps this was deliberate. The tourists might think it was an adventure to plunge into the dark little shop and unearth neglected treasures; they might feel that in a dusty and disorganized cave like this, the goods were sure to be undervalued.

Old Joe Green emerged from a dingy recess at the back, rubbing his hand through his dirty beard and glaring at Dan as though he resented the interruption. 'What is it this time?' he growled. 'You young fellers can't keep yer gear above a week.'

Dan grinned. 'I suppose you never lost any. Come on, Joe, where's your good rope in all this mess? Why can't you keep it shipshape in here?'

Joe obviously took his lack of attention to customers to extreme lengths. But when Dan eventually found what he wanted the old man knew the price of everything and would not be beaten down by a farthing. 'Careless again, I suppose?' he sneered as Dan paid over the money. 'Don't know how you young blokes mek a living. Not that it worries me, it's my profit when you have ter buy new gear.'

Dan reddened. 'It wasn't us that were careless. A dirty great steam trawler, one of the Bartlett fleet, ran us down in the night. I'd like to strangle that Bartlett! With him it's profit at any cost. Big boats, small crews and everybody watch out for himself. Them steamboats will be the death of fishing out of Brid.'

'Now look here, young Baker, it won't do to be talking folks down. You'll likely be asking

Mr Bartlett for a job one of these days. Don't let anyone hear you speaking ill of him. He's a real gent, is Mr Bartlett. I—know him personally, like. Have done since he were a lad.'

'Trust you to have a mate like him!' Dan heaved his gear onto a handcart and banged the door on his way out.

The nets and ropes had to be stowed in the boatshed that he shared with Robbie. That piece of business done, Dan drifted down to the water and leaned against the wall near to where his coble was tied up. It was good to keep an eye on the boat and also, if you wanted to know anything in the fishing community this was the spot. The place was quiet, but the tide was coming in and some of the lads should be back soon. A summer visitor in a flat cap wandered up to him. 'You look like a fisherman, son. What's the meaning of all them things over there? I'm a miner from West Riding, like. I know nowt about sea.'

Dan did his best to explain what the lobster gear on the quay was used for and went on to answer questions about the working life at sea. The man was amazed. 'Well, I never! I always thought miners had worst job. Now I know different. This here must be even more dangerous.'

While he was talking to the miner, Dan was keeping an eye open for any movement. He saw Bert Hardy look up and down the street before going into the chandler's shop.

During the next hour or so Dan spoke to several people but he did not see Bert Hardy come out of the shop again. This might be of interest; it was hard to say. In the intervals between chats, Dan thought about Hardy, a hard drinker and a morose, bad-tempered man. Fishermen were not often saints and Dan classed himself as a sinner, but Hardy was miserable with it. He seemed to have no friends.

'Yes, this is my boat, *Seabird*,' he said in answer to another query. She was rocking gently as the incoming tide lifted her. 'Cobles are mostly laid up for the summer while we go on the herring.' This seemed to leave the visitors more mystified than ever. Dan realized that if he wanted to stand about on the waterfront in peace, he would need to shed the gansey and wear a landsman's jacket.

The sun was in the west; it would be time for dinner at Seaview. Ma might need a hand. Dan shifted his position uneasily and looked out to sea. The conversation in the shop still niggled him. Why was Joe Green so keen on Bartlett? A coble was slipping quietly out between the massive stone walls of the harbour. It couldn't be Hardy, he was still in the shop, but it was Bert Hardy's coble, the twin of Dan's boat. His sails looked black against the sea and the big shape on board was

227

surely the owner. Hardy was going out . . . on what errand? How had he got out of the shop?

This needed thinking about. Dan went home, walking quickly with his swinging stride, wondering what he had seen. It wasn't going to help the investigation, but there was something odd going on here and he wanted to find out what it was. The coble owners were not usually putting to sea at this time of the year.

That night in the kitchen things seemed to be almost normal. Ma was knitting, Helen was doing the washing up and Dan was whittling a piece of wood, making fishing gear. You had to do something useful every day, even if there was no work. It was a good time to talk things over. 'Helen, what news have you got for us?' The lass was very quiet.

Helen looked over with a serious face. 'Ruth's improving, that's the main thing.' She shook her head. 'The police have been to see me again. They were going to take me back to the police station, but James got them to let me stay here and Mary said she would keep an eye on me.' The pleasant voice wavered a little.

'Good on you, Ma.' Dan could imagine her standing up to the fat sergeant.

'I am hoping Ruth will find some work.' Mary's hands were busy with the needles, but she was looking over at Dan. 'A lad has taken over the vegetable round with the donkey, so she's lost that place, and then you won't have any work for her until back end of year. Poor lass has to earn a living somehow. Likely she'll have to gut herring on the quay. There's usually a job for a quick fingered lass, although the Scotch boats fetch their own lasses with them.'

'Well, so far we've no herring to gut,' Dan said bitterly. 'Thanks to Mr Bartlett.'

Helen turned from the sink. 'I believe Ruth has found work, the other day. She came with us, with Ivy and me, to a farm. I think I told you about the Becks? When she saw them struggling with the hay, she offered to help them. So she's there—she's actually staying there and Ivy will take over her things. I think she'll like the life, and the folks will treat her well, there's a nice little room waiting for her. It was meant to be.' Thank heaven there was good news somewhere!

'That's grand,' Dan said briefly. The less said about Ruth the better, he seemed to imply. 'But about this jewellery . . . we've turned this house upside down and found nothing. I've been about the town and found nothing.'

Mary sighed. 'Well, it's a black cloud, you might say, hanging over us all. If the story gets into the *Bridlington Free Press* . . . well, Seaview might as well close. Folks won't be coming here.'

'Did you go up Church Street?' Helen asked

229

suddenly.

'Church Street? That's not so far from the harbour. But why Church Street?'

Helen picked up the tea towel. 'Because Ivy Cole thinks the diamonds might be somewhere there, near the harbour.' She paused, drying dishes busily. 'Do you believe in Ivy Cole?'

Well, that was a question. 'She's good with herbs,' Mary put in. 'And they say she can dowse for water . . . you've seen that, Helen.'

'Yes. That's what makes me think—she might know. Ivy sort of . . . dowsed. She held this pendulum over the map and she said: Church Street, or the harbour. She wasn't sure, she said honestly it was just a feeling. I walked down there, on the way home.' So that was why the lass had been late and why Dan had been needed in the kitchen. 'But there's nothing much . . . some tall old houses, one or two are boarding houses, and a public house that they call the Cockroach.' She screwed up her nose. 'It looks like a rough house to me.'

It was time to assert authority. 'That's interesting, but we haven't got much further, have we?' Dan favoured Helen with a stern look.

Mary said suddenly, 'Mrs White's is in Church Street.'

There was a gleam in Helen's eye as she said, 'The Spencers were staying at Mrs White's.' She grinned. 'I am prejudiced, because Maud Spencer tried to prove that I did it. And I think that idiot Simpson stayed there. He was here on the morning the jewels disappeared.'

'But White's is where people always go when there's no room at Seaview,' Dan said patiently. 'It doesn't prove anything. A lot of folks stay there.' He had another thought. 'James will be interested. Is he in tonight?'

When the dishes were put away and the kitchen set to rights, James was summoned. He seemed happy to be invited to drink his tea with them, but was still very subdued. Maud Spencer must have been a disappointment to him. He looked sceptical when Helen mentioned the pendulum. 'I can't really believe it,' he admitted. 'I think we'll have to leave that problem to the police, and hope they find the thief soon.'

Dan then explained what he had seen in the harbour and James was more interested. 'I've looked at the old houses near the harbour. It's possible that Hardy went out of a door at the back, of course.'

'But that row is built straight into the rock, there couldn't be a back door.' Dan had thought of that already. 'And I'm positive that he didn't come out of Green's. I wouldn't trust Bert Hardy. I don't know of a good reason to go out when he did, lobsters are over now.'

'Then—how about a passage that opens on to the harbour? They're very old houses, you know.' James sipped his tea. 'Hardy would

231

have had to swim to his boat, in that case . . . unless . . . there are several rowing boats tied up down there, one more or less wouldn't be noticed.'

It was strange that having lived here all his life, he had never heard of such a cellar. Dan frowned, trying to remember details of the harbour basin, the place he saw nearly every day, but seldom really looked at. It was nearly drained of water at low tide and surrounded by dark stone. 'Maybe there really is a passage that comes out near the harbour. I swear that Hardy never walked down the street, but I don't know what it means.'

'Don't be daft, lad, and keep away from Bert Hardy. Have nowt to do with him.' Mary stood up and folded her knitting away. 'I'm off to bed and I suggest you all do the same. Dan, you see that doors are all locked. Goodnight.' It was noticeable that when Dan was at home, Mary sometimes left him in charge.

*   *   *

When Mary had gone Dan stood up and stretched. 'I'm off down there, just to have a look round. Won't be long, don't wait up for me. I'll lock up when I come back, like a good boy.' He flashed a grin at Helen and slipped out of the back door, into the last of the long summer twilight.

'But it might be dangerous . . .' he heard

232

Helen wail as the door closed. Why did women always scare so easily? But James would take care of her; he smiled to himself in the darkness. James was—well, he was an office worker, after all. Used to soft indoor living and probably not much use in a tight spot.

A pale moon was rising and Dan could see fairly well as he slipped along the familiar path to the harbour. He was well used to night trips in the coble. Helen didn't realize that he was on home territory here and it was hardly likely to be dangerous, unless he fell into the harbour and drowned. Not many people did that when they were sober. From the fish quay at the seaward side of the harbour came the reedy sound of a mouth organ playing a Scottish tune, and occasional bursts of laughter. The Scottish summer fleet was trickling in after the herring and the lassies who came with them to 'gip' the fish were always laughing and joking. Dan had kissed one or two, but not often, because of their pervading smell of fish. He loved to copy their strange accents and expressions.

The investigator slid down cautiously into his rowing boat. The tide was coming in and would soon fill the basin, but there would be shallow water under him for an hour or so yet. In the faint glow from the moonlight he could see the rugged rockface where the water met the land. He moved along carefully. At first he saw nothing but smooth rock, but there was something darker up ahead. One section was overhung so that it was not visible from the road above, and a jutting shelf of rock hid it from the rest of the harbour. He had never thought to look round here before. Nosing round the shelf cautiously, Dan saw an iron grille about ten feet high, lichen-covered and blending into the rock so that it was hardly noticeable. There appeared to be a cave behind the grille. Right here in the harbour was something that he, Daniel Baker, had never seen before. He didn't know everything about Brid, after all.

Making the boat fast to a stanchion beside the grille, Dan tugged at the iron and felt it move slightly. It was suspended by thick ropes, but two men could probably shift it . . .

A sudden, dazzling beam from a lantern made him start and almost lose his balance. He had been spotted, even though he thought that the oars had made no sound and even though the niche was hidden.

'What do you think you're doing?' The deep voice was coming from above.

FIFTEEN

For a few seconds Dan held his breath. What now? Then he recognized the voice and laughed quietly. Trust old James to follow him, he wasn't like the other guests at Seaview, after all. James wanted to see action and he had proved to be handy at picking seabirds' eggs from the cliffs; he had strong arms and a cool head. Not really a typical office worker, then.

When the beam shone on him again, Dan gestured in the direction of the steps leading down into the water. 'Just the man! Come and help me to raise this door, James.' The writer clambered cautiously into the rowing boat and they glided back across the dark water to the grille.

Together, Dan and James tugged at the ropes holding the iron lattice until it moved slowly upwards on pulleys. Dan rowed the boat into the space behind the grille and James uncovered his lantern. By its light they could see a cave in the rock, with steps leading up in the direction of the town. This must be a secret entry, right under the nose of any authority that might be expected to take an interest. 'By golly, this beats all! I thought all the caves were round Flamborough,' breathed Dan. 'That's where the smuggling was supposed to be.' The boat nosed in and he looked round at the dripping walls and sniffed the dank air. 'Rotting seaweed, that's all. What do you think folks would want to bring in here?' It should have been full of contraband.

James peered at Dan in the dim light. 'This place is probably under water at high tide

. . . which means . . .' he broke off.

'Which means, Mr Kirby, that we'd better be off before the tide fills the cave. We might bump our heads on the roof, or be bumped off by—'

'Or we might run out of air, if the water goes right up to those steps.' James finished for him. 'Maybe this place is used by some who don't want to pay harbour dues, or excise tax. I'd better take you home, Dan; your mother would have a fit if she could see you now.'

Dan was still thinking. 'You sound like Helen. They could stand off out in the bay, far out, and somebody with a coble, say—like Hardy, he must have come out of here—could pick up the goods and fetch them in to the town. I suppose they can still make a bob or two on spirits or tobacco with no excise duty on them? Slip them in from Holland? If you avoided the quay, the only place where everybody loads and unloads, you could nose into the basin here as if you were tying up innocently. And then unload out of sight, in the cave—maybe after dark.' He laughed. 'And if it was a local like Hardy, nobody would look at him twice.'

'If we wait awhile, we might find out. It could make an interesting chapter in my story of working lives. But we'd better get out of here and watch from elsewhere, Dan. The water's rising, it makes me feel uneasy.' James was watching the water level against a mark on the wall.

'It's clever, you know. Right in the town, in full view but yet hidden . . . nowhere near the smugglers' caves . . . and operated by a man who's always about the harbour.' Dan nodded happily.

At that moment there was a clang and a loud splash; the boat rocked violently. Shaking off the water, both men turned and saw that the grille had fallen down and they were shut in the cave. 'Damn! We'll have to raise it again,' grumbled Dan, and paddled over to the iron door. Together they tried to move it, but the door would not budge.

'Next plan,' murmured James. He held the lantern up so that they could see the ropes leading to the pulleys that operated the door. As the tide came in, they could feel the gentle wash of water round the boat. 'We need to move it with the ropes.' But the ropes disappeared through a small hole in the rock and were taut; they could not be moved either way. 'The door must be operated from above,' he muttered.

Dan could feel panic rising, but he fought it down. 'Another plan,' he tried to mimic James's deliberate speech. 'We bang like hell on that door up there. Up the top of the steps. Do you see it?'

James held the boat steady while Dan ran up the steps and hammered on the door with the end of his oar. It was too strong for him to split the wood, an ancient, solid door with huge rusty iron hinges. Perhaps someone would hear them. 'Get ready to run past them and get out,' James told him.

They waited, but nothing happened. The water rose, taking the boat to a higher level. 'I reckon it must be Green's shop up there. Why don't he hear me banging? This must be the way Bert Hardy went out, so we have learned something at least.' Dan came back to the boat. 'All we have to do is get out.' We have to get out, and soon, he told himself. If I get out of here I'll never take advantage of a girl again.

'We'd better try to attract attention in the harbour, Dan. I'll wave my white shirt through the grille and we'll shout. There's a group down on the quay, they'll be able to do something.' James started to take off his shirt.

'I hope you're right. That's all we can do . . . but the lasses on the quay are making a fair amount of noise, they might not hear us.' Dan looked carefully at the roof, which was getting nearer, but there was no high water mark. It was all wet from the last high tide. The cave would be full of water soon; their chance of surviving would be gone. Dan felt like screaming, but he forced himself to keep still.

*   *   *

Ten minutes after Dan left, James, looking

apologetic, had gone after him. 'It might be good stuff for my book,' he had murmured and Helen thought it might help him to forget about his shattered idol, Miss Spencer. But as time passed, Helen began to feel uneasy. Something must have gone wrong; Dan had promised to be back soon. She must go down to the harbour, to see whether Dan's rowing boat was a clue to his whereabouts. The last thing he had mentioned was the harbour and a possible passage from above. That was probably where he had gone.

Should she tell Mary first? Better not, Mary would forbid her to go out after dark, and with good reason. The police would think it very suspicious, for one thing, if they caught her in the streets. Helen realized she had to be extremely cautious in her movements until the thief was found. She was more or less under house arrest, after all.

Apart from the law, Bridlington at night was not particularly dangerous, Helen decided. The visitors were usually quiet at night after a day in the fresh air, and many of the fisherfolk were sober and righteous people who went to bed early. But a young woman's reputation seemed to depend on her not walking in the dark alone. It was part of the bad luck of being born a girl. As a boy, Helen would have enjoyed much more freedom. *And I'd have made the most of it!* she told herself fiercely. No, she would just slip out, and if the men

239

were not about she would come back quickly. It would be easier to do something than to wait here, listening to the ticking of the kitchen clock.

Helen looked down at her neat black skirt and white blouse. This was not the way to dress if she wanted to avoid being noticed, but what could she do? Her eye fell on a basket of clean laundry that Mary had brought in that evening. She could borrow some clothes from Dan. Men certainly had all the luck: their clothes were much more practical than the long skirts of women. Helen struggled into a blue gansey and then into a pair of Dan's serge trousers, which were too long until she found his belt to hold them up with. She put on her walking-shoes and tied up her hair under Dan's cap.

What else might be needed? Helen took up Dan's whittling knife gingerly; it was very sharp and he had warned her not to touch it. But you never knew . . . She slipped it into the leather case on the belt.

Walking in the shadows, Helen went steadily down the street. Anyone who saw her might think it was Dan, or some other local lad. As she neared the harbour she could hear the shouts and laughter from the fish quay. Had Dan and James gone to join a party? It was easy to move quietly, keeping out of the light until she could see the quay. Sitting on upturned barrels, several girls were chatting and telling stories by the light of a small fire; one was playing a mouth organ. They had thick Scottish accents. There were no men among them. Of course, the herring fleet had put out to sea at the last high tide. These women were waiting to gut the fish that the men brought back. Dan and James were not there, of course.

Helen walked slowly round the harbour wall, her eyes straining to see in the darkness. After a while her night vision returned and the moonlight showed her the black water, with a few boats tied up. Dan's rowing boat had a white keel and it was not in its usual place. She looked carefully round the rock walls, but the boat was not there. Where could it have gone?

Across the land side of the harbour, Helen thought she did see something white. But it was not big enough to be a rowing boat. Was it a flag? It seemed to flutter, and then when the girls behind her stopped singing for a moment, she heard a hoarse cry for help. It sounded like Dan. He must be over there, and in some kind of trouble. But where was James? There was only one thing to do.

'Excuse me . . . I'm sorry to disturb you, but I need help.' Helen walked boldly into the firelight and faced the girls, who started up in surprise. 'Wey, laddie, what ails ye?' asked one burly lass, towering over Helen and looking at her curiously.

Helen gulped. 'Can you row a boat? There's

a man over the harbour there in trouble and I need to get over the water to him.'

The big woman looked her up and down. 'Ye're wearing a Bridlington gansey and ye canna row a boat? Shame on ye, laddie!' They all roared with laughter. Perhaps they had been drinking gin, Helen thought desperately. Would they be of any use in an emergency? Her heart sank.

'No, I borrowed the gansey. I'm a farmer. Please, can you help?' Her voice was higher than usual with nerves.

'Admit it, you're a lassie!' The big girl came closer, suddenly put her hand into the trousers Helen was wearing and to her embarrassment, made a grab. 'It's a lassie! Pity, she'd ha made a bonny lad. Right, let's find us a boat, come on, the rest of ye! Let's show these Yorkshire folk a thing or two.'

All the girls, five or six, ran down to the water with Helen. Two of them jumped into the nearest small boat and untied the mooring rope. 'Come on, then, what's your name, where we going?' Helen clambered awkwardly in, the other girls pushed off the boat and Helen pointed across the water to where she could still see the white flag.

'I'm Helen, and one of my friends is over there . . . or possibly two of them, in some sort of trouble. I don't know what has happened. Can you go any faster?' The boat was making erratic progress, with one girl to an oar at each

242

side, giggling as they went. 'And who are you?'

The big girl pulled her shawl closer with her free hand. 'I'm Morag and the wee one's Fiona, we're here for the herring, o' course.' Fiona, who was far from wee, laughed quietly.

'Thank you, Morag and Fiona.' They could now hear Dan and James, both shouting. 'Hurry up! Over here!' There was a ray of light from a lantern.

They bumped against the wall of rock, propelled by the tide. The white flag was pushed through a small grating, about a foot above the water level. 'Right, laddies, the Scots are here! Dinna worrit yerselves! We'll get ye oot o' there!' Morag called breezily, sounding just like one of Dan's imitations.

Morag tied their boat to the stanchion beside the cave and all the girls tried to move the grille, with no success. 'It's held by ropes,' Dan called, sounding quite calm. 'Have you got a knife? You girls got a fish knife?' But the girls had left their gutting knives behind.

Helen pulled out Dan's knife from her belt and handed it to Morag, who attacked the ropes with enthusiasm. She had big arms with muscles on them and she sawed through the ropes quite easily. Freed from the ropes the grating slipped, but not far enough for Dan and James to get out. It took the combined strength of the rescuers in the boat and the men in the cave to move the grille enough for them to wriggle free.

The water was up to the roof of the cave and the men were both gasping for air as they dragged themselves into the boat.

The rowing boat was very low in the water with two extra bodies on board. Dan and James were both wet and shivering. 'Just in time,' Dan said very quietly. 'And now, who do we thank? The Scotch lassies, and—I should know you, lad, but I can't quite see who it is.'

Helen laughed with relief. 'Let's just row slowly over to those steps, we don't want to swim home.'

James turned and looked at her in the faint light. 'It's Helen, isn't it? Good girl! If you hadn't come—'

'Helen!' Dan roared. He leaned over precariously and gave her a smacking kiss. 'I thought you were a lad in the dark. Never made that mistake before. Hey, that's my gansey you're wearing!'

'But for Helen ye'd be floating out to sea on the tide,' put in Morag cheerfully, pulling on the oar. 'We were all that busy crackin' and singin', ye ken, that we never heard or saw ye at all. But Helen here, dressed like a braw wee callant as she is, she came and got us. And,' she said with a look of admiration, 'she carries a canny knife, forby.'

'Yes, and I'd better have the knife back, thank you,' Helen said hastily. 'Thank you so much for your help, both of you. I'll come to see you again soon.'

'They would have to think of a way of thanking these cheerful lasses.

When at last they got back to Seaview Helen was relieved to find that Mary was still in bed. 'Don't tell her too much,' she begged. 'It will only worry her.' The men changed into dry clothes while Helen pulled the fire together and made them all tea and toast.

Both Dan and James were embarrassingly grateful for their rescue. When they were warm and fed, they looked at each other and smiled. 'It's good to be safe and home again. But I don't think we have thanked our rescuer properly.' James stood up. 'After you, Daniel!'

Dan swept her into a firm embrace, which gave Helen a melting feeling. Tired after the emotion of the night, for a moment she relaxed against him, savouring his warmth and the salty tang of the sea. 'Och, but ye're a braw wee lassie!' he told her in his imitation Scots. But then she remembered poor Ruth; Dan could be a split personality, one of them cold and calculating. She pulled away and was still blushing when James put his arm gently round her and gave her a chaste kiss on the cheek. 'We'll always be grateful, Helen. No other woman I know would have come down there to look for us. And you did the only thing possible to rescue us.'

'What would Mary say? Behave yourselves, both of you!' Helen gasped, her cheeks burning, but she was thankful that she had

245

arrived in time.

'So what did you find out?' Helen asked when they had all settled down again. Dan's clothes were quite comfortable and she had kept them on, but she was aware of his grin whenever he looked at her.

'There's a set of steps, must lead to Green's, and a door. We hammered on the door, but nothing happened . . . unless he heard us and that was why the grille came down.' An unpleasant thought: somebody had possibly tried to drown them. 'It must be a way in for goods I should think, and Green must be in it. Hey, maybe, just maybe the jewels went out that way, but we can't prove anything. We've lost the boat, too,' said Dan dismally. 'It might have been smashed up against the roof.' He thought for a minute. 'Or maybe not, it might just have scraped the paint.'

'Maybe they'll open the grille and let it out at low tide,' James suggested. 'Goodness, that was the closest call I ever saw, apart from an avalanche in Switzerland.'

The next morning the conspirators were all feeling tired, but they assured Mary that nothing very much had happened the night before. Late in the morning there was shopping to be done, so Helen was able to slip out with Dan, down to the harbour before she went to the shops. 'I mustn't be long,' she said guiltily. But she wanted to see whether Dan's rowing boat was in the harbour, and what sort

246

of wreck it was.

Dan himself was philosophical this morning. 'We're always fettling boats, we're used to it. But Green will know we've been in there. What will he make of it, I wonder? I'll have to tell him some tale . . .' he broke off and looked across to the fish quay, where a coble had just come in, towing another boat. A small crowd had gathered. 'What's going on over there? That looks like Hardy's boat. Come on, Helen, we'll have a look.'

Rather unwillingly, Helen allowed herself to be led down to the quay. The Scottish girls were not there and since it was fairly low tide there were only the two boats that Dan had seen. Hardy's boat was being made fast, but not by Hardy.

Dan went nearer. There was a still figure in the bottom of the boat. 'He's unconscious, I think,' Dan said. 'No, don't look, lass. He's dead.'

'Found him a mile out,' said the fisherman who had towed him in. 'Dead all right when we found him, that's for sure.' His mate shook his head. They had the haunted look of men who had travelled with a nightmare.

It was better to face the reality than to imagine it, so Helen looked down into the boat. Hardy lay on his back and the right side of his head was missing, just a mess of congealed blood. She turned away, fighting nausea. Bert Hardy had been unpleasant, he might even have been outside the law, but nobody deserved to end like this. It would possibly mean that his secrets had died with him.

'I'm going,' said Helen abruptly. 'Shopping . . .' She wanted to get away from the place, to forget what she had seen.

'Sorry, lass—I told you not to look.' Dan patted her shoulder. 'I'll just stay here a while and see what I can find out.' As Helen left she saw the police making their way down to the quay, and was glad they had not seen her there.

Poor Jessie! She had lost her father, and her livelihood as well. Jessie would not know what had happened. Would it be better if she heard the news from Helen, rather than from the police? It would not take long to run up to the street where the fisherfolk lived. If she thought too much about it she would not go . . . Helen turned resolutely up the street. The main thing was to ensure that Jessie had someone with her, one of the other girls perhaps.

Jessie was doing the washing outside in the yard, pounding the clothes vigorously in a peggy tub. She smiled to see Helen. 'It was grand that you found a place for Ruth!' she said happily. Jessie looked like her father, dark and solidly built, but she had a far nicer expression on her brown face.

Helen did not know where to begin. 'Jessie, I don't know how to tell you . . . but your

248

father has had—an accident.'

Jessie stopped pounding the clothes and her smile faded, but that was all. In a matter of fact voice she said, 'I've been expecting it for a long time, with the risks he takes . . . is he hurt bad, do you know?'

'I'm afraid—he's dead, Jessie.'

The girl stood quite still and silent, but large tears overflowed from her eyes and ran down her face. After a few minute she dashed them away with the back of her hand, and Helen offered a clean handkerchief. 'He's—he were a hard man,' she sobbed. 'But my ma loved him, and I tried to do the best for him I could. It were never good enough, of course, he went sour after she died.'

Helen felt the raw grief herself, like a lump of lead in her chest. 'Jessie, how can I help? Would you like me to fetch one of the girls?' She knew that the fishergirls always backed one another up if they could.

Jessie sank down on a stone wall, her head bowed. 'Yes, fetch Liza for me, will you? She and me went to school together.' She looked up at Helen through the tears. 'Thanks, lass. You did well to tell me before the cops arrive.'

'Where was he going? Do you know?' Helen asked innocently. It seemed mean to question a bereaved daughter, but the truth was important.

The girl sighed. 'He didn't tell me much, at all. But I think he was doing something for Joe

249

Green at the shop, delivering things out to boats at sea. He said he weren't going on the herring this season, he had bigger fish to fry.' She smiled faintly. 'Poor Dad took on too much, it seems.' She paused. 'I won't say nowt of that to police, no need to get him into trouble. It was mebbe a case of avoiding harbour dues, some folks don't like to pay.'

Eliza was shocked when Helen told her the news. She went round to see Jessie immediately, taking with her a smiling blue-eyed child who would probably do more to comfort the poor girl than anyone else could.

It was wise to get away before the police arrived; Helen had no wish to encounter the force again. As she walked round the harbour to the town she saw Dan's boat, neatly moored in its usual place and looking slightly battered, but still afloat. No doubt he would find it in due course. She looked across to the rocky outcrop that led to the cave, but nothing could be seen in the daylight. Whoever let out the boat had known to whom it belonged. But Hardy's death would cause such a stir that the exploit might be overlooked.

Helen sped round the shops on her errands for Mary as quickly as she could and arrived back at Seaview breathless. She expected a reprimand, but Dan had already told his mother the dire news and they had guessed that she would go to Jessie.

The peace of Bridlington had been

shattered by the robbery, and now by this violent death. Were the two connected? Was Hardy's death an accident? Some of the answers might be found in the chandler's shop.

SIXTEEN

'We agree, don't we, that Green's shop is at the centre of all this business,' Dan said to Helen at breakfast the next day. 'I should take a peek at the old villain—just creep in when he's not looking.' Mary was at the front door, seeing off a group of visitors; she always did this out of politeness, wishing them a safe journey, and they often promised to come back. People liked the personal contact that went with a small establishment.

'Don't take any more risks. I might decide not to rescue you another time,' Helen told him crossly. She was still shaken by the events of the last few days and not in the mood for more adventure.

'Ho, you're going to hold it over me, are you? Maybe you won't let even me go to sea?' Then Dan relented. 'Well, our skipper's doing repairs and we'll be back on the herring next week, I hope. But we still need to clear your name, my lass, and protect the good name of Seaview. The story hasn't got to the papers yet, but when the *Free Press* gets on to it we need to have some answers.' But by the time the yawl was seaworthy, Dan had not been able to do any spying, although he had dodged round the musty shop a couple of times and bought a few ends of rope.

Helen recovered her nerve after a few days. She decided to take matters into her own hands one evening when all the guests had elected to go to a concert with supper provided, which left the kitchen free for a change. She waylaid James in the hall and asked him for help. 'It's nothing risky, really. The Green shop is open until late, isn't it?'

James looked at her suspiciously. 'Well, yes, I've noticed that he sells to visitors in the evenings. But—'

'No buts, James. Say you'll help me.' Helen faced him squarely and James gave in. Mary was busy in the kitchen garden at the back of the house, and agreed that Helen could go out for an hour or so. What she did not know was that Helen then borrowed a spare set of Dan's clothes.

'No risk at all, James,' Helen assured him. 'Nothing like the cave. But I might be able to see something, some clue.' She was not sure what she might find in Green's living quarters, but there was no harm done if she slipped in and out quickly, while he was talking to James. In Dan's clothes she would not be noticed even if someone saw her coming out, and if Green saw her he would not know who she was. 'It's foolproof, I've thought it out.'

The writer shook his head doubtfully. 'I must admit that until you spoke the other night I didn't know you in Dan's gansey. It's quite a good disguise because it says "fisherman" and people tend not to look beyond that. But Helen, I'm not sure you'll find out anything useful. Joe Green won't have the jewels on display, now will he?' He smiled at Helen. 'I'm very concerned for your safety, my girl.'

He looked attractive when he smiled like that, but Helen was not going to be put off. 'Thank you, dear James. This is my plan.' It was such a relief to have him on her side after the painful business with Miss Spencer.

As instructed, some time later James sauntered down to the harbour and gazed into the dusty window of Green's shop. He stood as if in thought and then went in. Helen was there, leaning on the harbour wall in a good imitation of Dan. She watched James go into the shop and quietly wedge the door open so that the bell would not ring again. After a minute or two, she slipped into the shop. It was so easy to move in men's clothing; why did women put up with hampering long skirts? She could hear James talking loudly to Green at the far end, hidden by coils of rope hanging from the rafters. He was prattling about ships in bottles and other seaside curios; he was looking for a present for his aunt.

253

There were sharp smells of paraffin and pitch, new wood and old rope, and spiders' webs everywhere in the shop to make her shudder. Helen went to the left and pushed open the door of Green's private quarters. There she got a shock.

At the dingy kitchen table sat a burly man in an expensive suit, drumming his fingers on the table impatiently. Mr Bartlett! He had his back to her and Helen quickly slipped behind an open door that led into some kind of pantry, just in time before Green came shuffling back. They would surely hear her heart pounding; she tried to breathe quietly. It would not do to think about what would happen if she were caught, but at least she was in Dan's clothes. She was in a dark little space with a strong odour of mouldy cheese. What was Bartlett doing here? He was the last person one would expect to visit a dump like this. And yet . . . Green had told Dan to respect Mr Bartlett.

'I'm running out of time!' The big man spat out the words. 'Can't you leave the shop for a while? This is urgent!'

'Stupid tourist, can't make his mind up,' Green muttered. 'I've left him there, since you're so much in a hurry, but I'll have to go back soon. What's the matter, Mr Bartlett?' The hoarse voice had a note of apprehension.

'What happened, man? The diamonds didn't reach Amsterdam. *Where are they?* Fetch Hardy, I want to talk to him. He's got some explaining to do.' A chair scraped on the floor.

There was a silence. 'Well, I can't, yer see . . . I'm very sorry—'

'What do you mean, can't?' It sounded as though Bartlett was moving restlessly, pacing the kitchen and breathing heavily. 'You do as I tell you, Joe. Or else.' The voice was full of menace.

'Bert Hardy's dead, Mr Bartlett.' Green quavered. 'Dunno what went wrong this time. He's taken parcels out of here for years, no trouble, no questions asked. It was allus the safest route—'

'Dead? What do you mean? Can you prove it? He probably made off with them! They never got there, you idiot!'

There was a thud and a squeal from Green. 'Don't stamp on me toes, Mr Bartlett, I've got gout!' Helen winced in sympathy behind the door.

Bartlett seemed to control his temper with an effort. 'I've just had a signal from Amsterdam to say that the parcel has not been seen. They haven't heard from the boat, it never arrived. So what are you going to do about it? The diamonds are missing and I need them urgently. Do you understand, Green?'

'It was your trawler that he took them to, wasn't it?' Green was trying to rally. 'So your men might know what happened. How could I know? Bert came back with his face stove in and nothing in his pockets, as far as I know. His boat was towed into port by a lad who found it floating outside harbour. Nobody knows what happened, but everybody knows he's dead—half the town saw him.'

'What?' Bartlett shouted.

'Shush! The customer might hear you.' Green sounded nervous. 'Well, I don't know owt about it, but if Bert still had 'em cops will have found them by now.'

'I will find out.' Bartlett sounded vicious. 'Hardy was your contact, but you obviously can't be trusted. I will go after them myself. Dammit, man, everything depends on it! I will go out to the trawler, the same one that met Hardy. I've a rough idea where they'll be, their orders were to go back and fish . . . afterwards. You can find a coble, some reliable man who doesn't ask questions, to take me out tonight. Carry on here, and see what you can find out. 'I'll be back in time to go out with the tide. Hardy dead! I can't believe it.' Bartlett strode out, inches from where Helen lurked behind the door. Green scrabbled about for a while and at one point he took hold of the door into the pantry. Helen held her breath, but the man moved on.

Green went back into the shop and Helen could hear James carrying on at length about a painting of the bay in the evening light. 'A seascape,' he kept repeating. James led the shopkeeper to the back of the shop again, and Helen thankfully tottered out, feeling her knees weak with relief.

Helen and James walked back to Seaview separately and met up in the deserted sitting-room. Helen, back in her decorous housekeeper's dress, explained what she had heard. 'Bartlett knew that the jewels were being shipped out.' She shook her head. 'He was much nastier, harder than he seemed at Seaview.'

James looked at her with respect. 'You did well, Helen, better than Dan and I. Bartlett must have taken them himself, for some reason. Insurance? If he could claim insurance and then sell them in Europe he'd get twice the value. He must be short of money.' James was pacing up and down the room, his unruly hair standing on end.

'Would it not have been easier to sell them honestly, if he needed money?' Helen could not work it out. Why would he want to pretend it was theft?

'Well, yes, if his wife knew about the problem. It's possible he was keeping the money troubles from his wife, so he couldn't ask for the jewels. They had to appear to be stolen.' James smiled sadly. 'Well, it looks as though your two suspects, Maud and Simpson, are cleared. But we can't forget the ring she put in your room,' he added, half to himself. It was just as well that Maud had shown her unpleasant side before James got too involved with her. How long would he take to recover? It had been so hard, watching him under her influence.

Helen thought about Mrs Bartlett. 'I don't think the wife knew. She was genuinely upset, worried about what he might think. She's much nicer than he is, James. Mrs Bartlett was sure the diamonds had been stolen. I remember Bartlett went for a walk to the harbour, straight after breakfast that morning. He could have taken them to Green then.'

'The question is, where are they now? We are not much further on than Bartlett.' James sounded despondent.

'Dan's back tomorrow, he might think of something. If he knows one of the trawler's crew, for instance—he did say there were local men working for Bartlett.'

Helen laughed. 'I do feel much better, because at least we know something of what happened. But if we tell the police now, Bartlett will of course deny all knowledge and try even harder to blame me. Let's wait to see what Dan says.'

* * *

Dan came back from the second herring trip in a much better frame of mind and with money in his pocket, which he said was going straight into the bank. Helen managed to get James invited into the kitchen after dinner and they told Dan and his mother what they knew.

'It sounds as though you were taking risks,' Mary said severely. But they all knew that the threat of prison still hung over Helen; it was worth taking a risk to find out the truth.

Dan was quiet for a while; then he sat up straight and looked round. 'I've had an idea. Ma, you'll know but the others won't, that our boat *Seabird* was made by the same boat builder as Hardy's coble, *Seaspray*—and at the same time.' He stood up. 'An old bloke at Flamborough built them. Of course I bought mine second hand, but I went to see the old lad just before he retired.'

'Interesting,' said Helen politely. 'How does that help, Dan?'

'I'm not sure. But if we can get access to Bert's boat, we might see.'

James frowned. 'Won't the police have locked it up, as involved in a possible murder? Someone might have put the body in the boat after—after he died.'

Helen put in, 'When we were down at the harbour yesterday it was still tied up at the fish quay. It's handy there if the police want to look at it, I suppose.'

Dan glanced at Mary. 'We'll just be half an hour, Ma,' he said coaxingly. 'Washing-up's done, we'll all three go together. Just half an hour.'

Mary nodded unwillingly. 'But Helen

shouldn't make a habit of flitting round the town with you two, it'll get her a bad name.'

Twilight was settling over the harbour; the day-length had lessened a little as the summer went on. Helen walked along decorously with James and Dan led the way. There was no one about on the quay and the only boat there was Hardy's. 'Nice and quiet,' Dan said with satisfaction. 'We don't want to be gawped at.'

Dan swung down into the *Seaspray* and Helen saw with a shudder that blood still stained the bottom of the boat. How could there be anything left to see in an open coble with no decking? It was horrible; they should not have come.

'Aha!' Dan was feeling underneath one of the wooden seats. From his pocket he brought out a small key. There was a pause while he fished inside a compartment under the seat. 'It's the same as mine, good job he used the same lock. These boats have a little space for stowing things away, you can't see it and you wouldn't know it was there. I hadn't noticed until the old lad who built it told me and gave me a key. He was laughing to think that it had been there all those years without being found. Yes, and there's something here!' He dragged out a small sack. In the last of the light he unwrapped it and Helen gasped as a leather case was revealed. 'We've found 'em!' The diamonds were there, in Hardy's boat. They had been to sea and returned with his body.

Dan passed the parcel over to James on the quay.

'We'd better take them to the police station,' James suggested. 'Clear up the thing once and for all.' He peered in fascination at the jewels. 'That's the necklace Mrs B wore, I remember it.'

Dan shook his head as James wrapped the parcel in the sacking again. 'That was my first thought, but it would be dangerous. They would pin it on Helen, then. They'd say she had got cold feet and decided to turn them in. We're all from Seaview, the scene of the crime. They wouldn't believe us. We can't be involved. We'll have to get the coppers to make the find . . . they'll be so proud of themselves! We could get Jessie to tell them—'

'No!' Helen glared at him. 'Poor Jessie has enough to deal with. We can't ask her to help to prove her dad was a villain. That's thoughtless, Dan.'

A small voice from the dark said, 'But it doesn't matter now.' Jessie stepped out of the shadows, her black dress almost invisible in the dusk. 'I was—I was coming down to see the boat, to see if any of Dad's things were left in it, and you were there just before me. I saw what Dan found. But I don't understand what it means.'

Helen explained quickly about the diamonds and Jessie sighed. 'That was the sort of thing he was sometimes asked to ship out

261

from Green's. I picked up bits of stories when folks came to see him, but I tried to keep away from it. The less I knew, the better. Ay, Dan, I know about yon little box under the seat, but I don't have a key, of course.' She looked up at James. 'And who is this, please?'

'James is staying at Seaview, he's a good friend,' Helen said and noticed James' slow smile. 'He's the one who's writing a book. Now Jessie, are you willing to tell the police about the box and maybe try to find the key?'

'They probably have the key. It would be in Bert's pocket, and they will have a list of his belongings.' Dan locked the parcel back in the box and stepped ashore.

A sob escaped Jessie. 'I always thought he'd make a bad end. He was . . . a good seaman, and brave . . . but he took risks and he made his own rules.' She heaved a sigh and stood up straight. 'Well, he's gone and I have to carry on.' Helen thought that once the scandal had died down Jessie might make a better life for herself without the heavy hand of Bert upon her.

Dan drew Jessie away from the boat. 'No need for you to look there, lass, there's nowt else. Now, if you're willing, you could do us a great service. Just tell the police you've remembered about the little box under the seat and ask have they looked in it. They'll do the rest.'

They all walked slowly up the quay

together. 'For all we know,' and James was looking into the shadows as if someone else might be listening, 'your dad didn't know what was in the parcel. He was just supposed to be delivering it to a boat out at sea. That in itself is quite legal, although it might mean that somebody wants to avoid harbour dues.'

Helen shivered in the cool breeze off the water. 'I suppose I'm not completely cleared, then. Even if the Bartletts get their jewels back, there is still the question of . . . who took them?'

'Don't you know who?' Jessie asked.

'We assume that Bartlett himself took them to Green because he knows where they went, but we can't prove it,' Helen said grimly. 'And we don't know why he would do such a thing.'

'I'll try to find Johnny Fox. He's a hand on a Bartlett boat and he's often in the town. He might know something about his boss's affairs, you'd be surprised how seamen gossip! You and me have to do a tour of the pubs, James. But we'll take Helen home first.' Dan looked round. 'G'night, Jessie. It's hard for you, just now.'

*   *   *

Jessie walked slowly back up the hill from the harbour. It was nearly dark, too late to go to the police station tonight; it would have to wait until tomorrow. A strange kind of calm had come over her, as though Bert's death was

263

inevitable, it had to happen. It was the end of their old life, but grieving though she was, there was a faint light of hope in the distance. Jessie had a plan for her own life, and once the fuss was over and Dad was decently buried, she would be able to make a choice.

Jessie had felt very envious of Helen, with her nice clean work at Seaview. To get away from the stink of fish and to better herself as a maid at Sewerby Hall was Jessie's long-term ambition. That, and to avoid marrying a fisherman. Her mother's sister worked at the hall and had offered to speak for her about a job, but Bert Hardy would never allow it. He had kept his daughter at home to bait his lines, gut his herring and keep his house. But now it was over. Jessie could hardly believe it.

The little house was in darkness when she reached home, but Jessie was used to that. Dad had spent very little time at home, come to think of it. If he wasn't fishing or out on mysterious errands he was taking a pipe and a pint at the George. Jessie lit a candle, blew the dying fire into life and pulled the kettle over the hob for a cup of tea. She nearly dropped the kettle when a gravelly voice behind her said, 'I'll have a cup with you, lass. Just came to see how you was getting on, Jessie. It's a bad job about Bert, that it is.' A scruffy figure sat down uninvited in Bert Hardy's chair.

Jessie put out two cups with trembling hands. What did Joe Green want? Several neighbours had visited to offer help but this was not a sympathy visit, she was sure. 'Yes.' She could think of nothing else to say. The man looked sinister in the flickering candlelight, the dark eyes glittering above the beard that hid his face.

Green looked at her as though she was simple. He drank his tea in silence apart from the odd slurp and Jessie felt the tension mounting. After putting down his cup he sat with his hands on his knees, still looking at her. 'It's time you and me had a little talk, lass.'

'What—what about?' Jessie asked nervously.

With a sly smile, Green said, 'Well, you know what he was doing that night. Don't you?' he shouted suddenly.

'No, I don't.' Jessie moved to the door, but the man was there before her. He locked the door and put the key in his pocket. 'Now, don't make it hard for yourself. Bert worked with me, as you know. He would have wanted you to tell me. Where did he keep the . . . parcels he delivered for me? Where? Where do I look for a parcel that weren't delivered?' He grabbed her and dug his fingers into her breasts. Jessie struggled, but he was much stronger than she was. After a while, she stood still but the pain persisted.

'If you don't tell me it'll be the worse for you.' The hoarse voice was full of menace; the narrow, dark face with the raggy beard looked evil. Green held her tight against him, bruising her and the rank smell of his sweat seemed to add to her fear.

There was no choice; Jessie would have to tell him, and not the police, what she had just learned. Maybe it was in fact what Dad would have wanted and at least it would get rid of this horrible man. 'There's a sort of box, hidden under the seat in the boat,' she whispered. 'It'll be locked . . . that's where he kept things. But it will be locked,' she repeated. She wasn't going to tell him what was there, but he would soon find out.

Green sneered, but he released her. 'Locks are only for honest folk. Now remember, don't tell anyone, anyone at all, or I'll come after you. Do you understand?' He spoke slowly, mouthing the words. He drew her door key out of his pocket, then threw it in the fire as he went out.

With a shuddering sigh Jessie put a chair against the door and raked the key from the embers. She was far more vulnerable without her father. Bert Hardy was known as a fighter and no one had ever dared to lay a finger on Jessie. A live-in position at the hall was even more desirable now; you'd expect that maids there would be safe if they behaved themselves. 'I'll speak to Auntie next week,' she said aloud. 'I can wear Helen's dress if they want to see me.' It was good to have something else to think about.

At the police station, the sergeant and constable delegated to the jewels theft were both on duty that night. 'What do we do next, Sarge?' They had run out of ideas, since nothing could be pinned on the maid at Seaview.

The sergeant scratched his head. 'Nay, I'm fair baffled. That maid should have broken down by now, but we haven't got anywhere with her. Let's take a turn round the houses and down to the harbour. Get a bit of fresh air.'

Coincidence can be a strange thing, the policemen reflected afterwards. Honest Joe Green was spotted in the street, flitting through the shadows with something hidden under his jacket. He was a man who was always of interest, although he had kept out of trouble for years. From a doorway the police watched him go down to Hardy's boat. They heard the splinter of wood; the senior man held the constable back and they saw him find the parcel. Joe got halfway home to his shop before he was deprived of the diamonds by two large men in uniform who asked a lot of questions. The worst question, the one that filled him with dread, was: 'What do you know about Hardy's murder?'

'Nay, I know nothing. I were just getting

Bert's things out of his boat, to give to his daughter. Poor Jessie's that upset. I dunno what's in the bag, but it belongs to Jessie now. Bert's things, see. Bait and tackle and such.'

*   *   *

James and Dan spent very little time or money in pursuit of the Bartlett crew member; at the first pub they visited they were told he was at sea. Helen was quite relieved to see them come in soon after she did. 'I'm glad you're both sober and righteous, or sober at least,' she amended as she looked at Dan's cap, set at an extremely rakish angle.

'What next?' asked Dan, who seemed to be restless. 'I don't know what else we can do, except listen to the town gossip.'

'I'd better keep working on the book,' James announced. He looked at Helen. 'Have you any sketches for me, to give me some atmosphere?'

Dan wandered off and Helen went up to fetch her folder of sketches. She left them with James and went to find Mary in the kitchen. In a few minutes James came in to join them, looking pleased. 'These are excellent, Helen! Just what I needed. You really have talent, my girl.' He spread them out on the table.

Helen blushed and Mary seemed to be quite impressed. 'Well, I never!' She looked admiringly up at Helen and back to the

268

sketches. It was a relief to be praised for something, to forget about diamonds and dead bodies just for a while.

'I took extra drawing lessons at school, and I've kept doing it ever since,' Helen explained. 'And if you use a soft pencil and good paper, you can rub out lines you don't want and redraw them. James gave me the paper.' There they all were in a jumble: Jessie with her basket, Ruth and the donkey, Dan's coble in the harbour. Dan came in and leaned over them, fascinated.

James put the papers back in the folder. 'I sometimes wish we could redraw our lives,' he said a little wistfully. He looked at Helen with affection in his eyes. 'I'll keep these, if you don't mind. You're a grand lass, I can tell you've put in a lot of time with this. It's a great help.' Mary smiled complacently.

SEVENTEEN

Miss Eliza Burton tore another day from her calendar, measuring out her life in small squares of paper. There were only a few days to go before the summer holidays, when the schools would close and the weary teachers could go home for a rest.

'It's over twenty years since I started teaching here and I've boarded at Seaview since you opened,' she said to Mary as she went down the stairs on her way to school, the folder with marking under her arm. How many times had she gone up and down those stairs? 'One does get a little weary . . . although on the whole, I have enjoyed teaching.'

'You're not leaving, are you, Miss Burton?' Mary probably hoped not; the teacher knew she was a model guest, she was very quiet and she paid her bills promptly. A houseful of Miss Burtons would no doubt have pleased Mary Baker, especially since the trouble with the robbery. That sort of thing was bad for the house's reputation.

Miss Burton had taken care to look just the same as usual, her grey hair neatly coiled in a bun at the back of her head. She wore a middle-aged dress with a high neckline and sensible shoes, but under the modest bodice she was filled with a youthful sense of anticipation. Things were about to change, but until she was sure there was no point in telling Mary that she did hope to leave teaching soon. Think of it—this might be her last week of facing the class! In the neat folder, hidden between the school books, were the documents that would change her life.

The morning seemed very long, but at last the lunch hour arrived and Miss Burton hurried off to the bank in her brief hour of freedom to deposit her documents in safekeeping. It was the least she could do to honour her brother's memory. Poor Matthew had died of consumption during the winter, but his sister was sure that his business problems had caused his decline.

Before he died Matthew had given her some of his papers. 'I want you to know, Eliza, and anybody else who needs to know, what really happened.' He had rarely spoken of the failure, but it was obvious that it preyed on his mind, night and day.

'What did really happen, Matt?' she asked quietly. It might do him good to talk about his problems. His wife had died and Matthew lived alone, apart from a woman who came to clean for him. He'd refused to move in with his sister because of his illness.

The sick man looked at her with eyes that were unnaturally bright. 'Another man set out to ruin us. At first I thought we could beat him. There were four of us altogether, you remember: a syndicate, and we bought fish from the boats as they came in and sent it out to hotels, shops—anywhere with large orders. It was a good business and we paid a fair price.'

'Why would anyone want to ruin you? I should think you never did anyone a bad turn.' But perhaps he was suffering from delusions; it could happen in a grave illness. Miss Burton swallowed a lump in her throat.

Matthew laughed bitterly. 'He brought in large catches of fish in his boats and he wanted all the profit. He was desperate to enlarge his business by selling to the customer, and we stood in the way. So he and the thugs who worked for him assaulted our carriers and stole the orders. Usually they sold them elsewhere. They even took consignments that were going by rail, they collected them at the destination station. The customers were let down, of course. Hotels had no fish and no lobsters for dinner, and they were bound to blame us, the suppliers.' Matthew leaned back in his chair, exhausted.

Eliza Burton shook her head sadly. 'You never told me at the time. So I suppose he then took over.'

'Yes, then he offered to be a reliable supplier and the hotels started to buy from him. Soon after that, he put up the retail prices and gave the fishermen less. He got away with it, there was no competition. No one dared to stand up to him.' There was a silence and Matthew sipped from a glass of water. 'I have quite a lot of evidence, with names and dates of what happened. The lads who worked for us are witnesses, of course. They made sworn statements—here they are—and their addresses are all here.' He tapped the papers. 'I thought of taking him to court, but the rest of the syndicate were worried about what he might do—he'd threatened their wives and children.'

'Who is he? Do I know him? Is he still

operating?' It was a terrible story and Eliza could hardly sit still on her chair.

Matthew plunged on, ignoring the interruption. 'After Mildred died I had nothing to lose, but then this happened . . . he gestured at his wasted body. 'It's too late for me, lass, but I wanted you to know. I probably should have told you at the time, but—well, I suppose I didn't want to admit that I'd lost all my money and lost the business we built up over years. I'm too tired now to go over it, but you can read it for yourself. I don't ask you to do anything, you know, but I'd be happy to think you might take it further, one day. Talk to a solicitor, at any rate. The assault and theft were illegal, and I think it should also be against the law to operate a monopoly and hold the customers to ransom.'

She read the papers with dismay and for several weeks Miss Burton thought about her brother's story. Then he died and her grief was such that it took all her strength to get through the work at school. But as the summer came, she began to wonder how she could carry out Matthew's wishes. One warm night at Seaview as she lay awake a brilliant idea had floated into her mind. She would blackmail the man and exact revenge for Matthew . . . and even some money for herself. A little money, invested wisely, would allow her to retire early and begin to live her own life. It was a tempting thought.

The next day she typed a letter. Miss Burton demanded a certain sum in exchange for the papers, the evidence that could convict the man to whom she was writing. It was an elegant solution; he would not be buying her silence, but the hard evidence. She took great care to conceal her identity and location, but let him know what she knew. His reply was to be sent to her under a different name, care of a post office in Malton, a place where she was not known.

People would never believe that the quiet and respectable schoolteacher would carry out blackmail. 'But they don't know I was born under the sign of Scorpio,' she smiled to herself. The calm exterior hid fierce passions, and this time she felt the heat of revenge. She felt it that summer day as she walked to the bank and left Matthew's papers in a strongbox, to which she was given a key. It was time to take precautions.

After a week or two the man had replied, agreeing to her demand. So far, so good; now for the tricky bit. Would he send the money to the post office? He said in a note that he would be able to find it soon.

It had been a shock, of course, to meet the villain face to face. That night at Seaview, when she was introduced to the Bartletts, it had been difficult to keep calm. But she was reassured by their obvious wealth. William Bartlett had built his business by criminal

274

activity; but he looked respectable and prosperous. She had heard that he was a magistrate and a Justice of the Peace. The life he had built for himself would be brought down in ruins if the story got out—and Matthew had thought that there were probably other small operators who had been removed in the same way. He certainly would not want his criminal past to be known.

Having seen Bartlett, whose glance swept over her without any interest at all, Eliza Burton was even more determined to carry it through. The dramatic theft of Bartlett's jewels made Miss Burton wonder whether this was another act of revenge. She felt sorry for young Helen, upon whom the suspicion of theft was obviously weighing heavily.

On her last night at Seaview before the school holidays Miss Burton sat waiting with Mr Kirby for the summons to dinner. It was a fine evening and they were the only two dining. The writer seemed preoccupied; perhaps he was thinking about the beautiful young woman who had taken so much of his attention in the last few weeks. 'The Spencers left rather suddenly, did they not, Mr Kirby? Between dinner one evening and breakfast the next day,' she observed, thinking that he might know where they went. There was something odd about the Spencers.

James Kirby sighed. 'They did,' he agreed, but said no more. After a while he made an

275

effort to be sociable. 'It must be your last evening, Miss Burton. It's a cause for celebration—four weeks of holiday!' He looked at her. 'Would you care to join me in a glass of sherry? I know you don't normally take alcohol, but at the end of term perhaps it could be allowed.' He looked as though he needed a drink to cheer him up.

Mr Kirby was a kindly man and Miss Burton felt sorry for him. 'Very well, I will take a small glass, thank you.' James fished in the sideboard cupboard and brought out two glasses and a decanter. He poured them both a generous amount and they sat in the window, gazing out over the bay to where the evening sun lit the gleaming chalk of the headland, topped by the lighthouse.

A warm glow spread through Miss Burton with the unaccustomed drink. It was fine old sherry, rather dry; the glasses were crystal. 'This is not quite typical boarding house fare,' she smiled and, looking at James, noted that he seemed more relaxed.

'Not in the least, this is most civilized. Mary lets me keep a bottle or two in the cupboard for special occasions.' He had nearly finished his glass. 'Forgive me for being rather gloomy tonight, but I am very worried about poor Helen. The police are determined to find her guilty of stealing the Bartletts' jewels.' James added fiercely, 'I wish they'd never come here!'

'It is certainly most odd. And surprising that such a ruthless man should allow someone to steal from him. I can't think how it could have happened. No, no . . . very well, just a small one, then.' Miss Burton accepted another glass and looked round at the door, but there was no sign of dinner yet. 'Without food, I fear that the sherry will soon go to my head.'

'Do you know Bartlett?' James held the crystal glass to catch the light. 'To be honest I saw you looking at him once or twice during dinner when they were here, as though you remembered him from somewhere. Yes, I think he could be ruthless, all right.'

Miss Burton blushed a little. 'Mrs Bartlett seemed to be a very pleasant woman, not a bit like her husband. But my brother . . . he knew how ruthless Bartlett could be.' She put down her glass as the door opened and Helen brought in a tray of chicken and salad.

'Mary hopes you'll be happy with a cold meal and strawberries for dessert, it's such a warm evening,' Helen said apologetically. 'And because there's only two of you and it's not a hot dinner, she sent you a bottle of white wine.' Seaview guests expected a hot meal and three courses in the evening.

'Thank you, Helen,' James said genially. 'We've already had sherry, but it would be churlish to refuse Mary's wine. Thank her for us, will you? Now please don't worry, Miss Burton. You'll have no more duties today, another glass of wine won't hurt you.'

Eliza Burton could not remember when she had enjoyed a meal so much. James was pleasant company, the chicken was delicious and it was enhanced by a glass of cool white wine. She found herself telling James about her brother and his illness and she hardly noticed when the writer refilled her glass. 'And so your brother Matthew had dealings with Bartlett?' James asked persuasively. Soon he had the story, and it was a relief to tell someone the secret she had been carrying for so long. 'I would not dream of telling anyone else . . . please keep it to yourself,' she begged. 'But I hardly dare admit it, even to you, Mr Kirby. . .' The wine was making her head spin slightly, but it was a pleasant feeling. 'I have told Bartlett what I know and asked him for payment—to buy the documents from me. It will only be justice, after what happened to Matthew.'

James was suitably impressed; he gasped. 'You really did? Well, that's very interesting. We . . . have been trying to find out what really happened to the jewels and we have some evidence that the man might have taken the diamonds himself and tried to ship them overseas. We wondered why he might need the money and if he did, why could they not have been openly sold?'

Miss Burton suppressed a hiccup and took another sip of the excellent wine. The evening

278

light was fading out in the bay and far out she could see some of the herring boats returning to harbour. Suddenly, it all made sense. 'I did ask him for a rather large sum,' she said modestly, her eyes down, and James let out a laugh. Helen, coming in with dessert and coffee, thought how much more cheerful he looked tonight.

They ate strawberries in silence for a while, then Miss Burton said, 'The boats out there reminded me . . . it's the beginning of the season for herring and the profit is still to make, so he may have been short of capital, especially since he bought two more steam-trawlers during the winter. That was one of the last things Matthew told me.' Her eyes filled with tears. 'Poor Matthew was so frustrated. He said that Bartlett would ruin a lot more people, men like Daniel who go out in small boats. I believe Daniel has already had trouble from one of the Bartlett crews.'

'So it's possible that when Bartlett got your demand he decided to steal the jewels to raise the cash quickly.' James poured the last of the wine.

'And made it look like theft, so his wife wouldn't know about his murky past!' Miss Burton dabbed her mouth delicately with the napkin. 'We may have solved the mystery, Mr Kirby.'

'But we can't run down to the station and tell the police all about it, now can we? And

Helen is still in trouble.' James shook his head.

'And I haven't got my money, yet.' The wine had made her body relax and Miss Burton felt that it didn't matter very much, after all. She struggled to think clearly. 'Everything we do has consequences! My bad deed has affected poor Helen. Do you think I should confess to the police, James?' She had never called him James before, but tonight was different. 'I feel that I should do something to help the poor girl to clear her name. What a dreadful thing, to be wrongly accused!'

James was thinking. 'We should be able to tell the police enough without mentioning you, Miss Burton. It was brave—and really quite amazing that you took on Bartlett to avenge your brother.'

Sitting back in her chair with coffee Miss Burton smiled dreamily. There was one thing that she had left out of the account, one that she hardly admitted even to herself. One thing that made revenge even sweeter. Should she tell James? 'It was not just for my brother, you see. Will Bartlett was my lover, once. He was ambitious then, quite greedy. I was young, I loved his enterprise, his energy—ruthless people can be quite attractive, you know!' She smiled. 'Of course he didn't recognize me after all these years. I was a different person, then.'

'So you did know him, very well,' James said quietly. 'And it all ended in tears?' The young man looked so sympathetic; perhaps he was thinking of his attachment to Miss Spencer.

'We were to be married, but he dropped me very quickly when he met a rich woman who could put capital into his business. Matthew didn't know that; he would have wanted to kill Bartlett. She's dead now, so the Mrs Bartlett we met must be his second wife.' Miss Burton put her coffee cup back rather unsteadily in the saucer. 'Since this is confession time, I will tell you that when he left me, I was pregnant. I'd allowed him to seduce me. It is strange how you can fall in love with someone quite unsuitable, and be blind to their faults. I had to go away and the baby was adopted. It was agony at the time, but it's a long time ago.' James winced, but he nodded. They sat for a while and then she added, 'There is something about you, James, that makes me tell you secrets. But now, tell me: what happened to Maud Spencer? Was she involved in the theft?'

James took a small parcel from the table and opened it. Inside was a gold watch.

'They stole this from me in York and it has just come back in the post, with a letter, an apology; she regrets taking it and wants me to forgive her.' He sighed. 'It seems that the daughter—er—distracts the victim while her mother steals the goods. The mother is probably not deaf at all; it's a ploy to avert suspicion and possibly to eavesdrop on interesting conversations.' He looked uncomfortable. 'I admit I was stupid enough to fall for a pretty face, but all along I felt there was something not quite right about the Spencers. This week we found that Maud had actually put a ring in Helen's room and then told the police where to look for it. That made the case look very black for Helen.' He paused. 'I am not sure why she sent me the watch, unless it was to demonstrate how very naïve I am.'

Miss Burton was shocked. 'What mean tricks the woman gets up to! But what was her motive, I wonder, in trying to get Helen into trouble?'

James looked embarrassed. 'Jealousy.'

'I see.' The woman was a criminal, but she must have fallen for James. Who could blame her? Sitting there in the evening light, he looked very handsome. If she were younger . . . Miss Burton sighed. Helen would make a very suitable wife for James, she reflected, even if her social station was lower than his. They seemed to have a great deal in common. It was too soon to try to stand up, so she stayed where she was. 'We have had an interesting evening, you and I.'

*   *   *

The trawler steamed through the night, travelling north towards the fishing grounds, carrying with it a mixed bag of mortals, most of whom were full of hope. A good catch would put money in their pockets. Benny Turner was excited; it was his first trip and it had been hard to persuade his mother to allow it. Benny was on deck, watching the dark water. The experienced hands were getting the gear ready for action, and to keep Benny alert they had told him to 'look out for little boats.' The skipper was very keen to avoid them. He said he was worried about court action if they rammed a yawl and the little pests were everywhere; you couldn't see them until you were on top of them and with their sails down for fishing, they couldn't get out of the way quick enough. In the wide North Sea you would think there was plenty of room, but fishermen knew where to look for the feeding grounds and so they were often all in the same area.

The crew didn't openly talk about it, but Benny had heard a whisper that only a few days ago they'd run down a poor bloke in the dark and his mast had come down and stove his head in. Half his face was gone, they said. He was a bloke from Bridlington and they got another boat to tow him in, least said the better. Another accident at sea, and nobody to blame. But no wonder the skipper was jumpy. You wouldn't want that to happen too often.

Benny was keen to do the right thing, but if he saw nothing, how would they know he'd strained his eyes, peering into the darkness? So it was with relief that he spotted a tiny light bobbing about, seeming to wink on and off. He yelled to another man, 'There's a light out there on the left—I mean port bow!'

The skipper gave the order to slow the engines and a crewman said that they wanted to board. 'It's the old man himself, Mr Bartlett, by the signal,' he said. 'Wonder what he wants?'

'Owners sometimes like to come out and check up, just to make sure everything's right,' the skipper said slowly. 'But Mr Bartlett hasn't been out for some time.' He looked worried.

The big man was hauled aboard with difficulty but he obviously still remembered how to climb a rope ladder. In the lights on deck he looked a menacing figure, his big red face contorted with effort and also, it seemed, with anger. Bartlett was wearing the clothes of a fisherman but Benny could see that he was the owner. He looked round the deck and you could tell that he was checking on everything. He jerked his head at the skipper and they both moved forward, away from the crew. Benny kept watching the water with a vacant expression, but by straining his ears he could hear most of what they said.

'. . . happened to Hardy? Couldn't you do better than that?'

'Well, sir, it wasn't on purpose, you know!' The skipper sounded agitated. 'It seemed best to pretend that we didn't know he was hit . . . certainly you didn't want anybody to know it was your boat that did it. We got out of the area real fast, and we heard another boat took him in tow. At least there was no scandal . . . I have my reputation to think about, too.'

'So you didn't collect the goods?'

'No, sir, we didn't. Er—I didn't realize they were that important. Secret Government messages, I was told, but they could send them again, I thought.'

'I don't believe you. You're not that stupid . . . unless you panicked. I think you'd have taken his parcel and then rammed him, stands to reason.'

The skipper protested. 'Nay, Mr Bartlett. . .'

The listening Benny felt shivers down his spine when Bartlett hissed, 'Tell me the truth, man. Or else you'll never work for me again—or anyone else, for that matter. I'll break your arms and legs . . .'

The skipper was a big man but he sounded very small now. 'All right, Mr Bartlett. The truth is I did know he carried something valuable, 'cos of who was to meet us at Amsterdam later. We searched his boat afterwards but we couldn't find anything. Honest, that's what happened.'

Bartlett boiled over with rage. 'You dirty rat! You'll be off to Amsterdam or some other port as soon as you can to get rid of them, but meanwhile . . . I reckon the goods will be here. On this boat. And I will get them back, or it will be very painful for you.' He walked away.

'I will search the boat now.'

'Please sir, watch out!' the skipper called, but it was too late. In his rage Bartlett stormed down the deck and disappeared through an open hatch. There was a hoarse scream, then silence except for the throb of the engines.

Benny never forgot that night. The big boss had fallen down a hatch into the empty fish hold, right into the bottom of the boat, and broken his neck. If they'd had some luck with the shoals, if it had been full of fish he'd have had a soft landing; that's fate for you. Benny knew that fishing was dangerous, but not this bad. They said the boss was the richest man in Hull! And now he was dead, just like that. Nothing could be done except to lay him out as best they could, turn the boat slowly round and head off back to Hull. The skipper would have a lot of explaining to do; there would be an inquest, for sure.

Benny was not sure whether he wanted a life at sea, after all.

EIGHTEEN

'Summer's over, you'll soon be going home to your papa and mama. Are you sad, Helen? I'm in—inconsolable, is that the right word?' Daniel was his usual teasing self, but it was true that Helen's time at Seaview was nearly at an end. By October, most of the visitors had disappeared and the little town was settling down already into its winter quiet. It was time to go home.

'Probably not the right word, Dan. You're bound have someone to console you. Now leave me in peace, we have work to do. There could be thirty or forty guests at the party tonight.'

The Saturday evening party had been booked by James about a month before, at a kitchen conference with all hands present. 'The publisher said that the book will be printed by October,' he said happily. 'We must have the celebration before Helen goes home, of course. She has been a great help to me. So, if it's convenient, Mary, we could invite a few people to a buffet supper on the night of the hunter's moon. In some places it was the traditional time for an autumn feast.' He looked pleased with the idea.

Mary smiled. 'They always used to have dinner parties at the full moon when I was in service, so the guests could see their way home. Ay, well, hunter's moon is the one after this—we have the harvest moon at the moment.'

A party at Seaview would be a good way to round off the summer. Only a writer would think of mixing up the social classes for an event like this, but of course James mixed with everybody. It was amazing that the book was to be published so soon, but here it was: *Working Lives*, and they were about to celebrate its appearance. Helen had been promised a copy and she could hardly wait to see it.

Dan came up behind her and slid his arms round her waist. 'You'll be the belle of the ball, lassie! And then you'll leave me. I will cry on your shoulder if you like.' He kissed her behind the ear and Helen felt the familiar shiver of excitement. The villain was at his most persuasive, but she went on polishing glasses. Dan was not serious; it was just a game.

Under the large white apron Helen was wearing a new dress from a Bridlington dressmaker, rather more up to the fashion than the rest of her wardrobe. The dark pink suited her complexion and the fitted waist emphasized her figure without being too daring.

James came in and Helen breathed a silent sigh of relief. 'Will you give me a hand with the boxes, Dan? The books have arrived.' With a meaningful look at Helen, Dan went off with James, who had an aura of suppressed excitement about him. It must be a wonderful moment for him, the result of so many months of work. She sighed again; would she ever achieve anything like this?

Mary was surprisingly serene when she came through from the dining-room. 'We're

288

nearly ready,' she said happily. 'There's no dinner to worry about, the buffet is all done . . . where's the smoked salmon, love?'

The last of the sunset was fading and the hunter's moon was rising over the sea by the time the guests began to arrive. Helen offered each of them a glass of fruit punch but Miss Burton refused hers, with a rueful look at James. 'I'd better not, thank you, Helen.' She took a glass of lemonade. Miss Burton had stayed at Seaview over the weekend to attend the party but Helen could see that she was not going to let her hair down; the bun was firmly in place and the black dress was forbidding in its respectability.

James took a glass and whispered to Helen, 'We'll get the speeches over first, before the food. My goodness, you look very fetching in that dress, Miss Moore!'

James himself was almost elegant, his unruly hair smoothed down and a crisp white shirt emphasizing his tan.

Helen looked up in surprise as Mrs Bartlett came in, quietly dressed in black but with a warm smile for Helen. 'I've been thinking of you, my dear,' she said so that no one else could hear. 'That jewel business . . . how you must have suffered. We now know that poor William was trying to sell them, no doubt he would have told me about it, but for the accident. I am still trying to come to terms with it all. The police now know everything, of course. But I was touched to be invited tonight.'

For a moment Helen was speechless. She'd had no idea that Mrs Bartlett was invited, but it was good to hear from her that the truth was now known and the last lingering doubts about Helen's honesty had been dispelled, even from the musty offices of the Bridlington police station. Then good manners prompted her to say quickly, 'We were all very sorry to hear of his sad death, Mrs Bartlett. Thank you for thinking of me. It was good of you to come tonight.'

Even more of a shock was in store; Helen's father and mother came in, all smiles.

'I didn't think I'd see you until next week!' she gasped.

Dan was mingling with the guests as to the manner born, looking very handsome in a well-fitting suit and James's quiet glow of success had replaced the haunted look he had worn for most of the summer. Dan looked after the neighbours and local people. Ivy Cole was among them, bringing a sheaf of aromatic herbs for the food table. She ushered in a shy little trio, John and Martha Beck and their young helper, Ruth. 'Good to see you—I've invited as many of the people who figure in the book as I could,' James explained. They were followed by a couple of fishermen in their best suits and a pretty girl in a green dress.

Dan had been talking to Ivy and Ruth, but when the girl in green appeared Helen saw him move round the room until he stood beside her. His admiration was obvious and Helen could see why. Her glossy black hair curled softly round her face and the high cheekbones gave her a distinguished look. She moved gracefully and she radiated enjoyment. Dan handed her a drink and stayed by her side.

It's a good job I'm not in love with Dan, Helen told herself. But he'll have to watch out for James, he's very susceptible to pretty young women! She suppressed a giggle. Then she looked again at the pair. 'Good heavens—it's Jessie!' Suddenly Helen recognized the green dress as the one she had been given; now it was worn by young Jessie Hardy, no longer a fishergirl but looking bonnier and happier than they had ever seen her. The change in her was amazing. Did Dan realize yet that he was chatting to Bert Hardy's lass?

The next time Helen had a moment to look over to where Jessie stood, she was talking to Ruth. As Helen watched Ruth crumpled up; she slid slowly down the wall and onto the floor. Helen and Dan both moved forward to help her; the poor girl came round after a minute and was most embarrassed, but most of the guests had the good sense to keep away. Mary took her off to the kitchen for a dose of sal volatile, poor Ruth looking just as pale as she had been in the summer.

Helen looked at Dan and Jessie, who were both concerned. 'What happened, do you think?'

'Poor lass isn't strong, yet, you know. And it's hot and crowded in here,' Dan suggested.

'You're right, it was probably that,' Jessie agreed. 'I just mentioned that my dad was killed in an accident, like. It seemed to give her a shock. The next minute, she was on the floor. And she'd had nothing to drink,' Jessie added earnestly. 'We haven't seen her for weeks, so she wouldn't know about Dad.'

James was trying to get the guests to sit down. Chairs were arranged in the sitting-room in rows, with a space at one end for the speakers, but people were too busy talking to move and the volume of noise was high. In the interlude, Helen slipped into the kitchen to see Ruth, whom she found looking embarrassed.

'I'll just go and check on the food,' Mary said. When they were alone, Helen looked at Ruth. 'What's wrong, love?' she asked gently. 'You can tell me.'

Ruth shook her head wordlessly, and there was a silence. But then she raised her eyes. 'It's only fair for you to know, Helen. Jessie told me—told me that her father's dead . . .' Her thin shoulders shook with sobs. 'The shock . . . but it's such a relief, Helen. I never thought I could be free.'

292

It was a minute or two before Helen understood. 'So it was Hardy who . . . tormented you?' Ruth nodded. 'It's all over, Ruth.' Bert Hardy, ruining the poor girl's life all those years. He was a selfish brute and he deserved to die, she thought fiercely. She held the poor girl until Ruth was calm again, and then gently changed the subject and asked about the farm.

'It's lovely, Helen, working there. The animals . . . I've got a little cat of my own. I'm going to stay there, they are grand folks and they do need help.'

Helen stood up. 'I've got to go now, love, but I'll see you later in the evening. And I'll come to see you at the farm when I can.' She too felt that a weight had been taken from her. Dan was not the rapist; Dan was what Ruth had called him, a free spirit. She should have known better than to suspect him of causing Ruth's downfall.

Back in the big room, the speeches were about to begin. A representative of the publisher started off the proceedings with a rather boring speech about new trends in book publishing.

'Realism is the thing, ladies and gentlemen,' he boomed. 'And it is here . . . pages from real life in this book.'

Next, James took the floor and Helen noticed a journalist from the local paper take out his notebook. 'This occasion is a celebration of the people of Bridlington, the workers who keep society going,' he said, with a smile at the subjects of his book. 'I hope you will be happy with the book and I'm pleased that so many of you are here this evening.' He picked up a copy and Helen craned her neck to see what it looked like. His next words shook her to the core. 'I think, and I hope you will all agree, that the book owes a great deal to the illustrations that bring the subjects to life.' He smiled at Helen. 'The artist is of course Helen Moore, and our engraver worked from her drawings. Thank you, Helen. I have a great deal to thank you for!' He stepped forward and handed her a copy of the book, then kissed her cheek. 'Thank you for so much,' he murmured in her ear. 'I wouldn't be here at all if it wasn't for you.' The applause was deafening and Helen blushed.

A spokesman from the town said that the book would put Bridlington on the map, once and for all. He hoped that many copies would be sold and as he was the bookseller, Helen hoped he would see to it.

When copies had been distributed and everybody moved into the dining-room for supper, Helen confronted James. 'I had no idea! Why didn't you tell me?' she demanded. Her sketches were all there, nicely framed and with a page for each: the cobles sailing into the bay, Jessie in her bonnet and boots, Ruth with Moses the donkey and the rest. 'I can't believe this is my work.' There on the printed page their work, the sketches and the words, somehow seemed so much more professional.

James passed her a glass of sherry. 'Get this down you, as Mary would say. We wanted it to be a surprise . . . but I wasn't sure whether they could be ready in time, so I sent away the drawings just after you gave them to me. At the last minute it was all done and it seemed a good idea to have everyone here, before we all go home for the winter. This book belongs to you as much as to me.' He grinned at her happily. 'I am so glad you like it.'

Helen stood clutching the book in its elegant red cover, caught between laughing and crying. Her mother came up and gave her a kiss. 'We never knew how much talent you had, Helen. We're so proud of you!' She stood back and looked at her daughter. 'You seem to have grown up, somehow, this summer.'

Her father beamed, then looked at someone behind her. 'And who is this young man?' Daniel slid an arm decorously round Helen's waist before he introduced himself and her father laughed. 'I must say you don't look at all like a fisherman!'

Dan took the book from Helen and turned the pages until he came to the drawing of a young man in a gansey, beside his boat. 'That's the real me, sir. Part coble owner, of course. Not just a deck hand.'

'Deck hands don't usually wear suits like

yours,' the older man reminded him lightly and Helen caught her mother looking at Dan with a benign expression. He'd obviously charmed her, too. Mary had often said he was good at chatting to ladies.

People were talking in groups and the food was beginning to circulate; Helen felt that she should be on duty. But the middle-aged man from the publishing house gently detained her. 'I'm glad you like the book, we're very pleased with it, Miss Moore. It should sell well. And now, I am sure you're very busy tonight, but some time in the future we would like to talk to you about the illustrated children's book you're planning—what was it James called it— "Jolly Pirates"?'

Good heavens, he knew about the pirate book; she had only suggested the idea to James as a joke, one day when he was looking sad. 'Well! Yes . . . I haven't got very far,' Helen stammered. Helen Moore, book illustrator, it was an amazing idea. All those hours spent drawing for her own pleasure had resulted in this achievement, for herself and James. It opened up new possibilities for her, beyond going home to work in the dairy. She circled the room with trays of savouries, floating on air.

It was quite late when the noise died down and people began to make their way home. Helen's parents were staying at Mrs White's and would take her home the next day; they lingered, talking to James. Feeling subdued, Helen helped Dan to wash the dishes for the last time. 'I might come and visit you one day,' Dan told her cheerfully.

'You don't ask whether I want to see you!' Helen was repressive. What would his mother think? Mary had been trying to keep them apart all summer. But Dan just laughed, a confident young man who was sure of his welcome anywhere. It would be interesting, she supposed, to see him in her own environment and away from the sea.

'How did you find Jessie?' she asked him mischievously.

Dan blushed, just a little. 'I didn't know her at first. My goodness, she's changed. Jessie's got away from the fish, you know. She's training as a maid at the hall and I reckon she'll do right well. A nice young lass, our Jessie.'

When the dishes were done, Dan offered to escort the Moores to Mrs White's boarding house while Helen put the rooms to rights. It was very quiet in the house; Mary had gone to bed, worn out she said by the excitement. At last Helen looked round the tidy sitting-room with approval, took off her apron and then slowly collapsed on to a sofa. She picked up a copy of the book and had started to read James's account of a trip in a coble when a shadow fell across the page. James sat down beside her, exactly where he used to sit beside

Maud. They smiled at each other.

'Helen Moore, book illustrator.' James echoed her own thoughts. 'It's the sort of career that you can develop even while you're living at home on the farm.' He thought for a moment. 'Although I suppose your summer by the sea gave you plenty of new subjects.' He looked thoughtful. 'We've been so busy that I haven't had time to look ahead. I've just realized that this is it, Helen, the end of the summer. You're going home and so am I. I shall miss you very much, my girl.'

They sat in silence for a while, and the sadness, the finality of it came stealing over Helen. Perhaps it was a reaction after the excitement of the evening? But there would be no more talks with James, no more cosy chats in the kitchen with Mary. She would miss the sense of anticipation when new guests arrived —and the relief when some of them left. It was all over; the summer was gone, with all its ups and downs. Would she ever see James again? He was a friend, a real friend and she was going to lose him. A tear slid down her cheek and she realized that through it all, she had never wept at Seaview. This was the wrong time to start.

James took her hand. 'Helen, come out with me for a few moments, it's a beautiful night. I'm sure Mary won't mind.'

'Mary's in bed . . . I'll get my shawl.' Helen joined him at the door and together they stepped into the velvet night. There was only a slight breeze off the sea and the air was crisp and clean. A deep-yellow moon sailed above them, its light reflected in a shining path across the water.

'Let's walk on the beach . . . the tide's going out, we won't get cut off!' Helen smiled, remembering poor Lancelot. They wandered along, hand in hand; James's hand was warm and firm in hers, an assured clasp. Goodness, I will miss James, Helen thought. But it was selfish to be so sad when James was happy with the success of his book. Helen made an effort. 'Thank you, James, for everything. The publisher wanted to talk about the pirate book and I'd love to do something like that . . . you've given me so much encouragement.'

'And when it comes out, send a copy to Lancelot!' James laughed. 'But seriously, I hope we will be able to work on more projects together. A farming book, for instance . . . workers on the land.' He looked down at Helen. 'You gave me that idea. I have to thank you for so much, Helen. Even for my life, you know. And for . . . er . . . bearing with me over that Maud Spencer affair. I do regret it . . . I wasted a lot of time with Maud.'

'I worried for you, James, I felt you would be made unhappy.' Helen's eyes were on the curling breakers out there over the rocks, shining in the moonlight. Over the bay, the cliffs of Flamborough gleamed white, gashed near the base by the mysterious smuggler's caves. What a beautiful place; she had seldom seen the bay by moonlight.

'You did? Then—do you care about me at all, Helen? I've always thought you were—you and Dan were quite close.' James looked suddenly animated.

Helen laughed quietly. 'Dan is fickle, his mother says. He's a charmer, but—well, I must have grown up a little this summer, I've managed to resist him. We've had good times and bad, all of us. But Dan and I are not—close.' The moonlit bay was part of Dan's world; she was turning her back on the sea, its beauty and its terror. 'I love it here, but I'm not the right girl for Daniel.' Another thought struck her like a warm glow. 'Yes, I do care about you, James. I have cared about you all the summer.'

They stopped and looked at each other. 'Good!' James said. 'There's hope for me, then, in spite of my mistakes.' There on the beach, in full view of the sleeping town, James Kirby gathered Helen in his arms and kissed her. For the first time she was close to him, feeling his warmth, relaxing, tasting the sea salt on his lips. She felt deeply content.

'On such a night as this. . . .' he murmured against her hair. 'I'm falling in love with you, Helen, just as I'm going to lose you. You've been so patient with me! We've been friends and we worked together well, but is there a chance at all that you might learn to love me? That you might want to spend the rest of your life with me?'

There was a feeling deep inside Helen that this might be a very important moment in her life. On impulse she reached up, put her arms round his neck and kissed him experimentally, as though she was trying to make up her mind. Then she leaned back in his arms and looked at the handsome face in the moonlight; the eyes were kind, the mouth curved in a smile. 'James, it is possible. But such a magic night, James, can go to your head. Wise girls are careful not to promise too much. We've had a wonderful evening, so much success! Shall we wait until the morning? When the sun comes up, things may look different. You're a . . . successful man and I'm a—a domestic servant.' This sudden transformation of partly stuffy Mr Kirby had taken her by surprise; he had never flirted with her, as had Dan.

'You are a lovely girl and a talented artist. The night of the hunter's moon is a special time, Helen. Tonight is ours . . . the start of our future. Now, Miss Moore, let us plan to meet again soon. There's so much we can do together!'

Helen looked back over the footprints they had made and then into the distance to the shining sands ahead, yet to be trodden, like their journey through life. Too many words would spoil the moment, so she said gently,

'Yes, James, we will meet again.' The moon shone on them benignly as they walked at the edge of the waves, looking out over the restless sea.